A WING AND A PRAYER

1990, Blackpool. Thirty-three-year-old Helen Burnside is shocked when she learns that her beloved Great Aunt Alice has died of a sudden heart attack, and even more surprised when she is bequeathed her Yorkshire cottage. Although they were close, Alice was an enigmatic figure, estranged from most of her family. What led to the long-held animosity between Alice, her mother Ada and her sister Lizzie, and why did she leave Blackpool for Yorkshire all those years ago? Moving into Alice's cottage, Helen uncovers a series of devastating family secrets. But as she pieces together the truth about her aunt's life, it seems her own is about to go in a new direction.

MARGARET THORNTON

A WING AND A PRAYER

Complete and Unabridged

MAGNA
Leicester

First published in Great Britain in 2019 by
Severn House Publishers Ltd
London

First Ulverscroft Edition
published 2020
by arrangement with
Severn House Publishers Ltd
London

A catalogue record for this book is available
from the British Library.

ISBN 978-0-7505-4796-3

Published by
Ulverscroft Limited
Anstey, Leicestershire

Set by Words & Graphics Ltd.
Anstey, Leicestershire
Printed and bound in Great Britain by
T. J. International Ltd., Padstow, Cornwall

This book is printed on acid-free paper

1

The phone rang just as Helen was putting on her jacket, ready to dash out to the car and drive to the pub where she worked a few evenings each week. She was often last minute; a few more seconds and she would have gone. She was tempted to ignore it, but it might be important. It might even be Alex . . . but that was very unlikely.

'Hello,' she said, somewhat impatiently, as she picked up the phone from the small table in the hall.

'Hello, Helen . . . It's Mum.'

'I'm just on my way to work, Mum, and I'm running late. What is it? Can't it wait?'

'I'm sorry, love. I knew you'd be dashing off about this time, but I'm afraid I have some bad news.'

Helen felt the blood drain from her face. 'What is it?'

'It's Aunt Alice. She's had a heart attack. I'm sorry, love . . . I'm afraid she's gone. It was so very sudden.'

Helen felt her eyes fill with tears, and she sat down on the chair at the side of the table. 'Oh, no! How dreadful! But she wasn't ill. She was perfectly all right the last time I saw her, about ten days ago. Does Gran know?'

'Yes, it was your gran who phoned to tell me. Alice's next-door neighbour was concerned because there were two bottles of milk on the doorstep and Trixie was miaowing outside. The back door was open so Nora was able to get in . . . and she found her; in the fireside chair, just as though she was asleep.'

Helen felt the tears running down her cheeks. 'Oh . . . how very sad. I can't believe it. You say she'd had a heart attack?'

'Yes, apparently so, but there will have to be a post-mortem. She hadn't been ill — well, not ill enough to go to the doctor. Nora rang for the doctor at once, of course, and that was what he diagnosed: a sudden massive heart attack. He called for an ambulance, and it's all under control. But your gran and I will be going over there tomorrow. Your gran's her next of kin — she's her only sister — so we'll have to go and see to things; the funeral and everything, you know.'

'She wasn't very old, was she?'

'No, only seventy-one. Not old by today's standards. Your gran's seven years older than Alice, and still hale and hearty, but you just never know . . . Anyway, I'm sorry to give you such bad news. You were always Alice's favourite, you know. And, of course, she never had any children of her own.'

'Never even got married, did she? I often wondered why that was, Mum?'

'Oh, lots of reasons I suppose, love. Your gran would never say much about her. There was something of a rift between them after Aunt

2

Alice went back to live in Yorkshire. But, like I say, she's her next of kin.'

'Would you like me to drive you over there, Mum? I could get some time off work.'

'No thanks, love. I'm quite a capable driver, and I'm my own boss; I don't have to ask for time off work. And your dad will be fine on his own for a few days.'

'Look, Mum, I'd better go,' Helen said. 'I'm late already. Ring me when you get to Yorkshire and let me know what's happening. I can't take it in yet about Aunt Alice . . . I shall miss her so much.'

'We all will, love, but I know how close you were to her. Bye for now. Drive carefully . . . or might it be better if you didn't go to the pub tonight?'

'No, I'll have to go. Don't worry; I'll be careful. Bye, Mum, and take care of Gran.'

'Will do. Bye, love . . . '

Helen brushed the tears from her cheeks, picked up her car keys and went out to where her red Volkswagen was parked outside her ground-floor flat. Not a new car, but not very old either. It was a 1987 model, three years old, that she had bought a few months ago when she'd received a pay rise. She was saving up for a deposit to buy a flat of her own, but she felt that the car was a small luxury that she deserved. She would have her own place all in good time, and she was quite happy where she was at the moment, in a tree-lined avenue near Stanley Park. It wasn't too far from the estate agency where she worked during the day, on Whitegate

Drive, one of the main roads leading out of Blackpool.

Helen Burnside was thirty-three years old, unmarried — although she had not been short of boyfriends, one or two of whom she had thought might even be 'the one'. She was on her own again now, having parted from Alex Barker two weeks previously. It had not been working out, and they had decided to call it a day. Helen was now having slight regrets, but she was damned if she was going to admit it. He must make the first move if he was so inclined. If not, then she would move forward. In the paraphrased words of a song from one of her favourite musicals, *Oklahoma!*, many a new day would dawn before she looked back at the romance behind her.

It was only a few minutes' drive to the Wayside Inn in nearby Marton, where she worked three nights a week and occasional weekends, to supplement her savings towards a home of her own.

'Sorry I'm late,' she called after parking her car in the car park, which was not too busy early in the evening. 'Mum rang just as I was coming out. It was bad news, actually, so I had to stop and talk to her for a few minutes.' She was talking to Betty Ainsworth as she was taking off her jacket in the family room behind the bar.

'Don't rush,' said Betty. 'I can see you're upset, and we're not busy at the moment. Sit down and tell me about it. Has . . . has someone died?'

Helen sat down on the settee and Betty sat beside her. 'Yes,' answered Helen. 'My Aunt

4

Alice has died, very suddenly; it was a heart attack. She's my great-aunt, actually, my mother's aunt, but I've been very close to her, especially these last few years. She had a hip replacement about three years ago, and I went over to Yorkshire to look after her for a while. I was between jobs at the time, and it seemed to be the obvious solution for me to go and stay there. She insisted that she should pay me, because she would have needed a carer otherwise. And it worked very well. I was sorry, in a way, to leave Yorkshire to come back home, but we've been in close contact ever since.'

'You say this happened suddenly? She hadn't been ill?'

'Apparently not. She recovered well after the hip operation. She lived on her own, but she was very independent and very fit, so it's a tremendous shock.'

'Whereabouts in Yorkshire did she live? I know it's a very big county.'

'She lives . . . lived . . . in a little village called Thornbeck, on the road between Pickering and Scarborough. She'd lived in Yorkshire since the early fifties, a few years before I was born. It was a bit of a mystery why she left Blackpool. No one seems to want to talk about it. My mother never says much, but maybe she doesn't know much about it. Aunt Alice made a life for herself over there. She had her own little cottage that she rented at first and then managed to buy . . . '

Helen's reminiscences were cut short when Jeff Ainsworth, the landlord, put his head round the door. 'We're getting busy out here. We could do with a hand when you two have finished your nattering,' he said, but with a grin on his face.

'Oh . . . I'm sorry, Jeff,' said Helen, jumping up at once.

'Helen has suffered a bereavement,' said Betty quietly. 'An aunt she was very fond of.'

'I didn't realize,' said Jeff. 'Take your time, of course, Helen. Betty and I can cope; Bob's gone down to the cellar but he won't be long. Just come when you're ready.'

'I'm OK,' said Helen. 'Really I am. Anyway, I'll be better keeping busy tonight instead of sitting around and moping.'

And, indeed, she was busy throughout the evening, serving drinks and simple bar snacks — crisps, sandwiches, meat pies and sausage rolls. No cooked meals here; it was a small, homely place, popular mainly with the locals, and didn't try to compete with the larger establishments that were opening up in the area.

Helen's memories of her great-aunt returned, however, after she had driven home at eleven o'clock that blustery March evening.

She parked her car in its usual spot on the road outside the house. The occupants of the upstairs flat, who had been in residence there longer, had the use of the garage. Helen didn't mind; it was easier for a quick getaway in the mornings.

Her flat was, for the moment, all she could wish for, comprising a living room that was quite spacious, a bedroom, small kitchen and bathroom. It was fully furnished, albeit in a mish-mash of styles, some dating from the thirties and others

6

in the so-called 'contemporary' style that had been popular in the fifties, when the whole idea of furnishing was changing drastically after the stringencies of the wartime period. Helen had added her own personal touches — bright cushions and rugs and covers, pictures and photos, her CD player and the piano from home, as she was the only one who played.

Her accommodation was very desirable compared with many of the flats that were on offer. The rent was not cheap but she was doing well in the career that she had not exactly chosen, but in which she had found herself. She was quite careful, though not miserly with money, and the extra she was earning with her evening job was being put to one side for the time when she found a place of her own to buy.

Helen made a cup of Horlicks, which she usually found helped her get to sleep. She sat up in bed to drink it and to read the latest Inspector Wexford book by Ruth Rendell. But this time the intricacies of the plot failed to wholly engage her mind. She put it to one side and switched off the bedside lamp, then tried to compose herself for sleep.

She was trying to accept that Aunt Alice was no longer there, but it was hard to believe that such a lively and young-looking person could so suddenly be gone. Memories of her were poignant. A busy and active little lady, no more than five foot two in height, with hair that had once been golden, faded to an attractive ash blonde, and bright blue eyes that had lost none of their sparkle.

Helen knew that the Fletcher family had once lived in Yorkshire, in the mill city of Bradford, but had moved to Blackpool in 1921. It remained a mystery as to why Alice had returned there in the early fifties . . .

★   ★   ★

Alice was the younger daughter of Albert and Ada Fletcher. Her sister Elizabeth, always known as Lizzie, was Helen's grandmother. Albert had served in the trenches in the First World War and, to Ada's relief and some surprise, had returned. Alice was born in 1919, but Albert had suffered as a result of poison gas and had died in 1920, a victim of the Spanish flu epidemic that was sweeping through the country. Ada was left a widow with one-year-old Alice, and Lizzie, who was then eight years old.

Ada was not rich, but she was not poverty-stricken either. She and Albert had both worked for several years in one of the many woollen mills and had not married until they were in their mid-twenties. With the help of her parents, and with the money she had managed to save, Ada had decided to start a new life for herself and her daughters.

Blackpool was becoming known as the leading seaside resort in the north of England. Ada remembered the happy holidays she had spent there as a child, and so she decided to try her hand as a seaside landlady, as many more women were doing at the time.

She scraped together enough for a deposit on

a three-storey house in the part of Blackpool known as North Shore. She worked hard, putting in long hours at the boarding house, and she expected her daughters to do the same. When they left school at fourteen, Lizzie in 1926 and Alice in 1933, they both worked alongside their mother, helping with the cooking and cleaning, and serving at the dining tables. As it was a family concern there was no need, in Ada's opinion, to employ extra staff, except on rare occasions. Each year, before the start of the holiday season, around Easter time, the house would be given a good spring clean, from top to bottom, and at that time Ada would agree to employ a woman to help with the heavier duties of scrubbing and polishing and washing the paintwork.

Ada did not consider that her girls might want to pursue a career — or at least an occupation — outside of the boarding house as some of their school friends, whose parents were not in the holiday business, were able to do. It was true, though, that many young women found themselves in the same position as Lizzie and Alice, working for a small wage that amounted to scarcely more than pocket money. After all, they had their bed and board, and it was Ada's view that that was sufficient.

Helen's memories of Ada, her great-grandmother, were very vague. She had died in 1961 at the age of seventy-five, when Helen was four years old. She had seemed, in hindsight, to be a very old lady compared with Helen's grandmother, Lizzie, who was now seventy-eight, a spry and energetic woman. But Grandma Ada, of course, had been born in the last century when Queen Victoria was on the throne, and the ideas and opinions of that generation had remained with her.

She had apparently ruled her two daughters with a rod of iron. She had been unable, however, to prevent Lizzie from marrying in 1933 when she was twenty-one. She had 'come of age' and no longer needed parental permission. Lizzie had married Norman Weaver, a local lad who attended the church where the Fletcher family occasionally worshipped. It was understood, though, that Lizzie would continue to work for her mother, and she and Norman would have their own private rooms in the boarding house. It was convenient, also, that Lizzie's new husband was such a handyman. He was a painter and decorator by trade, and he soon found himself painting and wallpapering the boarding house bedrooms during the winter. But Ada, parsimonious though she could be, had to agree that he should receive the appropriate payment.

It was in one of the newly decorated bedrooms that Megan, Helen's mother, was born in 1934. They all lived there throughout the Second World War; then in 1946 Ada finally decided that she had been a seaside landlady for long enough. She had not bargained for the houseful of RAF recruits that had been billeted there during the war years, and she did not have the heart to build up the holiday trade again. Her decision was a great relief to Lizzie as well. She was still subject to her mother's demands and ideas, although Norman made sure that his mother-in-law did not always get her own way.

They were all in agreement, though, about the house that they bought in Bispham, in a residential area, a few miles further north of their present home. The semi-detached house was only a few minutes' walk from the sea, something that Ada had insisted on. She had lived close to the sea all the time she had been in Blackpool but had hardly ever had time to walk along the promenade. She took a stroll there, along the cliffs when it was not too breezy, every day until she died in 1961 following an attack of flu and bronchitis.

And so Lizzie and Norman were on their own at last. Megan was now married to Arthur Burnside and they had their own semi-detached house in the same area; not too far away but, on the other hand, not too near, as Arthur remarked to Megan.

Megan was the only daughter — the only child, in fact — of Lizzie and Norman and, as such, had felt constricted at times and not allowed the same freedom as some of her school friends. Lizzie had been brought up by a mother who was born in the Victorian era and who had never lost her strait-laced outlook on life. And neither, deep down, had Lizzie. She disapproved of the goings-on of teenagers, as the youngsters of the day were being called. Lizzie was aware, too, that there was so much more she could have done, other choices she could have made, if she had not been restricted to a life spent working in a boarding house.

She was determined that Megan should have choices in her life that she herself had been denied. Megan attended the girls' grammar school which was in itself regarded as a great achievement by her parents. Lizzie would have loved her only daughter to go to college or university and become a teacher or solicitor or something with 'letters to her name', but Megan resisted all attempts to persuade her to do so. Instead she left school at sixteen and started work in a bookshop in the town centre.

Reading, above all else, was her favourite pastime and this job suited her perfectly. She was promoted in a year or two from a junior assistant to a senior one and then to chief buyer. She continued in this position until 1957 when her daughter, Helen, was born and then, three years later, her son, Peter.

She had married Arthur Burnside in 1955. He was a teacher of English at a local secondary modern school and had often visited the book-shop to buy books for what was his consuming interest as well as his job. Lizzie consoled herself that even though her daughter had not become a teacher herself, she had married one.

When Megan returned to work after both their children had started school it was not to a bookshop but to a market stall. Her great friend Anne, whom she had known since their school-days, had told her that there was a good profit to be made from second-hand books. And so, working together, they had rented a stall in a town-centre market and started in a small way. Their business had developed over the years as more and more people discovered their stall. They accepted only books that were in a good condition. Some of them, indeed, seemed almost as good as new and could be sold at a price that compared favourably with brand-new books. Others that were dog-eared or slightly soiled were sold at a bargain price.

They expanded as time went on and now sold greetings cards and items of stationery. Their hours were flexible to fit in with their domestic arrangements, and the two part-time women would fit in as and when they were required.

Megan, too, had been shocked to hear of her Aunt Alice's death on that March day in 1990. She had known that Helen would be distressed at the news; she had been surprised but pleased at how her daughter and her aunt had become so close in recent years. It was a closeness that Megan had never really felt towards her aunt. Alice had left Blackpool to make a new home in Yorkshire and a new life for herself in the early 1950s. Megan had never known why, although she had guessed — or at least half guessed — at the reason.

Her own mother, Lizzie, had been very close-lipped about her sister's movements. They had visited Aunt Alice in her new home a few times each year, but it was as though Lizzie had felt obliged to do so. Megan was always aware of a certain lack of warmth between her mother and her aunt. She knew there had also been animosity between her aunt and her grand-mother, Ada, although this had mellowed somewhat by the time the old lady died.

Alice had been friendly enough towards Megan, who was only fifteen years her junior; but it was Helen, and later Peter, who had captured Alice's interest and affection, Helen more so than her brother.

Megan reflected now, as she prepared to make the journey to Yorkshire the following day, that Helen would be grieving sorely at her great-aunt's death, whereas Lizzie seemed to be taking the news of her sister's demise in her stride, as was her way. When Megan's father had died a few years ago Lizzie had coped with it all in her usual matter-of-fact manner. She now lived alone, facing life stoically in the way she had learned from her mother.

2

Helen received a phone call from her mother to say that she and Lizzie were now settled in Aunt Alice's cottage and would stay there for the next week or so, possibly longer. They had been in touch with Alice's solicitor and were making arrangements, along with the funeral director and the vicar of the local church, for the funeral.

Helen had been to see how her father was coping in her mother's absence.

'Oh, you know me, love, I'm fine,' said Arthur Burnside. 'I can manage on my own; cook myself a meal an' all that. Maybe not as well as your mum, but I'm coping. I'm what you might call a modern man. What about you, though? I know Alice's death has come as a shock to you, hasn't it?'

'Yes, it has,' said Helen, 'but I'm coming to terms with it now. I came to know her pretty well when I stayed with her, the time she had her hip operation. We chatted quite a lot about the time when she was a girl, living in the boarding house. But I felt there were certain things she was secretive about. And I didn't pry; she had a perfect right to keep things to herself if that was what she wanted. She had made a lot of friends in the village and she was involved with the local church. She seemed to be very well liked there; there was always someone popping round to see her.'

They heard a few days later that the funeral was planned for the Wednesday of the following week; a service and burial at the church, followed by a lunch for those who wished to attend at one of the village inns.

'I shall get a day off school,' said Arthur. 'Possibly two days, so I will drive you there if you like. There's no need for us to take both cars. We'll set off early on Wednesday morning; the drive takes about three hours. And maybe we'll stay overnight if we don't feel like coming back the same day. Your mum and gran are staying at Alice's cottage, but I'm sure there'll be room for us to squeeze in there as well.'

'Peter and Linda will be travelling from Skipton, which is a good deal nearer,' said Helen, 'so they'll go back the same day. They're leaving the children with a neighbour.'

Helen's brother, Peter, had been transferred to Skipton by the bank he worked for, and there he had met and married Linda. He was now aged thirty, and they had two children, a boy and a girl aged five and three respectively. Helen took no notice when people made comments that her brother was leaving her far behind. She would get married when — and if — she found the right man.

Helen dressed with care on the morning of the funeral, having risen at seven o'clock to make sure she was ready when her father came for her. She knew there was a new idea regarding a funeral service; to regard it as a celebration of the life of the deceased person rather than being sombre and sad. Sometimes the person left instructions stating they wanted their friends and family members to avoid dark clothes, but as far as she knew her aunt had not made any plans for her funeral. She had probably assumed that she would be around for several more years.

Helen knew, though, that she must stick to the more conventional dress. Her gran would be horrified if she turned up in the sort of clothes that she preferred — bright pink or red or turquoise; colours which she felt enhanced her pale complexion and fairish hair, to which she added golden highlights from time to time. She wore short skirts too, but not miniskirts, which were no longer fashionable.

She considered that the just-above-the-knee-length navy blue skirt and jacket she sometimes wore at the office would be acceptable; she did not possess any black clothes at all. With the suit she wore a white T-shirt top, and she would don a soft navy beret if it proved necessary to wear a hat in church.

Her father, too, was soberly dressed in his best charcoal-grey suit, rather than the casual attire of sports jacket and grey trousers that he wore at school.

They were on the road soon after eight o'clock, and after leaving Lancashire they took the road over Blubberhouses moor, and then via Thirsk and Helmsley to the expanse of moorland known as Sutton Bank. It was a route that Helen had taken many times before, and she loved the wild open scenery and the vastness of the sky, but this time the journey was tinged with sadness.

They arrived soon after eleven and made their

way to Alice's cottage in the centre of Thornbeck. There was a tiny stream running through the village, little more than a culvert, and the cottage was in a row of similar ones overlooking the stream. There was a minuscule front garden where crocuses were blooming and the short path led to the green painted door with its shining brass handle and letter box.

Arthur parked near the village green — there was no room in front of the cottages — and Megan, who must have been looking out for them, opened the door at once.

Helen had prepared herself for the cottage to feel strange now her aunt was no longer there, but the place still felt warm and welcoming, as though some vestige of her presence remained.

The family members gathered in the living room where a fire was burning in the grate. Alice had had central heating installed a few years ago, but a fire added warmth and cheer. Her black and white cat, Trixie, was sitting on the rug. She looked round and miaowed pitifully when she saw Helen, then went towards her and rubbed up against her legs. She remembered Helen from previous visits, when she had made a fuss of Alice's feline companion.

'She's missing Alice,' said Megan. 'She can't understand what's going on, and she keeps miaowing and looking at us so sadly. We'll have to find her a good home; perhaps one of Alice's friends might take her.'

'I'll take her home with me,' said Helen at once. 'She knows me and she'll soon settle down.'

'Well, that's a solution, I suppose,' said Megan. 'I know Alice would want her to be well-cared-for.'

Helen's brother, Peter, and his lively young wife, Linda, five years his junior, had already arrived. It was good to see them again despite the sad circumstances. Peter, like his father, was soberly dressed in a grey suit. Linda, however, was wearing a deep-red trouser suit. Helen guessed that their gran would disapprove both of the colour and of the trousers. She was of the generation that believed men should wear the trousers and women should keep to ladylike skirts. Land girls had worn trousers during the war, but Lizzie disliked the modern trend which regarded them as stylish and fashionable garments for women.

Linda, however, did have a tiny black feather hat perched on top of her blonde hair, so maybe that was her way of conforming to tradition.

Lizzie was dressed entirely in dark clothing. She had taken off her heavy black coat with the fur collar, and her dress was grey with white edging to the collar and cuffs, and pearl buttons down the front of the bodice. It was quite stylish, but not very flattering to Lizzie's pale complexion and her iron-grey hair, which was almost covered by her black felt hat.

Helen thought that her mother looked very smart, as she always did. Megan's suit consisted of a black and white hounds-tooth jacket and a knee-length black skirt. It had not been bought especially for the funeral — Helen had seen it several times before — but it was very suitable for the occasion, worn with a pale lilac jumper. Megan's mid-brown hair was greying now at the temples, but she disguised it with a coppery tint.

'You look very smart, Mum,' Helen told her. 'Will you be wearing a hat?' she asked in an undertone.

'Yes, I thought it would be best to do so,' she replied, 'or else your gran will be telling me off. I've brought a mauve beret that will match my jumper. You look very nice yourself, love. It's a sad day, though, isn't it?'

'Yes, very sad. You arranged for the flowers, did you?'

'Yes, a long wreath of lilies and carnations and some spring flowers from you and Dad and me. Your gran wanted one of her own. And Peter and Linda had ordered theirs locally. There'll no doubt be others as well. Alice was very well liked by the people here. I always think it's a shame how the flowers are left to wither on the grave, but at least it shows that people loved her and will remember her.'

The funeral cars arrived just before midday for the short journey to St Michael's parish church opposite the village green. Helen, though trying to be brave, was unable to swallow for the lump in her throat, and she felt tears welling up in her eyes as she looked at the coffin. It was covered with a mass of flowers, pink, yellow, white, mauve and deep purple. There were wreaths, large and small, at the side as well, tributes of love and respect for a dear friend.

There was room for all six family members in the large saloon car. When they arrived at the church there was a crowd of people waiting there who had come in their own cars or walked; the village of Thornbeck, though well-populated, was also quite well contained.

The vicar shook hands with them, adding a quiet word of condolence to Helen, whom he remembered from her previous visits, especially from the time she had cared for her aunt.

The Reverend Martin Crosby, a middle-aged man with a wife and grown-up family, had been in the parish for many years, and had known Alice as well as he knew many of his parishioners.

He led the procession of mourners into the church that had served the community since before the time of the Reformation. It was a squat grey stone building with a tower and its own graveyard, well-tended by the verger and not overgrown as were so many country churchyards. Crocuses and early flowering daffodils fringed the path, although the tall trees were not yet showing much sign of greenery.

The coffin was carried by four men of the congregation, followed by the family and the rest of the mourners, Alice's closest friends and other acquaintances who had known her from her good work in the parish.

Lizzie and Megan had planned the service — insisting that they would like it to be a simple one as Alice would not have wanted a lot of fuss. The vicar had played his part too; he knew which were Alice's favourite hymns and he also chose the appropriate bible readings. Lizzie and Megan had realized that he knew far more about

Alice than they did.

It was the vicar who gave the eulogy, saying how Alice had been born in Yorkshire but the family had moved to Blackpool when she was a very young child. She had lived there for many years, being a worker in the holiday trade for which Blackpool was famous. Then, in the fifties, she had returned to Yorkshire, to her roots and to where, he guessed, her heart had always been.

He spoke of the many friends she had made over the years in the village and the church community, of her work as a member of the church council and as an honorary member of the Mothers' Union, as she had had no children of her own. She had worked hard at coffee mornings and at occasions such the spring and Christmas fairs, and would be sorely missed for her talent at flower arranging and as a member of the church choir.

Helen, glancing round surreptitiously, noted that the church was tastefully adorned with floral displays. Vases of spring flowers, lilies, tulips and daffodils with sprigs of pussy willow stood on the altar — which the vicar preferred to call the Communion table, his churchmanship being low rather than high — and on the font and window ledges. Despite the chill emanating from the stone walls and floor, there was an air of comfort and cheer from the russet-toned oaken pulpit and the pews with their flat cushions and kneelers of rich red. The midday sun, shining through the stained-glass windows, cast a dappled light on the heads of the congregation.

Throughout the service, though, Helen was

constantly aware of the coffin standing forlornly in the chancel, covered with its mass of flowers, and the realization kept coming back to her that she would never see her aunt again.

They rose to sing the last hymn, 'In Heavenly Love Abiding', before the vicar led the mourners, following behind the coffin, to the graveside. It was a poignant moment as the coffin was lowered into the ground and the family members symbolically scattered earth on the top. Helen felt her tears brimming again as the vicar spoke of the sure and certain hope of the Resurrection. She reflected that her aunt was now at peace, which was what people always said on such an occasion, although in her view it was many years too soon.

It was only a few minutes' drive or walk to the Cherry Tree, the inn where the buffet lunch was to be held, on the other side of the village green. The vicar had issued an invitation to anyone who wished to do so to gather there for an informal lunch.

Helen had visited the Cherry Tree before. She and her aunt had sometimes had lunch there, and she recalled that she had been there with Alex, and her aunt, when they had driven over to see Alice just before last Christmas. Helen had broken her resolve and had phoned to tell Alex of Aunt Alice's death. She felt that she should do so because he had liked her aunt, and she had also wondered whether he might see it as an opportunity for him to suggest that they might try again. But although he had been sympathetic and genuinely sorry at the news, he had not made any overtures about them getting back together. Since then her mind had been occupied with other matters, and thoughts of Alex had receded to the back of her mind. In fact, she now believed that she might be well and truly over him.

The funeral party had been given a private room at the Cherry Tree. It was a typical, popular country inn with a low ceiling and oaken beams, and uneven stone floors covered in part by brightly coloured rugs, which one had to be careful not to trip over.

A cheerful fire burned in the open hearth; the late March day was cold although it was now officially springtime. The buffet lunch, consisting of soup and sandwiches, pork pies and sausage rolls, with trifle or apple pie to follow, was laid out on a long table for everyone to help themselves.

Helen looked around and guessed there were up to thirty people there. The six tables, covered with red and white checked cloths, each held six. Some tables were full and at others there were three or four people. She had not been to many funerals, only those of three of her grandparents — Lizzie was the only one left now — and she felt as she always did at such occasions. The gathering inevitably became a time for chatting with friends, some that you may not have seen for a while; then there would be camaraderie and laughter as people relaxed. Helen thought it seemed so ironic that the main person, the reason why they were all there, was missing. She reflected that her aunt would have loved such a gathering of friends.

When they had finished the very satisfactory meal they circulated, talking to first one group and then another. There were several whom Helen knew from her previous visits. The vicar, who preferred, informally, to be called Martin, and his wife, Patricia, had been good friends of Alice. Nora and Bill, Alice's next-door neighbours, a couple around the same age as her, said what a lovely, friendly neighbour she had been. They had looked after Trixie, her cat, until Lizzie and Megan had arrived, and were anxious to know what would happen to her now. Helen said that she would take her back to Blackpool and hoped that she would settle down there.

She met the owners of the row of shops adjacent to the village green, where Alice had done her weekly shopping. When Alice had first come to live in Thornbeck, she had worked at the village store that had sold groceries and almost everything else. It had also been the village post office. Alice had worked there as an assistant along with the owners, Clive and Edith Meadows. When Clive had died in his fifties, from the bronchitis from which he had long suffered, Alice had gone into partnership with Edith, and they worked there until they both retired in their early sixties. The store had been taken over by a consortium and was now a busy Spar shop.

Alice and Edith had remained close friends and had sometimes gone away on holidays together. Edith was another person who would miss her very much.

There were several others from the community who offered their condolences to Helen,
whom they had met before, and to Lizzie and
Megan.

Robert and Pamela Kershaw were a couple in
their late forties with whom Alice had been
friendly for many years. They ran a market
garden just outside the village. She had been a
babysitter for them when their children were
small, until the two of them became teenagers.
She had become a sort of unofficial extra
grandma to James and Jennifer, who were now
both away at college.

'The children were very distressed to hear
about Alice's death,' Robert told Helen. 'They
would have been here today if it were possible,
but Jennifer is doing her teaching practice and
James is taking exams.'

'We've been very sad too,' said Pamela. 'I
know she had turned seventy, but that's not very
old these days, is it?'

'And I shall miss my trips over here,' said
Helen. 'It's become a home from home to me. I
love Yorkshire, just as my aunt did.'

Megan came over just then to speak to Helen.
'Excuse me interrupting,' she said. 'Mr Fothergill
wants to know when it will be convenient for us
to go and see him, about Alice's will, you know?'

Helen said goodbye to Robert and Pamela and
rejoined her family. Mr Fothergill was Alice's
solicitor whose premises were in Pickering, the
nearest town of any size. They agreed to meet
there the following morning at nine thirty. Peter
and Linda would not be there as they were

travelling back home to Skipton after the funeral, but it was agreed that Lizzie, Megan, Arthur and Helen would attend.

3

Helen had not even thought about what her Aunt Alice's will would contain. It seemed wrong, somehow, to think about Alice's money and her worldly goods being left to someone else. Why could she not have been spared a few more years to enjoy them herself? But this was the way of it; Aunt Alice's last will and testament had to be discussed with the family. Helen knew, though, that if someone died without leaving a will — intestate, she thought it was called — it could cause no end of trouble. Everything would most likely go to the next of kin, which in Alice's case was her elder sister, Lizzie.

It was doubtful that Alice would have left a great deal of money, although there was her house, of course. Helen had gathered, from overhearing conversations over the years, that when her great-grandma Ada had died the money she left had been divided between her two daughters, Lizzie and Alice. There had been a rift of some sort in the family, but Ada had done the right thing in making sure that Alice was left the same amount of money as Lizzie. The house where Ada had lived with Lizzie and Norman was in Ada's name, bought following the sale of the boarding house, and it was only right that it should go to Lizzie, as it was her home.

Mr John Fothergill was the son of the practice

Fothergill and Son. Mr Cuthbert, his father, was almost eighty years of age now but liked to keep his eagle eye on everything, and he came into the office a few mornings or afternoons each week.

It was Mr John, however, who was in charge on that morning at the end of March. The office was on the main street of Pickering on the second floor of the building up flights of steep stairs. Helen was surprised at how well her gran coped with the stairs. She was a little out of breath when she reached the top, which was only to be expected, but so were the rest of them. Megan rang the bell and the secretary, a grey-haired, efficient-looking woman of fifty or so, showed them into the office, then disappeared into her own domain next door.

It was a large, rather soulless room with brown paintwork, a rather worn brown and green carpet and faded yellowish wallpaper, with sepia prints of Yorkshire scenes on the walls.

Mr Fothergill was seated behind an enormous desk and stood up as they entered, shaking hands with them all. He invited them to sit on the four leather chairs prepared in readiness. Helen thought he looked a typical solicitor although, in truth, she had not met any, only read about them in books. He seemed like a character out of Dickens, Mr Wemmick, perhaps. He wore a grey pinstripe suit, a white shirt with a stiff collar and a black tie. His shrewd grey eyes looked out from behind rimless spectacles with gold frames. He was balding on top and he, too, looked to be in his mid-fifties. When he smiled he looked far less stern and intimidating.

29

'My father and I were sad to hear of your loss,' he said, 'and surprised, too. Alice was a sprightly lady, and we had the pleasure of dealing with her affairs for many years, my father at first and now myself.'

He had all of the papers ready in front of him. 'It is all fairly straightforward,' he said. 'Miss Fletcher was not a wealthy woman; on the other hand she was careful and had made a couple of rather good investments, at our advice. So, all told, the sum should amount to something in the region of ten thousand pounds, maybe a little more.'

'Then there will be the sale of the house and the contents?' questioned Lizzie, which Helen thought was a little premature.

'I will be coming to that later,' said Mr Fothergill, looking over the top of his glasses at Lizzie, a hint of a smile on his lips.

'So . . . there are a couple of bequests.' He went on to read: 'To St Michael's Church, the sum of five hundred pounds; and five hundred pounds each to Jennifer and James Kershaw, to be held in trust until they reach the age of twenty-one. The remainder to be divided equally between my sister, Elizabeth Weaver, my niece, Megan Burnside, my great-niece, Helen Burnside, and my great-nephew, Peter Burnside.' Mr Fothergill took a deep breath before he went on. 'My house, number eight Bluebell Cottages, and the contents therein I leave to my dear great-niece, Helen, in recognition of her loving care for me and the lasting friendship we have enjoyed.'

There were gasps of surprise, possibly the loudest one from Helen herself. She also heard a 'tut' from her gran. A scarcely audible one, but a sign of displeasure nonetheless. Helen could tell from the expression on the older woman's face that she had not imagined it.

'Well, I can't believe it!' said Lizzie, shaking her head.

'Why not, Mother?' retorted Megan. Then looking fondly towards her daughter, she said, 'It's no more than you deserve, love.'

'Hear hear,' echoed her father. 'You've been very good to your aunt, and I know you wouldn't have expected this.'

'I certainly didn't,' said Helen. 'I can't quite believe it myself.'

'Well, you'll have all the trouble of selling it, won't you?' said her grandmother. 'And I shouldn't think that will be easy. I've always thought it must be damp with that stream right outside the door.'

'Of course it isn't damp, Gran,' said Helen. 'It's only a culvert; it's so shallow it's not even fenced off. No one could drown in it. You could hardly get your feet wet.'

Lizzie sniffed. 'Of course, you know best, don't you? You always do.'

Helen was astonished at her gran's reaction. It was so unlike her, but she knew there was something that had happened years ago that had caused a bitter resentment between the sisters, although she had thought it might have been forgotten by now.

The atmosphere in the room had changed.

31

There was an uncomfortable feeling and a few moments' silence as Megan looked daggers at her mother.

'Could we proceed, please?' said Mr Fothergill, seemingly the least fazed of them all. He had no doubt experienced similar reactions before at the reading of a will.

'Miss Fletcher was quite certain that this was what she wished,' he said with a brief smile at Helen. 'She was very fond of you, my dear, and she said that as she had no children of her own — or grandchildren, of course — she looked on you as the granddaughter she had never had. I know the sale of the property might not be easy, with you living so far away, but I can put you in touch with an excellent estate agency — there is one a few doors away from here — and they will be able to deal with it all for you.'

'Thank you,' said Helen. She gave a little smile. 'As a matter of fact, I work for an estate agency myself, so I doubt that anyone could pull the wool over my eyes.'

'Well, fancy that!' said Mr Fothergill. 'I had no idea. As you say, you will know exactly what is going on.' He straightened the papers in front of him. 'There is still some work for us to do, collating the various amounts in bank accounts and bonds. We will send the four of you the cheques in due course. You will inform Mr Peter Burnside of his legacy, won't you? And we will inform the vicar of St Michael's Church of the bequest, and also Jennifer and James Kershaw.'

'And who are they when they're at home?' asked Lizzie.

Megan cast another exasperated glance at her mother, while Mr Fothergill, ignoring her rudeness, answered Lizzie's question.

'Jennifer and James are the children of Robert and Pamela Kershaw. They — the parents, I mean — run a market garden just outside the village. I know your sister has been friendly with this family. Indeed, she had many such friends in the village, but she could not leave bequests to them all. I believe this family were rather special to her.'

'First I've heard of them,' remarked Lizzie.

'Well, I know them, Gran,' said Helen. 'Robert and Pamela sing in the church choir, as Aunt Alice did, and I think that was how she came to know them. Their daughter, Jennifer, is at teacher training college in her final year, and James is in his first year at university. Aunt Alice used to babysit for them when they were little.'

'Yes . . . ' Mr Fothergill took up the story. 'Robert and Pamela Kershaw no longer have any close relatives nearby, and so your sister offered to look after the children if they wished to go out for the evening — babysit, as they call it.'

'And I suppose Aunt Alice became quite close to them,' said Helen. 'Another instance, perhaps, of the grandchildren she didn't have. As she seemed to have thought of me,' she added quietly.

'Quite so,' said Mr Fothergill, straightening his papers again. 'I think that concludes the business, unless you have any questions?'

Megan looked at her mother, who shook her head. Megan spoke for them all. 'No, I don't think so, Mr Fothergill. It all seems very straightforward. Thank you for all your trouble, and for explaining it so clearly.'

He nodded a trifle curtly. 'My pleasure and, once again, I am sorry for your loss.' He shook hands with them all and saw them off the premises.

'Well, we'd best get back and have a cup of tea before we set off for Blackpool,' said Lizzie. 'I think they could at least have made us a cup of tea.'

'It was just a business meeting, Mother,' said Megan. 'Perhaps they don't go in for such niceties.'

'Well, I'm only saying it would have been nice,' countered Lizzie. 'And no doubt he'll be sending us his bill.'

'Along with our bequests,' said Arthur. 'Well, not for me, but then I wouldn't expect it. But we've never argued about money, have we, Megan? It's share and share alike in our house. I must say I'm very pleased at what Alice has done for our Helen. She's a good lass and she deserves it.'

'Thank you, Dad,' said Helen.

They spoke very little after that until they were back in Thornbeck.

'Now, are you going to invite us into your house, Helen?' said Lizzie as they walked up the path, Arthur having parked the car on the other side of the stream.

'I think Mum has the key,' replied Helen quietly.

'Come along,' said Megan breezily. 'I'll put the

34

kettle on, and I'll make us some sandwiches before we set off. Sit down, Mother. Helen and I will see to everything.'

'Take no notice of your gran,' she said as they busied themselves in the kitchen. 'She'll get over it. I really don't know what she's so resentful about. I know she's the next of kin, but Alice has done what she thought was right, and your dad and I agree, and I'm sure Peter will as well.'

'I don't want it to cause any trouble,' said Helen, 'and I do appreciate what Aunt Alice has done. I'm just . . . flabber-gasted; it's incredible.'

They ate a quick snack lunch from plates on their knees. Trixie the cat, who had come in with them when they returned, purred as she rubbed against Helen's legs.

'Did you say you were taking the cat back with you?' asked Lizzie, who was behaving a little more graciously now. 'She seems to like you, doesn't she?'

'Yes, that's what I said,' replied Helen, a little distractedly.

'Did Alice have a cat basket to carry her in?'

'Yes, she had a sort of carrier thing to put her in when she went to the vet. It's under the stairs where she kept her Hoover.'

'And I dare say you'll have to come back here before long, won't you, to see about selling the house?' Lizzie went on.

'Er . . . I'm not going to sell it, Gran,' said Helen.

'Do you mean you're going to let it out to folk?' said Lizzie. It seemed as though she was trying to make up for her fit of pique. 'It can be a load of trouble, you know, having tenants.'

'No, Gran, I'm not going to let it either,' said Helen. She paused for a moment, then she smiled at them all. 'I'm going to live here.'

'What?' exclaimed her grandmother. 'Why on earth would you want to live here? You live in Blackpool.'

'Well, this is a surprise,' said her mother, rather more reasonably. 'You need to think about it carefully, love. You've got a good job in Blackpool, and you're doing well there.'

'I work at an estate agency,' said Helen. 'I know I'm doing well, but it's not an unusual sort of job. There are estate agencies all over; probably a few more in Pickering as well as the one Mr Fothergill mentioned. And there'll be plenty in Scarborough — that's not too far away. I shouldn't have much difficulty in finding another job.'

'Would you really like to come and live here?' asked her father. He sounded less surprised and more able to understand what his daughter was saying. 'I agree that you would get another job; you're very experienced, but it would be a big step to take.'

'Most of your family are in Blackpool,' said her mother. 'Your aunt and uncle and cousins on your dad's side, as well as us.' Although Megan was an only child, Arthur had a sister and a brother. 'And you have so many friends there.'

'And what about that boyfriend of yours?' said her grandmother. 'Alex . . . isn't it?'

'Oh, that's all over, Gran,' said Helen. 'We're not seeing each other now. We decided it would be better if we called it a day.'

'Goodness me!' said Lizzie. 'I don't know! How many young men are you going to meet before you make up your mind! All this chopping and changing!'

Helen exchanged a glance and a half smile with her mother. Megan raised her eyebrows but neither of them spoke. Helen was pleased that her mum — and her dad — were quite modern parents.

'It wasn't like that in our day,' Lizzie went on. 'You met a nice young man, then you got engaged, and married after a year or two. Then you made the best of it. You didn't change your mind if things started to go wrong.'

Helen knew that her gran would disapprove most strongly if she knew about certain things. Helen had not actually lived with Alex, nor with another couple of young men she had been friendly with before him. But Alex had stayed the night at her flat a few times, just as she had stayed at his place on a few occasions. Her mum seemed to know but had made no comment, but Gran would be horrified.

Helen said, in answer to her gran's remarks, 'Well, maybe I want to be very sure, Gran, before I get married, then there would be less chance of it going wrong. And as for coming to live here, I was intending to buy a place of my own quite soon instead of renting, and now . . . I don't need to look any further. I always liked this cottage, and I like the village and the countryside round here.'

'I agree that there's nowt wrong with

Yorkshire,' said Lizzie. 'I was born here — well, in Bradford — and so was Alice. But like your mum says, your family and friends are in Blackpool.'

'Well, it's not a million miles away, is it? Only a few hours' car journey. And Peter and Linda and the children are in Skipton, so I'll be able to see more of them.'

Megan looked at the clock on the mantelshelf. 'We'll have to be heading back soon if we want to get home before teatime. I'll cook us all a meal when we get back; you as well, Mother, and Helen, before you go home. There's some bacon and sausages in the fridge here that need using, and there's a fresh loaf and a fruit cake.' She laughed. 'I take it you're not moving in here now, Helen?'

'No, there'll be a lot to sort out first, and I'll have to work two weeks' notice . . . And I think I'd better leave Trixie here. There's no point in taking her to a new home, then bringing her back again. She's had enough upset, losing Aunt Alice. I'll just pop next door and ask Nora if she'll look after her for a couple of weeks until I come back . . . '

4

It was Easter time when Helen returned to Thornbeck; a preliminary visit to take stock of things before she went to live there. Daffodils as well as crocuses were now blooming in the cottage gardens, where soon there would be swathes of bluebells, after which the cottages were named.

The trees in the churchyard and in the gardens of the larger houses in the village were bursting into bud, showing early signs of their bright springtime green.

Helen's decision to move had caused a great deal of surprise and some concern, not only among her family members, but also with her friends and colleagues.

'Well, that's come out of the blue,' said Carl Pritchard, her boss at the estate agency. 'I had no idea you were thinking of making a move.'

'Neither had I,' said Helen. 'It has come out of the blue for me as well. I would have been looking for somewhere to buy sometime soon, as you know, but suddenly . . . there was Aunt Alice's cottage all ready and waiting for me.'

'But I thought you would want a self-contained flat or a small semi or terraced house, not a country cottage?'

'Yes, so I did, but when I found out that Aunt Alice had left it to me, I realized that that was the answer. I have a feeling that she would want me to live there.'

'Well, you will have a good reference from me, I can assure you, although we will be sorry to lose you.'

There had been much discussion as well with her parents who had her best interests at heart. Her grandmother was keeping quiet after her initial outburst.

'Well, you're certainly old enough to know your own mind,' said her father, 'and I suppose with you being in the business yourself you can tell if the place is structurally sound?'

'Yes, I'm sure there are no major problems,' Helen assured him. 'No damp, no woodworm, and the roof seems in good order. It's a bit old fashioned inside. I would want new kitchen fittings, and a new bathroom, eventually; but I've already got the money I've saved up to buy a property. I know I'm . . . very fortunate.'

Helen felt her eyes misting over again as she thought of her Aunt Alice's premature death. She would much rather have her aunt still there with them than be going to live in her empty house.

'We'll miss you such a lot,' said her mother. 'That goes without saying, but we know you'll keep in touch. As you say, it's not all that far for us to pop over for the day. We won't keep pestering you, though; you have your own life to live. No doubt you'll make new friends there . . . But you're involved in so many things here, aren't you? Your amateur operatic society, and your evening classes.'

'It's quite a lively community, Mum. I'm sure there'll be all sorts of things going on. I might join the church choir, if they'll have me! Aunt Alice was in the choir.'

'But you've never been much of a churchgoer, have you, not since you stopped going to Sunday school. Christmas and Easter, maybe, like your dad and me. Although you were confirmed, ages ago.'

'There's no reason why I shouldn't start going again though, is there, Mum? I used to go to church with Aunt Alice. She was singing in the choir, but she introduced me to some people in the congregation and I used to sit with them. They made me very welcome. And there may well be other things going on in the village or nearby, like the operatic society here.'

'Yes, I'm sure you'll be able to make a new life for yourself there,' said Megan. 'You've never been a shy sort of girl.'

'I'd like you to come over quite soon after I've settled in, Mum, to help me to sort out Aunt Alice's things — clothes and personal stuff. I'm dreading doing that; it'll be very upsetting. Most of it will have to go to charity shops, I suppose. But there may be some things that you would like, you and Gran. She had some nice china and cut glass, and pictures. All sorts of things that you could have to remember her by.'

'We'll see, love,' said Megan. 'I agree it's all very sad. There's a saying, isn't there, that you come into the world with nothing and you take nothing out. But we must try to look to the future. Alice wouldn't want us to be miserable . . . '

Helen worked her notice at the estate agency,

and then drove over to Yorkshire on Saturday morning. It was now mid-April and the next day would be Easter Sunday.

She had possession of her flat in Blackpool until the end of the month as there was still a good deal of sorting out to do. There were several large items of her own that would have to be transported by a removal firm: her piano; bed linen, towels and cushions; her CD player and music collection; music books and several shelves of novels and non-fiction books. Not to mention her clothing and a vast array of shoes and handbags.

She took a case full of clothing in the car and enough food to see her through the weekend. She wanted to spend a few days there to get the feel of the place — to get used to being there on her own without Aunt Alice — and to tell the people she knew that she would soon be living there. Unless word had already been passed round via the local grapevine — she had told Nora and Bill next door of her intention and had not told them to keep it to themselves. So it might well be that her appearance would not be too much of a surprise.

Helen felt that she would like to be part of the congregation at St Michael's Church for the Easter Sunday morning service. As her mother had reminded her, she had not been a regular churchgoer for several years, but she had a feeling that her aunt would want her to be there and it would be a good opportunity to establish herself as a member of the community.

Trixie jumped over the fence from next door

when she saw Helen in the garden. The cat rubbed herself against Helen's legs, miaowing, as if to say hello again. Nora had refused to take any payment for looking after her so Helen had bought her a big Easter egg filled with chocolates.

'She doesn't seem quite so lost now,' said Nora. 'She really missed your aunt at first, and it's best to keep her here in her own home. Cats are pretty independent creatures, though, aren't they? So long as there's somebody to feed them and make a fuss of them — when they feel like it — they're quite content.'

For her part, Helen was glad to have the cat's company. The cottage didn't feel so empty with her there.

The church bells rang out on Easter Sunday morning, and Helen entered the church a little timidly and sat in a pew near the back. One or two people noticed her and smiled and nodded. She knew the lady who came to sit next to her. Alice had introduced her as Madge Pearson, a fellow member of the Mothers' Union, about the same age as her aunt. Helen told Madge, in a quiet voice, that she would soon be coming to live in her aunt's house.

The woman smiled as if, perhaps, she already knew. 'I thought you might, my dear,' she said. 'We will all be pleased to have you with us.'

Many of the congregation were elderly, as was the norm in so many churches these days, but there were younger folk there as well, and Helen hoped there might be a group of some sort that she might join.

As the choir processed round the church at the start of the service, singing 'Christ the Lord is risen today', Robert Kershaw noticed her and smiled, and so did his wife who was with the women choristers. The service was joyous and uplifting. Helen knew all the hymns and sang along tunefully.

'You must join the choir,' Madge whispered to her. 'With a voice like that they'll be delighted to have you. I can't sing for toffee! I've a voice like a crow, but I like a nice hymn.'

Helen thought it was true that Madge was a little out of tune but what did that matter? The lady was worshipping God as well as she could, and He wouldn't mind how she sounded.

The sermon was about new life and looking towards the future with Jesus as our guide. Helen was pleased that she had been confirmed when she was in her teens, and so was able to take part in the service of Holy Communion. The wine was in a large silver chalice, wiped clean after each usage, which evoked a feeling of unity, rather than drinking from tiny individual glasses, as was the practice in some churches.

Coffee was served in the nearby church hall after the service.

'You'll come and join us, won't you?' said Madge, and Helen agreed that she would.

A team of ladies was busy in the kitchen, pouring out coffee behind the serving hatch. Not all of the members of the congregation stayed for coffee; some went home to see to their Sunday roasts. Several people came to say hello to Helen and to say how pleased they were to see her.

They stood or sat in little groups around the room, moving round to speak to first one and then another.

James and Jennifer Kershaw, home from college, said how nice it was that Helen was coming to live in Alice's cottage, and how surprised they had been to hear of her bequests to them.

Helen noticed that Jennifer and James referred to her aunt as Alice. But then, why not, she asked herself. Maybe they had called her Aunty Alice when they were small, but after all she was not a relation, just a courtesy aunt. And younger people calling older ones by their Christian names was becoming more the norm nowadays. Helen's father now called his mother-in-law Lizzie. Helen doubted that her gran really approved of this — she was a stickler for respect and the old-fashioned ways — but she had never voiced her disapproval.

Helen would never have dreamed of referring to her aunt as Alice, not to her face. She was 'Aunt Alice', or sometimes Aunty, as she had been when Helen was a little girl.

'I know she was very fond of you two,' she said to the brother and sister. 'She used to babysit for you, when you were little, didn't she? And I don't suppose she knew many children or teenagers. She could have had grandchildren, of course, at her age, but she had never married.'

'Why was that? Do you know?' asked Jennifer.

'No, I don't know,' replied Helen. 'No one in my family seems to know either, or they don't want to talk about it. I have wondered if she had a fiancé — or a young man at least — who was killed during the war. She was in her twenties during the war years, but I'm only surmising.'

'She was an attractive lady,' said Jennifer. 'Always smartly dressed, and she had her hair done regularly. And she took an interest in everything that was going on, not just in the village but all over the country. I remember she used to talk about politics with our dad.'

'I think Mr Jenkins who owns the antique shop was rather sweet on her,' said James. 'We know she used to go in the shop quite frequently, and she had a few nice pieces that she'd bought there; unless they were gifts, of course.'

'Now, now. Don't gossip, James,' said his sister. 'We don't know, do we? Alice could be very secretive when she wanted to be. Most likely they were just good friends. She had a lot of friends.'

Their mother, Pamela, came to join them. 'Would you like to come and have lunch with us, Helen?' she asked. 'There's a large chicken in the oven — seeing that it's Easter — and there'll be plenty for all of us. And the vegetables are all prepared to go in the microwave.'

'Thank you,' said Helen. 'It's very kind of you, but I won't, if you don't mind. Another time, perhaps? Madge — Mrs Pearson — asked me as well, but I said no. There are things I must see to while I'm here, and I'd like to make a start this afternoon. I've got a nice pork chop for lunch, so I won't go hungry.'

'When are you going back?' asked Robert, who had now joined the little group.

46

'Probably on Wednesday. I need to go into Pickering on Tuesday to see Mr Fothergill; the office will be closed tomorrow. And I want to scout around and see if there's any chance of me finding a job here.'

'There are three estate agencies that I know of in Pickering,' said Robert. 'I hope you find something suitable. And when are you moving here for good?'

'At the beginning of May, all being well. I'm looking forward to it.'

Helen found that she really was looking forward to the move. Everyone was departing now to go home and eat their Easter Sunday lunch, or dinner, as some of them called it. Helen walked back across the village green and opened the door of the cottage that was already starting to feel more like home.

She grilled her pork chop and made some chips and put a handful of frozen peas in a pan of boiling water. She dined at the small table in the kitchen, finishing off her meal with a good slice of the Simnel cake topped with marzipan that she had bought from a local bakery back home. All Helen's meals were simple ones, unless she was entertaining a guest — or several guests — as she had sometimes done in her flat.

Glancing round the kitchen she decided that she would, in due course, have it re-fitted. Aunt Alice already had a fitted kitchen with blue Formica cupboards and worktops, a small Formica-topped table and a stainless-steel sink. Helen fancied pinewood units and a table to match, with a couple of wheel-backed chairs to replace the not very comfortable stools. She would also like a more modern electric cooker to replace the rather ancient gas oven. She already had her own microwave oven which would come with the rest of her belongings — an essential item for when she was in a hurry, as she so often was.

The kitchen floor had at one time been stone flagged, as the cottage dated back to the early Victorian era. It was now covered with blue and yellow linoleum tiles. Helen thought she would like a kitchen carpet eventually for a little warmth, for this was the coldest room.

Fortunately the cottage had been modernized over the years. There was gas-fired central heating throughout, as well as a fireplace in the living room. The living area was the only downstairs room apart from the kitchen. An annexe which had been built on at the back housed a bath, washbasin and toilet. The WC had once been at the end of the garden, shared with a neighbour, and baths had been taken in a zinc tub in front of the living-room fire.

Upstairs there were two bedrooms, and a tiny box room which had been converted to hold an extra toilet for night use. Alice had always occupied the front bedroom overlooking the village green. The back bedroom, for guests, and where Helen had always slept, overlooked the back garden and beyond that a coppice and the gentle slope of a hill. This was altogether a gentler part of Yorkshire. The hillier, more rugged regions of the moors and the dales lay to the north, towards Cumbria, and to the west where the road over the Pennines led to Lancashire.

Helen had decided she would still use the back bedroom for herself. Alice had furnished it, most probably with Helen in mind, with furniture of light oak in a traditional style which never looked dated. There was a good-sized wardrobe, a chest of drawers, and a knee-hole dressing table. The carpet was leaf green, and the curtains had a floral pattern of yellow and green, very spring-like and toning with the yellow bedspread.

A set of bookshelves held a selection of paperbacks: mysteries by Agatha Christie and Ngaio Marsh; contemporary novels by Catherine Cookson and Maeve Binchy; and, surprisingly, a large number of Mills & Boon romances.

Helen smiled to herself, knowing how much her aunt had enjoyed losing herself in one of these escapist novels. She had confessed to Helen that she knew they were 'not real life', but she liked to imagine herself on the French Riviera, on a cruise ship on the Nile, or even in a sheik's tent in the desert.

'And it all turns out all right in the end,' Alice had once said. 'That's what I like: a happy ending. You don't always get that in real life . . . ' Her aunt had paused reflectively when she had made that remark. Helen had waited, not saying anything, but Alice had not elaborated. 'I know I'm not so young any more,' she had said, 'but I was, once upon a time . . . '

Helen unpacked the large suitcase she had brought, putting her clothes in the wardrobe and chest of drawers. The wardrobe contained some of Alice's summer clothing and shoes, which Helen carried into the front bedroom and placed on the double bed. She felt a lump in her throat again but she told herself to get on with the job. Her mother would come and help her eventually, in her more matter-of-fact way, to dispose of everything.

Alice's bedroom was furnished in a more old-fashioned style with some of the items she had acquired when she bought the property. Furniture of a highly polished reddish-brown wood, and a Lloyd Loom basket weave chair which matched the deep pink carpet and curtains. On top of the bed, over the pink bedspread, was a plump satin eiderdown of a dark raspberry shade, the sort that was seldom seen in these days of duvets, but Helen guessed it would be equally as warm.

There was a small fireplace, as there was also in Helen's room, a relic from the days when people lit fires in bedrooms. It was no longer used, of course, but it made an attractive feature with its floral tiles and an arrangement of dried flowers and leaves in the grate. On the small mantelshelf there was a Royal Doulton figurine of a lady in Edwardian dress — there were several other such pieces in the display cabinet downstairs — a small cut-glass vase, and a photo, black and white, of course — of Alice and her sister Lizzie taken many years ago. Helen had seen it before, but now she took it down to look at it more closely.

The two girls looked happy together, their arms around each other's shoulders and smiling into the camera. Helen guessed it might have been taken by one of the visitors to the boarding house; the striped awning to keep the sun off the paintwork was behind them. Alice was slim and what might now be called petite with straight fair hair reaching to her shoulders. Lizzie was an inch or two taller and slightly plumper, with short dark curly hair. Helen thought it dated back to the mid-thirties, before the war started. Lizzie was married by that time but still lived and worked at the boarding house. Alice looked about fifteen or sixteen, the age when she, Helen, had been studying hard at school to get good grades in her GCEs, whereas she knew that her aunt at that age had been working her fingers to the bone cleaning and cooking and doing the washing-up for a houseful of visitors.

She put the photo back with a sigh and turned to the dressing table. There was a lace-edged runner on which sat a hand mirror, hairbrush, clothes brush and comb, all backed in pink enamel. There was also a floral china tray containing odds and ends of hair grips, buttons and safety pins; a cut-glass powder bowl; and a bottle of Alice's favourite perfume, Coty L'Aimant.

Helen idly opened the top drawer. It contained her aunt's underwear: vests, nightdresses, petticoats, bras and panties, not very different from the ones that Helen herself wore. She closed the drawer quickly. It seemed wrong to be rooting about in her aunt's personal belongings. She would wait awhile. It was too soon, and the pain of her loss had re-surfaced.

51

The middle drawer contained jumpers, cardigans and T-shirts, and again she left them to be dealt with another time.

She opened the bottom drawer. Scarves, gloves, tights. A box which contained handkerchiefs — Alice had always preferred hankies to tissues. There was another box, too: a tin box with a picture on the lid of King George VI and Queen Elizabeth in their Coronation regalia. When was that? Back in 1937, if Helen remembered correctly. A long time ago. Helen had known only the present queen and the younger royals, Charles and Diana, and Andrew and Fergie, although the Queen Mother was still around.

Helen put the box on the bed and, despite her misgivings and a feeling that she was snooping, curiosity got the better of her.

5

With a slight hesitation, Helen removed the lid to reveal the contents of the box. She could see at a glance that they were mementoes. As she took out first one, then another, and laid them on the bed, she felt that she was prying, that these were private, personal things that her great-aunt had treasured. At the same time, she felt that Aunt Alice would not have minded her seeing what was inside the box. Maybe she had even wished Helen to know something of her earlier life. Had it not been so, she could have destroyed them, for Helen soon realized that these articles dated back almost fifty years, to the time when Alice was a young woman in her early twenties — ten years or so younger than Helen was now.

There was a bundle of letters; not a large bundle, only a dozen or so, tied up with a red ribbon. A rose that might once have been red but was now brown and wrinkled and had been pressed to preserve it. A small leather-bound book of poetry. Helen was not surprised to see it was the selected works of the Romantic poets. There were silken markers between several of the pages. She knew she would have to discover later on which poems her aunt had loved to read.

There was a black and white photograph, not a snapshot but more of a studio photo, of a young man in RAF uniform. Helen found she was not surprised at this. She smiled to herself but also felt a tear in her eye. She had always felt, deep down, that there must once have been someone special in Alice's life.

He was an attractive-looking young man, early twenties, she guessed, the age that her aunt would have been in the early years of the war. She knew that the boarding house where her gran, Lizzie, and Alice had worked for their mother had been an RAF billet during the war years, as were most of the hotels and boarding houses. So it was hardly surprising that the younger unmarried daughter would form a friendship with one of those young men.

She looked at the photo again, thinking that he resembled somebody that she knew. Then she realized he had a look of that young man from *Brideshead Revisited*. Not the blond one; the dark one. What was he called? Yes, Jeremy Irons. He had the same sort of lean features and a humorous intelligence in his eyes. He was smiling for the camera and looked happy and carefree with his cap worn at a jaunty angle. The two stripes on his sleeve denoted that he was a corporal. Her Aunt Alice's sweetheart, she guessed. She turned the photo over and saw that this was true. The bold handwriting read: *To my darling Alice, with all my love, Tony.*

Helen wondered what had happened to him, and what had happened to Alice. Clearly there had not been a happy ending for the two of them. But Alice seemed to have found contentment and a quiet happiness in her life all the same.

In the corner of the box there was a brooch: the RAF crest between two silver wings. She had seen similar ones on those antique programmes that were so popular on the television. It was a keepsake given by airmen to a loved one: a wife, mother or sweetheart. She knew, though, that Alice had not worn it, at least not recently.

There were a few other mementoes in the box. A tiny perfume bottle, almost empty, of dark blue glass, bearing the name Evening in Paris, and a georgette handkerchief in shades of pink and blue with a powder puff fastened in the middle. It smelled musty, and Helen thought it was a strange sort of thing, but they must have been all the rage at one time.

She drew out a tiny celluloid doll wearing a feathered skirt, the sort that might have been won at a fairground, possibly at Blackpool Pleasure Beach. And a little china model of Blackpool Tower emblazoned with the words: *A Present from Blackpool.* Helen knew it was an item of Goss china which had become very collectable. There were a few postcards of views of the town that visitors would send home, but these had not been used — a view of Stanley Park lake, one of the Tower Ballroom, and the clifftop gardens along the promenade at Little Bispham. An eclectic mixture of odds and ends, no doubt holding many treasured memories.

Helen knew that she must read one of the letters. She drew it out of the envelope hesitantly. It was addressed to Miss Alice Fletcher, 20 West Street, which she knew had been the address of the boarding house in North Shore. The address at the top of the letter was that of a camp in Lincolnshire. Reading the letter, Helen realized that Tony had been transferred from the Blackpool billet to a camp where he was having further training to become a member, presumably, of a bomber crew. Helen only scanned the letter, feeling that it was too personal for her to devour it avidly, as she might do with a romantic novel. The letter began, *My darling Alice . . .* She could tell that this young man had loved Alice very much and was missing her acutely. A sentence near the end read: *Before very long I will be 'coming in on a wing and a prayer', as it says in the song. I know I will be in your prayers, as you will be in mine.*

The song struck a chord in Helen's mind. She was sure she had heard it sung; could it have been sung by Vera Lynn? Her songs and those of Anne Shelton and Bing Crosby, the Glenn Miller orchestra, and many other wartime melodies were still played frequently on the radio. Just as the wartime films were shown on the TV over and over again. It seemed that the generation who had lived through that time never seemed to tire of seeing them, and the younger generations learned a lot that they didn't know about, although Helen guessed that it was often glamourized.

'Coming in on a wing and a prayer . . . ' She hummed the tune to herself; she had a good memory for words and for tunes. She only needed to hear a song once or twice and she retained it in her mind. How did the song go? 'With our full crew aboard, and our trust in the

Lord, we're coming in on a wing and a prayer.'

But unless she was very much mistaken, Helen thought that her aunt's boyfriend Tony — or had he been her fiancé? Somehow, she didn't think so — had been one who had not returned.

She glanced at a couple more letters. They were all in the same vein; mainly memories of their time together and expressions of love. Not much about the training he was undergoing or the flights over Germany. No mention of comrades who had been lost, although there surely must have been some. In one of the letters he had given Alice his home address, in case she should ever need it, he had said. Helen learned that his name was Tony Sinclair, and his home was in Malton, near York. So he was a Yorkshire lad, too, just as Alice had become a Yorkshire lass again, choosing to return to the county of her birth.

Helen was thoughtful for the rest of the day, unable to concentrate on anything but the contents of Aunt Alice's box and the nostalgic letters. She knew that she must find out more about Alice and the young man, Tony. She had a feeling her aunt would have wanted her to do so.

She wondered whether her mother, Megan, knew anything about Alice's boyfriend, Tony. The dates on the letters were 1942 and '43, so presumably Alice had not met Tony until the middle years of the war. Alice would then have been about twenty-three or -four, and Megan would have been nine or ten. Old enough to be aware of what was going on, but she had not mentioned it to Helen.

Helen's grandmother, Lizzie, must certainly have known about what was happening, but she had always been very secretive about her younger sister. Helen knew there had been a rift and a certain animosity between the two sisters, although this seemed to have mellowed as the years had gone by.

Helen thought she might have an inkling as to what the secrecy had been about, but she must be careful not to jump to the wrong conclusion. She would ask her mother when next she saw her. With the discovery of the box of mementoes and the letters, surely she would tell Helen what she knew of Alice's love affair. She returned the box to the drawer for the moment, knowing that she would return to it and try to learn more of the secrets it held.

The next day was Easter Monday, and a bank holiday, so Helen decided she would treat it as such for herself. Her time was her own now. She had two weeks in which to sort out everything for her move, to try to find some employment and to enjoy a bit of leisure time.

She decided she would visit the city of York. She had been there a few times with her aunt and once with Alex. It was a lively, bustling city, and was always crowded with both locals and tourists, whatever the time of year. It would be particularly so on Easter Monday but what did it matter? There would always be room for one more.

She took the road across the Vale of York, the towers of the Minster appearing on the horizon when she was a few miles away from the city. It was best to explore York on foot, it being almost impossible to negotiate the narrow streets in a car. She parked in an empty space she was lucky to find near the station and the Railway Museum which housed all manner of engines and carriages.

The sun was shining but there was a nip in the air as she set off across the Lendal Bridge into the heart of the city. In the Minster garden the trees were bursting into leaf and the flower beds were bright with red and pink tulips, daffodils and hyacinths. As Helen strolled around she felt a lightness in her heart and a quiet joy in her surroundings that she had not known since her great-aunt's death.

★   ★   ★

There was so much to see in York, far too much for one day. It was a higgledy-piggledy sort of place in which one could easily get lost were it not for the frequent signs pointing one in the right direction. Much of the merchandise for sale in The Shambles area could be classed as 'tat', but there were some attractive goods as well amid the melee of souvenir ashtrays, purses, pens and paperweights. Helen found a pictorial map of the Minster and the surrounding area etched on copper. Probably quite a modern one but done in an olde-worlde style surrounded by a simple black frame. She decided she could afford it, and it would be a nice focal point over the fireplace in her new home.

On Tuesday morning she drove to Pickering to

see Mr Fothergill. She felt it was only right to tell him that she had decided to come and live in her aunt's house rather than to sell the property. He was busy with a client but was able to see her after a short wait, and seemed genuinely pleased to see her and to hear that she would soon be living in Thornbeck.

'You told me that you worked in an estate agency in Blackpool?' he said.

'Yes, that's right. But I've finished there now, and I'll be looking for a job when I've moved here.'

'I thought about you the other day,' Mr Fothergill said now. 'The young lady who works at Montague and Price — the estate agency a few doors away — is leaving soon to take maternity leave. I didn't know, of course, that you would be coming to live here, but I thought to myself that you would be just the sort of young lady they would be hoping to find.'

Helen could scarcely believe what he was saying. 'But that's wonderful, Mr Fothergill,' she said. 'I haven't even started looking yet. Do you think . . . ?'

'I'm certain, my dear. You go along and see them and tell them that I sent you. Alan Price is a good friend of mine. Mr Montague doesn't come in very much now, but it's an old established business.'

'I have a reference here from my last place,' said Helen. 'Thank you very much, Mr Fothergill. I shall go and see Mr Price. This really seems too good to be true.'

Mr Fothergill shook hands with her. 'Goodbye

for now, my dear, and good luck, but I have every confidence I will be seeing you again before very long.'

Helen guessed that Alan Price might be about the same age as Mr Fothergill, in his early fifties, but much more modern in appearance, as though he belonged in the nineties rather than in the previous century. He was quite attractive in a foxy sort of way with pointed features and dark ginger hair. Helen introduced herself and told him why she had come. He shook hands with her vigorously then dashed around briskly, pulling out a chair for her and asking an assistant if she would be so good as to make them a pot of tea.

'We haven't advertised the vacancy yet,' he told her. 'It's only a temporary post, but one never knows what might happen, and it's always best to employ someone who has been recommended.'

'I have a reference here,' said Helen, producing it from her bag.

He read it swiftly, and then nodded as he handed it back to her. 'That's fine, just fine . . . When could you start?'

Helen gasped. 'You mean . . . you want to take me on?'

'Of course; it doesn't take me long to make up my mind.' He turned to the young woman who was working quietly behind a desk. 'This is Paula. She'll be leaving us at t'end of next week to await the birth of her baby, won't you, my dear?'

'Yes, that's right.' She smiled at Helen. 'We all get along well together here.'

The other young woman assistant had returned with the tea. 'Thank you, Jill,' said Mr

Price, taking the tray from her and putting it on the counter. 'Now, this is Helen, and she will be our new member of staff.'

It was decided that Helen would start there during the first week in May, after she had moved and more or less settled in her new surroundings. Paula, whom Helen judged to be about seven months into her pregnancy, had spent much of her time showing prospective buyers around the houses and flats that were on offer, and it was hoped that Helen would be able to do the same when she was more acquainted with the area.

Feeling in a celebratory mood and not quite believing her luck, Helen treated herself to lunch — steak and chips, with a glass of red wine — at a nearby restaurant, then spent the afternoon exploring the town where she would be working. It was a small but busy and prosperous market town. There were no department stores, but plenty of shops catering for all tastes and pockets. She felt somehow that this was the right place for her, and that Aunt Alice would have been delighted.

When Helen returned to Thornbeck at the beginning of May her mother accompanied her to help get everything more or less shipshape before she started working at the estate agency. Megan stayed for a couple of nights and together they unpacked all the tea chests that had been brought by the removal van, putting everything in its correct place.

'A place for everything, and everything in its place,' said Megan. 'That's what your gran always says.'

'She's got over the shock of me inheriting all this, has she?' asked Helen.

'Oh, I think so,' replied Megan. 'None of us had thought about what Aunt Alice's will would contain. We didn't expect her to go so soon, did we? Anyway, this is what she wanted, and I'm sure it's right. One would have expected your gran to go first — she is seven years older — but it shows that we can't take anything for granted. Now it's up to you, Helen, to make a new life for yourself here. We shall miss you, but I know you'll settle down and make new friends. You seem to have a few already.'

'Yes, so I have. Everyone was very welcoming when I came at the Easter weekend.'

There was a surfeit of pots and pans, crockery, china, cutlery and ornaments that had belonged to Alice, much of it more to Megan's taste, and certainly to Lizzie's taste, than Helen's.

'Take whatever you would like, Mum, for you and Gran,' said Helen. 'I shall keep a few nice things to remember Aunt Alice. I've always liked those Crown Derby birds.'

It was a sad task packing Alice's clothes, shoes and handbags into suitcases and boxes for Helen to take to the charity shops in Pickering when she started work in a couple of days' time. They loaded Megan's car with bed linen and towels, kitchen utensils and some rather delicate china. There was a Royal Albert tea service lavishly decorated with red and pink roses, and one of Shelley china with a delicate blue design of forget-me-nots.

Helen had debated with herself whether or not

to tell her mother about the box of mementoes she had found. In the end she decided she would do so. The photograph might jog her mother's memory. She brought the box down the evening before Megan was due to return home.

'I want to show you this, Mum,' she said, opening the box of treasures. 'It was in Aunt Alice's bottom drawer. I felt as though I was prying, in a way, but she could have destroyed it, couldn't she, if she didn't want anyone to see it? It seems as though she had a boyfriend, one who meant quite a lot to her; there are some letters as well.' She handed her mother the photograph. 'He was called Tony Sinclair, and his home was in Malton, so he was a Yorkshire lad. Do you recognize him? I guess he was billeted at the boarding house that Great-grandma Ada had.'

Megan looked startled for a moment. 'Good gracious!' she said. 'After all this time . . . ' She looked keenly at the photo then shook her head. She turned it over and smiled sadly as she silently read the words: *To my darling Alice.*

'How very sad,' she said. 'No, I don't recognize this young man, but then it's not likely that I would. I suppose I would have been about . . . what? Seven or eight at the time, depending on when it was. There were RAF men billeted there for most of the war years, one lot following another as they finished their training.' She laughed. 'I was much too young to appreciate having a houseful of fit young RAF blokes! But it seems as though Alice may well have made the most of it. She always seemed so quiet and shy, though. But I do remember something . . . '

'What is it, Mum?'

'Well, I remember that Alice was taken ill. The war had been going on for a few years; it might have been 1942 or '43. Anyway, she was sent to stay with some relations in Yorkshire until she was well again. Grandma Ada's sister and her family, I think, but I was never told much about it.'

'Then she came back to Blackpool?'

'Yes, eventually. I suppose I didn't take a great deal of notice. I was always told not to be nosey, so I didn't ask. I know Grandma Ada was very tight-lipped about it, and so was my mother. I didn't think much about it at the time, but over the years . . . well . . . I suppose I've put two and two together.'

'And Gran — your mother, I mean — she's never said anything, even now?'

'No, I told you there was a rift in the family and nobody talked about it. So I tried to put it to the back of my mind, for Aunt Alice's sake really. She had made a new life for herself and seemed to be very happy.'

'There's an obvious answer, though, isn't there, Mum,' said Helen, 'as to why she was sent away? Poor Alice! It was such a scandal in those days, wasn't it? Dear me, the poor girl . . . '

'Don't you think we might be jumping to conclusions, Helen?' said her mother. 'I know what you are thinking, and I suppose I am as well. But there's no proof, is there? Nothing to say that . . . that she had a child. It doesn't mention it in any of those letters? I presume you have read them?'

'I glanced at them, Mum, that's all. I didn't want to pore over them, you know? But I could tell they were very much in love, Alice and this Tony. And I wonder why she went back to Yorkshire? You say it was in the early fifties?'

'Yes, before you were born. She didn't live in Thornbeck at first. I think she lived somewhere near Bradford. But she was in Thornbeck for the last . . . twenty years or so, as far as I can remember.'

'Do you think she went back to Yorkshire to find out about her child? I presumed he — or she — would have been adopted. And did she find him . . . or her? She settled down there very well, didn't she? And she was very happy. Oh . . . I do hope she found what she was looking for . . . '

'I've told you, Helen, we're jumping to conclusions. And is it any of our business anyway? It was all water under the bridge, as far as I was concerned, until you unearthed all these secrets. But I do intend to ask your gran about it. I've never understood all the secrecy, and I think it's time she told us what she knows. As I say, Helen love, it's a long time ago; more than fifty years since the war started. I was only five years old. Memories fade as the years go by.'

But Megan found as she looked back that the memories were still there, though hidden away at the back of her mind. But the more she thought about those wartime years the clearer the memories became.

6

Megan was five years old when war broke out on 3 September, 1939. She recalled a popular catchphrase by a comedian of the day, often heard on the wireless: 'The day war broke out my missus said to me . . . ' This always raised a smile to give a touch of humour to the grim outlook, although in the early days of the war nothing much happened. There was a feeling of anticlimax among the adults, and the children were puzzled as to exactly what was going on.

Megan had been attending school for several months, but now it was the long summer holiday. The new school term had not started because of the advent of war. They had all been issued with gas masks. Megan had gone with her mother to the nearby church hall to collect theirs. Young children had one that looked like Mickey Mouse, in red and blue, but as Megan was five she had an ordinary one like the grown-ups. It had a nozzle like a pig's snout, with air holes so that you could breathe. It was made of rubber. You stuck your chin in and pulled the straps up over your head. There was a little window so that you could see, and when you breathed out it sometimes made a rather rude noise.

When the school term started a few days later one of the first lessons they learned was the air-raid drill. When they heard a bell they put on their gas masks, the teachers as well as the children, and trooped out to the makeshift air-raid shelter that had been built in the playground. It was quite good fun really, a nice little break from lessons, and the boys thought it was hilarious to see who could make the rudest noise.

If there had really been an air raid they would have heard a wailing sound that went up and down. They did in fact hear it a few times during those early days, but it was always a false alarm. Then the 'all clear' siren would be heard, a sound all on one note, which meant that the danger was over.

Megan lived with her parents, Lizzie and Norman Weaver, in a boarding house in the north of Blackpool. She knew that her grandma, Ada, was the one in charge — the landlady — but Megan's mother worked there, and so did Aunt Alice, her mother's younger sister. Megan's dad was a painter and decorator, and the three of them had their own rooms on the first floor. Megan remembered a warm and cosy living room with a coal fire, comfy chairs, and a table in the window where they would dine on Sundays and when Daddy came home from work at teatime.

Sometimes during the week Megan and her mum had their midday meal downstairs with Grandma and Aunt Alice. They had a rather larger living room which they always called the 'kitchen'. It wasn't really a kitchen, as Megan realized when she was older. The meals were cooked in what they referred to as the 'back kitchen' at the rear of the house, overlooking the backyard, the coal shed and the outside lavatory.

Lizzie and Norman had a nice bedroom at the front of the house, and Megan was supposed to have her own little room nearby. But in the summer when the house was full of visitors she slept anywhere there was a spare room. That was usually up in the attic as those rooms were not considered suitable for visitors. Megan didn't mind though; she loved it up there. The roof sloped down to the floor — you had to be careful not to bump your head — and there was a tiny window from where you could see Blackpool Tower in the distance.

The visitors' rooms all had a washbasin, but at the time the war started there were no bathrooms in the house, not even for the family. There was a toilet on each landing as well as the one in the backyard. Megan had a chamber pot with a design of pink roses which went under the bed in the attic room. She had a bath once a week in a large zinc tub in front of the fire in the kitchen. She supposed the grown-ups did as well, although she had never really thought about it. It was not until after the war when they went to live in a semi-detached house that they enjoyed the luxury of a bathroom. But that was the way things were for many folk and, by and large, they did not yearn for what they knew they could not have.

On that memorable day, the third of September — it was a Sunday — the family all gathered in the kitchen: Grandma Ada, Aunt Alice, Lizzie and Norman, and Megan. She knew there was going to be a war. The Germans had been causing trouble and the men of Britain would be joining the army and going to fight them. Megan knew about fights. There were often fights in the playground among the bigger boys and they usually got into trouble. But this was going to be a real war with guns and tanks and aeroplanes dropping bombs. Looking back on it, it was hard to say how the children had gained so much information and why they were not frightened to death, but they did not appear to be. Megan, at least, was happy and felt safe in the bosom of her family.

They all sat round the wireless set, a large wooden cabinet with a cut-out sunray design, and they listened in silence to the voice of the prime minister, a man called Neville Chamberlain. It was quite a long speech, and Megan gathered that he had been waiting for a message that had not arrived, and so the country was now at war with Germany.

'So now we know,' said Grandma Ada. 'Well, it's what we've been expecting, isn't it? Go an' make us a cup of tea, Alice, there's a good lass. And there's a bottle of brandy in the sideboard cupboard; we'll have a tot of brandy in it an' all. I save it for emergencies, but I reckon this is one, if anything is.'

Alice, who was used to obeying her mother's commands, scurried into the back kitchen, and Lizzie found the brandy bottle at the back of the sideboard cupboard. While the grown-ups sipped their tea and talked about what it all might mean to them, Megan sat quietly, as she had been brought up to do, dressing her favourite doll, Betsy, in some different clothes, with one ear tuned to what the adults were saying.

'I suppose the next thing that'll happen will be us looking after a houseful of evacuees,' said Ada. 'We've no visitors in, and I reckon we've seen the last of 'em for goodness knows how long. They'll not let us sit pretty with twelve empty bedrooms.'

'Nor would we want to, Mother,' said Lizzie. 'We've all got to do our bit, and we'll get paid for doing it, won't we?'

'Oh aye, I suppose there'll be an allowance, but it might be not as much as we get from the visitors. Mind you, they always get a jolly good deal; three meals a day and a nice bedroom with a washbasin, all for three pounds a week.'

'And I shall have to do my bit an' all,' said Megan's dad. 'I'm young and able-bodied, so I guess I'll have to go and join up.'

'Hey, steady on, lad,' said Ada. 'You're not all that young. You'll be thirty next birthday, won't you? That's not young for a soldier. They'll be wanting the lads of eighteen to twenty-one. Just wait till they send for you. Your time'll come, if it lasts that long. It might well be over before you can say 'Jack Robinson'.'

'And it might not, Ma,' replied Norman. 'They said that about the last war, didn't they? 'It'll all be over by Christmas,' they said. And it lasted five years.'

'Heaven preserve us!' said Ada. 'Don't say that's all we've got to look forward to! Five years of war! It doesn't bear thinking about.'

'It won't last so long this time, Ma,' said Norman. 'We'll have a better army; it was a shambles last time. And there'll be the Royal Air Force, and the Navy. We'll be better prepared. We'll soon send those Jerries packing, you'll see.'

The very next day a woman from the WVS called to ask if Mrs Fletcher would be willing to take evacuees who would be arriving from Liverpool in a day or two. It was more or less obligatory, but Ada asked for younger children accompanied by their mothers. She did not like the idea of looking after unaccompanied school-aged children. At least this lot would be supervised by their mothers.

The powers that be decided that their quota would be ten mothers with fifteen children, ranging in age from one to four.

Megan watched them arriving as she looked through the window of their first-floor living room. Her mum had been down to the church hall to meet them and to show them the way to their new home.

Megan was used to having visitors in the house, people who had come for a week's holiday at the seaside. There were a few who came back each year and sometimes, if her mother felt they were trustworthy, she would allow Megan to go with them to the sands, to make sand pies and castles and to paddle in the rock pools. Mummy was usually too busy to take her, so it was a treat for Megan.

But these new people were not the usual visitors. They had left their homes because it was feared that the Germans would soon start dropping bombs on Liverpool and other big cities, so they had come to a place of safety.

They were a mixed crowd of people. Some of them — both the women and the children — were what Megan's mum would call scruffy while others were quite clean and tidy. They all had gas masks in cardboard boxes slung around their bodies; the women carried cases and bags and one or two had babies in their arms, and there were a couple of younger children in pushchairs.

After that Megan didn't see a great deal of them because they had their meals in the dining room that the visitors had used, with a section at the end where there were easy chairs and settees, a wireless set and a piano, so that they could relax in the evenings.

They were waited on at the tables at first by Lizzie and Alice, then a few of the more enterprising women said they would like to help. They made a rota for serving, clearing away and helping with the washing-up. Most of them wanted to pull their weight. After all, it was not supposed to be a holiday. But it became clear that some of them regarded it as such.

'Can't be bad, can it?' Lizzie heard one woman say to her friend. 'A couple of months at the seaside an' no work to do; no good-for-nothing husband neither.'

'Your Bill's joined up, hasn't he?'

'Aye, but there's nowt much happening at the moment. No bombs dropping like they said there'd be.'

'No, we'd best make the most of it here. We'll have to go back if this bore war carries on much longer.'

That was what the current situation was being

called: the 'bore war' or the 'phoney war'.

'And I don't know as we're any better off with young kids and their mothers,' said Ada. 'They're letting 'em run riot! I've had to lock the piano to stop them little beggars thumping on it. At least if the kids were on their own we might be able to control 'em.'

'I doubt it, Mam,' said Lizzie. 'They've got lads of six and seven next door, and Jean says they're running wild. They've had no discipline at home, that's the trouble . . .'

Their new guests were not all feckless and unruly, though. One woman in particular stood out from the crowd with her polite manners and her well-behaved little girl. Some of the other women thought that Elsie Wilson was 'lah-di-dah' and considered herself a cut above the rest of them, but mostly they agreed with her when she said that they should help with the chores and not expect to be waited on. It was Elsie who had suggested a rota, 'to get 'em off their backsides', as Ada put it.

The school term had started, but the local children were attending only in the mornings. The schools were not large enough to cope with such an influx of evacuees, and so for the time being the local children had lessons in the mornings and the newcomers in the afternoons.

Some children thought this was a great idea, although the parents were not too happy about it. Megan wasn't keen either; she enjoyed going to school, and everyone at home was too busy so she had to amuse herself.

And so it was that one afternoon, when she

was at a loose end, she met Mrs Wilson and her little girl, Shirley.

'Hello, dear. You're Megan, aren't you?' said the lady.

Megan nodded and smiled. 'Yes, I am.'

'Well, I'm Mrs Wilson, and this is Shirley,' said the lady. 'We're just going for a walk on the prom. Would you like to come with us?'

'Yes, please,' said Megan eagerly.

'Well, go and ask your mum if it's all right,' said Mrs Wilson.

Lizzie had agreed readily, and that was the first of many outings that Megan enjoyed with her new friends. That first afternoon they walked northwards as far as the boating pool, a favourite haunt for the children. There were paddle boats, swings and slides, and a kiosk that sold ice cream and fizzy pop. That afternoon they rode on the automated animal ride. Megan climbed on to the back of a giraffe and Shirley chose an elephant. They whizzed around the track, waving to Shirley's mum every time they passed her. Then she bought them both an ice cream.

The two girls soon became good friends but, alas, it all came to an end. The 'bore war' was continuing and the evacuees started to drift back home. By Christmas they had all left Ada's boarding house, and it was the same in nearly all the lodgings in Blackpool. Elsie Wilson promised to keep in touch, and Megan said she would send postcards to Shirley. And so they did, for a while . . .

'By heck! It's to be hoped we get compensation for damages,' said Ada, when they had all departed. 'There's scorch marks on the tables, would you believe, where they've stubbed out their cigarettes. And holes in the sheets where the little beggars have shoved their feet through. Mind you, I admit that some of 'em were getting a bit worn. And umpteen broken cups and glasses, and I shall need a new carpet for the stairs where they've all traipsed up and down.'

'Hold your horses, Mother,' said Lizzie. 'I doubt if we'll get anything yet. And I reckon we'll be having the RAF billeted with us now the evacuees have gone.'

'Aye, I suppose so,' said Ada. 'At least they'll be old enough to know how to behave themselves.'

Sure enough, early in the new year of 1940 twenty RAF recruits were billeted there, as they were in the majority of boarding houses and hotels in the town. Blackpool became the main training ground for the RAF in the north of England. It was an ideal location with the long stretch of sand where they drilled and did their bayonet practice. The various parts of the Winter Gardens complex — the Indian lounge, the Baronial Hall and the Empress Ballroom — were used for lectures and training sessions, as were some of the larger hotels.

Ada had been sceptical at first, but she soon came to enjoy having a houseful of boisterous young men. It was a big adventure to them at first, and they enjoyed the camaraderie and fun when their day's training was over.

Ada had always been known for serving jolly good meals. The visitors said so, and so did these lads. They tucked into the shepherds pies, hotpots, sausages and mash, rice puddings and apple pies. Ada smiled and laughed a lot more now, pleased at their good-humoured banter and teasing. It had been a big disappointment to her that she had never had a son, so these lads, rather late in the day, were making up for it.

Lizzie enjoyed the company of these new lodgers as well. She was an attractive young woman, dark-haired and with a pleasing rounded figure. She was not averse to a bit of flirtatious teasing and saucy remarks. They knew she was married and that they must keep their distance, but there was no harm in chatting.

Alice was shy, much more reserved than her sister. She was pretty, too, with long fawn hair, delicate features and a slim figure. She was not confident, though, with people she did not know, so Lizzie was the one who got the attention.

Megan did not see a great deal of the new arrivals, although you could not fail to be aware of their presence. Every evening you could hear their laughter and their strident voices raised in a chorus of 'Bless 'em all', or 'Roll out the Barrel', accompanied on the rather out-of-tune piano by one of the lads who could play.

Ada had unlocked the piano again and didn't mind how they used it. 'Poor lads,' she said. 'Let 'em enjoy themselves. They'll be in the thick of it before long.'

They stayed there for only a few months, then they were sent elsewhere for further specialized training, and other new recruits took their place.

In February Norman decided he would join up.

'If you join the RAF they might let you stay here, Daddy,' said Megan.

'No, love; that's not a good idea,' he told her. 'Anyway, I'm going to join the army. I shall be a soldier, not an airman.'

He told Lizzie he felt guilty with all those lads in the house, 'all doing their bit for King and Country. I don't want somebody handing me a white feather.'

'Oh, they'll not be doing that this time,' said Ada. 'Wait till you're called up, Norman.'

But he would not listen. He enlisted and was sent to a camp in the south of England.

'I doubt if he'll see active service,' said Ada. 'Not for a whit at any rate.'

She was proved right because in May the troops who were fighting on the Continent suffered a severe setback. After losing ground with the Germans they were forced to flee to the coast of France. The name Dunkirk was soon on everyone's lips.

When Megan looked back on those wartime years her mind was a jumble of memories. Some were quite clear; others she had almost forgotten. After all, it was fifty years ago.

She remembered the retreat from Dunkirk. She had watched pictures of it on the Gaumont British News at the Odeon cinema. Soldiers had been stranded on the beaches in northern France, and lots of little ships and boats had sailed across the Channel to bring them home to England.

Everyone was very proud of the British soldiers, and they were treated like heroes, although Megan realized in later years that it had been a defeat, not a victory, and that the future had looked very grim at that time.

The new Prime Minister, Winston Churchill, was often on the news at the cinema. He had a face like a bulldog and smoked a big cigar. He said our country would never be defeated, and everybody tried to believe him. You would often see Adolf Hitler as well, the man who was causing all the trouble in Germany. He was a small man with sleek black hair and a little moustache. The boys at school mimicked him, lifting up their right arms and saying, 'Heil Hitler'.

Megan also remembered that her Aunt Alice had gone out to work for the first time in her life. She had always worked for Grandma Ada in the boarding house, but as the war continued, all the women who were not married had to go and do some sort of work to help the war effort. They could join the army or navy or RAF — although they would not do any fighting — or go to work on a farm as a Land Girl. Or they could work at a munitions factory helping to build aeroplanes and tanks.

Alice chose to work at a branch of the Vickers-Armstrongs aircraft factory. The main factory was at Squires Gate, near Blackpool, on the road to St Annes. There was a nearer one, however, over near the bus station in Talbot Road, a few minutes' walk from her home, so Alice decided she would go and work there.

She set off each morning looking very different, in trousers and green overalls and a turban covering her hair. She had not wanted to go at first. She was timid and had never learned to stick up for herself.

Thinking about it, so many years later, Megan realized that going out to work, especially doing war work, had been the making of Alice. She had become a very different person, although it had not happened all at once.

Megan had not recognized the photograph of the young RAF corporal, but she knew that her aunt had made new friends at work, and had gone out in the evenings, to the cinema and the dance halls, things she had not done before. It was very likely that she had become friendly with some of the RAF lads who had stayed there; obviously there had been one who had become very special to her.

Megan had not known anything about this. As a child of eight or nine she had been told nothing at all. She had known only that Aunt Alice had gone away for a rest because she was poorly, and had come back several months later, very pale and subdued.

Other memories surfaced from the depths of Megan's mind as she thought about those wartime years. Her father had joined the army and was granted leave every few months. He remarked each time he saw her how much she had grown. As he was stationed in the south of England it was quite easy for him to get home, although he said it was a long and weary journey on crowded trains.

He did not go overseas until 1944, at the time of the D-Day landings. He was in the second wave of troops who crossed to France and, fortunately, he returned safe and sound. Many of the fathers of Megan's school friends were in the forces, and they often had special efforts at school to help the soldiers, sailors and airmen: raffles and jumble sales, and competitions for the best designed poster for 'Dig for Victory' or the 'Squander Bug'. They were encouraged to defeat the Squander Bug by saving up their pennies to buy sixpenny savings stamps, the money going to help the war effort.

Megan was sure that her mum missed her dad; she said that she did, and Megan missed him very much. Mummy chatted a lot more to the airmen now that Daddy was not there. She had thought very little about it at the time, but, looking back on it, certain memories became clearer and more meaningful.

It would have been a couple of years after her dad had joined the army that her mum had become friendly with the sergeant who was in charge of the men at the billet. He was Sergeant Whittaker, and her mum called him Alan. He sometimes came to their room upstairs and had a cup of tea with her mum, and when Megan had gone to bed she could hear them talking and laughing in the room next door.

It was only in later years that Megan recalled how lively her mum had seemed when Sergeant Whittaker was around — she looked prettier, with a touch of lipstick and her hair nicely combed.

He had gone, though, after a few months, as they all did. Megan had never heard of him again, and she had almost forgotten about him until now.

She smiled to herself. She could not possibly ask her mother about her friendship with the sergeant, but she would most certainly ask her about the young corporal with whom her Aunt Alice had been so friendly. Surely it was time that all the secrecy came to an end.

7

'Oh, so that's all come to light, has it?' said Lizzie when Megan told her about the box of mementoes that Helen had found, especially the photo of the young airman. 'Well, I can tell you, it's best forgotten, Megan, like it has been for years. We never talked about it. Your gran wouldn't let anyone mention it so there's no point in dragging it all up again now.'

'But Aunt Alice didn't forget, did she?' said Megan. 'She obviously loved him very much, as he loved her.'

'Well, that's as may be, but what does it matter now? Just forget about it, Megan, and tell Helen to forget about it an' all.'

Megan looked keenly at her mother. 'Alice had a baby, didn't she?'

'Yes, she did, and it nearly killed your gran, the disgrace of it all! Not that anybody ever knew outside of the family. Folks may have guessed there was summat up, but we never breathed a word, we were so ashamed of her.'

'Why, Mother? It was wartime. That must have happened to lots of young women.'

'That doesn't make it right, does it? Oh, I know folks reckon nothing much to it nowadays. Young lasses jump into bed with somebody they've only just met, but it was different then. Well-brought-up girls were expected to behave themselves.'

'Did she have a boy or a girl?' Megan was determined not to let the matter drop. 'And what happened to it? I mean . . . to him or her?'

'I don't know what she had. Happen your gran knew, but she never said. I told you, we never talked about it. Alice went to stay with your gran's sister, Aunt Maggie, near Bradford till it was all over, and the child was adopted.'

'Poor Alice! And what happened to the young airman? Do you remember him? He was called Tony Sinclair.'

'Oh aye, I remember him all right, and we knew Alice was friendly with him. She'd had one or two boyfriends; she came out of her shell when she went to work at the factory and started to meet other young lasses. Then he went to a camp down south. I think he was training to be a wireless operator, so he probably went on a bombing raid and never came back. We never heard of him again. That's all I know and all I'm telling you.'

'I do think you might have told me before, Mother. It must have been dreadful for Aunt Alice.'

'Aye, maybe it was.' Lizzie's eyes softened momentarily. 'But she got over it, didn't she? She was happy enough living in Yorkshire.'

'Why did she go back there? Do you think she tried to find out about the baby? Or about Tony and what happened to him?'

'Alice wanted a fresh start, and I suppose you couldn't blame her. Things weren't right between her and your gran. When we left the boarding house she went to lodge with a friend

84

she'd met at the factory. She worked in a shop for a while, then she upped sticks and went to Yorkshire. She lived in one or two places there, then she settled in Thornbeck.'

'And she made it up with Gran? I suppose Gran forgave her eventually, did she, for straying from the straight and narrow?'

Lizzie was aware of the hint of sarcasm in her daughter's words. 'It wasn't summat to be taken lightly, Megan,' she retorted. 'But we all got along better as the years went by. It was all a long time ago . . . so just forget about it and tell Helen to do the same. There's no point in dragging up the past; goodness knows what you might find.'

All the same, Lizzie doubted that Megan would heed her words and, more particularly, neither would Helen. She was a law unto herself, that young woman.

When Megan had gone home and Lizzie was alone that evening the memories flooded back — right back to the time when they had moved to Blackpool to live at the boarding house . . .

Lizzie had always hated her name. Her proper name, Elizabeth, was a good, dignified name — the name of queens — but no one ever called her by it.

'Come on, our Lizzie,' her mother would shout. 'Get a move on washing them pots. We haven't got all day . . . ' And that was before she left school and had a full-time job working for her mother.

Nowadays Lizzie was quite a fashionable name. Young women didn't mind being called

Lizzie, or Liz. Liz Taylor, of course, had helped to boost the popularity of the name. At the time Lizzie was born, in the early years of the century, and before that, in the Victorian era, it had been customary to shorten names, or to make them more ordinary. Sarah became Sally, Ellen or Eleanor became Nellie, and Margaret became Maggie.

As Lizzie Fletcher she had worked like a slave for her mother, and so had Alice. Lizzie's mind went back to the early years, during the 1920s. The houses were then referred to as lodging houses, and visitors brought their own food to be cooked to their own requirements. At that time there were no washbasins in the rooms. Hot water was carried upstairs every morning and evening, and each room had a washstand with a large jug and basin. There were no bathrooms, but fortunately there was a lavatory — or WC — on each landing. By the time the war started in 1939 washbasins had been installed, and the visitors no longer brought their own food. They were, however, provided with three meals a day: a cooked breakfast, midday dinner, and 'high tea'.

The summer of 1939 had been a particularly busy one. The continuous sunshine had tempted record numbers of visitors to Blackpool and to other seaside resorts. Ada said it had been one of the best seasons she had ever known, but numbers began to dwindle as the rumours of war became a reality.

Lizzie recalled that the evacuees had been an unruly lot, apart from a few helpful ones, and they had been glad to see the back of them. The RAF recruits, though, were a different kettle of fish. They had breezed in like a gust of fresh air, bringing new life and a spirit of joviality to the place. Lizzie unashamedly enjoyed their company, although she had to watch her Ps and Qs under her mother's eagle eye.

'Don't forget you're a married woman, our Lizzie,' her mother would remind her.

Norman had joined up early in 1940 and Lizzie realized, with a feeling of guilt, that she didn't miss him as much as she should. They had been married for seven years, and Megan was now almost six years old. They were happy enough together, but Lizzie had never been head over heels in love with her husband, and she suspected that neither had he been with her. She had met him at a church social evening, although he had always been around with the rest of the lads she knew, and after a couple of years they had got married. She was twenty-one and did not need her mother's permission. Lizzie admitted to herself that she was marrying partly to get away from her mother's iron-fisted control.

They agreed that they would live in the boarding house rather than in a place of their own, provided that Norman continued with his own work as a painter and decorator and played no part in the running of the business. Norman was easy-going and usually agreed with what Lizzie decided.

'It makes sense anyway, love,' he said to her. 'Your mam won't charge us rent, and we'll have our bed and board. Can't be bad, eh?'

It did afford them the privacy they needed, and it was convenient for Lizzie not to have to travel to her place of work. Also, her mother was always available to look after Megan if ever Lizzie and Norman wanted a little time on their own.

Ada loved her granddaughter, and she was always more lenient and affectionate towards Megan than she had been to her own two daughters. After Lizzie's marriage, Alice became more dominated than ever by her mother, and did not have the spirit that her sister had to stick up for herself.

Lizzie was relieved that Norman was safe — or as safe as he could be — in his camp down south, and she had adjusted to her life without him.

It was early in 1942 that Lizzie met Alan Whittaker. He was the sergeant in charge of the billet and therefore came into closer contact with Ada, the landlady, and her second-in-command, Lizzie, than did the rest of the men, regarding the rules and regulations and the conduct of the recruits. There had, however, been very little trouble. The RAF lads were pleased to have such a good billet — above all, good food — and they found the pleasures that Blackpool offered were a welcome diversion from the arduous training programme and thoughts of the terrors that might lie ahead.

The news had been grim for a while. Following the debacle of Dunkirk, the Blitz had begun in earnest. The Battle of Britain raged in the skies above southern England; there had been the destruction of Coventry, and London and other big cities were bombed nightly.

Very little happened, though, in the skies above Blackpool. The dropping of a bomb on Seed Street, a row of terraced houses near to North Station, had been an isolated incident, but it had caused several deaths and destruction of property.

'Happen they were trying to bomb your factory, Alice,' commented Ada, but the munitions factory had not been affected. 'Or happen North Station just across the road. Anyroad, we're all safe, thank the Lord.'

Alan Whittaker commented to Lizzie that it was probably a pilot getting rid of his last bomb, maybe aiming for — but missing — the sea before heading back home.

'Although there's a theory that Blackpool will not be targeted,' he told her, 'there are thousands of us RAF blokes here, and a few bombs could get rid of a whole lot of us. But Blackpool Tower is a good landmark; the pilots know exactly where they are and they use it to turn round and head back across the Irish Sea. And I've also heard that Hitler regards Blackpool as a great holiday resort for the Germans to inhabit once they've won the war!'

'Fat chance of that!' replied Lizzie. 'Especially now.'

For it seemed that the tide had turned. Following the bombing of the American naval fleet by the Japanese at Pearl Harbor, in December 1941, America had entered the war.

It had been feared, during the early years, that Britain would be invaded, that it was only a matter of time, but no one was allowed to say so. Defeatist talk was frowned upon and could be a punishable offence, although mutterings went on in some quarters.

'I won't have that sort of talk in my house,' Ada had declared. She had asked Lizzie to write out, in her best copybook printing, the words spoken by Queen Victoria to the troops during the Boer War.

Please understand there is no depression in this house and we are not interested in the possibilities of defeat. They do not exist.

This framed quotation had been hung in the dining room where all the lads read it and took it to heart. It was still there a year later as a reminder that Britain would be victorious, and that, indeed, was now beginning to seem more likely.

Sergeant Alan Whittaker was rather older than the rest of the recruits. He was twenty-five, and Lizzie at that time was twenty-nine. He was tall and dark-haired, not conventionally handsome — his nose was rather long, and his teeth in his wide mouth were a little crooked — but he had a winning smile and shrewd grey eyes that could be either serious or light-hearted.

Lizzie often chatted with him when she served supper to the men in the evenings; a cup of tea or coffee and a biscuit for those who had remained in the billet. Many of them, of course, were out enjoying themselves in Blackpool's many cinemas or pubs or the three ballrooms.

Alan, more often than not, was sitting by himself engrossed in a book.

The lads who stayed in had various ways of spending the evening: playing draughts or dominoes or chess, for a select few. Ada had bought a chess set and a darts board at a jumble sale for the entertainment of her RAF lads. She regarded them as her special responsibility and it seemed there was little she would not do for them.

One thing that was not allowed in the billet was alcohol, and this was the rule in most houses. If they wanted to drink there were scores of pubs, and if one or two of them occasionally returned home a little merry Ada would turn a blind eye. They managed to have fun, though, singing around the piano. 'Run Rabbit Run' was a great favourite, and so was 'Lili Marlene', which had been pinched from the Germans. Or they joined in with Vera Lynn or Anne Shelton — the Forces' Sweethearts — on the wireless, singing along, though rather less tunefully, to the heartrending songs 'We'll Meet Again' or 'Silver Wings in the Moonlight'.

'What are you reading?' Lizzie asked Alan one evening in February as she handed him a cup of tea.

'Oh, one of my favourite murder mysteries,' he replied. 'I've read it before, but it's such an intriguing plot that I'm reading it again.'

He showed her the green paperback Penguin book of The ABC Murders by Agatha Christie.

'I like Agatha Christie, too,' said Lizzie. She sat down on the chair opposite him; all the other men had been served and her work was finished for the moment. 'I haven't read that one but I've read a lot of the others. I think *Murder on the Orient Express* was the cleverest one. I'd never have guessed who done it. And it turned out to be all of them!' She put a hand to her mouth. 'Oh, gosh . . . I hope you've read it or else I'll have spoiled it.'

'Yes, of course I have. It's a classic. I think it will always be her most famous one. What else do you read, Lizzie, as well as murder mysteries?'

'Not a great deal, I'm afraid. I like a nice romance or a family story, and my woman's magazine I get every week. I don't get much time to read, and if my mother sees me reading, she says, 'Get your head out of that book, Lizzie. There's all this work to be done!''

Alan grinned. 'She keeps your nose to the grindstone, does she?'

'You can say that again!'

'I know you both work very hard. This is a jolly good billet. I know all the lads think so.'

'Yes, I suppose it is; and you lads bring out the softer side in my mother. I know she wishes she had a son rather than us two girls, and now she's got a houseful of lads to look after.'

'I'm sure she appreciates you, though she may not show it. Your sister goes out to work, doesn't she?'

'Yes, she works at the munitions factory. I'm real glad she had a chance to get away from Mother's apron strings. She wouldn't say boo to a goose before, but the factory has given her a taste of freedom, and she's making the most of it.'

'I don't blame her. She's a pretty girl . . . and so is her sister,' he added rather coyly.

'Thank you, kind sir!' Lizzie felt herself blushing a little. 'I don't get much chance to dress up though, nowadays, like our Alice does. And there's Megan to see to, of course.'

'Yes, she's a bonny little girl. How old is she?'

'She's seven, nearly eight. Do you have any children, Alan?'

He chuckled. 'None that I know of.'

'What?' She looked puzzled for a moment, then she grinned.

'No . . . I'm not married,' he said. 'I did have a girlfriend, but she joined the Land Army and . . . well, it sort of fizzled out.'

Lizzie nodded. 'That's a pity, but I supposed it happens sometimes. What was your job before you joined the RAF?' She hoped she wasn't being too nosey. 'If you don't mind telling me,' she added.

'No, why should I? I ran a garage with my father, in Sheffield. I was quite good on the mechanical side, so I was in charge of repairs and the maintenance of the vehicles. And that's what I'm doing here; they put you to the job you're most suited to, but it's aircraft engines rather than cars. In fact, I'm a trainee instructor now because I took to it quite easily.'

'So you'll be part of the ground crew, will you, instead of flying? Although I know it's just as important.'

He shrugged. 'Who can tell what we'll end up doing? We all have to play our part, one way or the other.' He stopped as Ada entered the room.

'Hey up! Here comes the boss,' he said in an undertone.

Ada sometimes came in around ten o'clock to see what was going on. She started stacking the empty cups and saucers on a tray, casting an enquiring glance in Lizzie's direction. Lizzie, however, did not jump to her feet as though she was doing something wrong.

She smiled at Alan. 'It's been nice talking to you,' she said.

'Same here,' he replied with a wide grin. 'I'll lend you this book; I think you'll enjoy it.'

'Thank you,' she said, then on a sudden whim she added, quietly, 'Come and have a cup of tea with me in my room sometime . . . if you would like to. It gets a bit rowdy down here, doesn't it? You know where I am, don't you? On the first floor, at the front.'

'Yes, it says 'Private' on the door. Perhaps tomorrow evening?'

'Yes, why not? It's Alice's turn to help with the suppers tomorrow night.' Alice had agreed that she would help out occasionally in the evening when she was not 'gadding about' as her mother put it, and she always did so on Thursday evening.

'I'd better go and help Mother now,' Lizzie went on. Ada was talking to two lads at the other end of the room and did not hear their conversation.

Alan grinned again, and she noticed the laughter lines around his eyes. He winked. 'She can't very well sack you, can she?'

To her surprise her mother did not admonish

her. 'I'm glad you were talking to the sergeant,' she said. 'I sometimes think he looks a bit lonely, poor lad . . . Anyroad, come on, Lizzie. Let's get these pots washed before we go to bed.'

There was a tap on the door the following evening at about quarter to nine. Lizzie was pleased to see Alan there with a couple of books in his hand. She had changed from her working clothes into one of her Sunday skirts and a red jumper which went well with her dark hair. She had put on a smear of red lipstick, then blotted it so that it didn't look tarty.

'I'm not too early, am I?' he said. 'I guessed your little girl might be in bed by now.'

'Yes, she is,' said Lizzie. 'Come on in, Alan. Megan usually goes to bed around half past eight. She's a good little girl and she never complains about it . . . Not that it would matter if she was still up,' she added, trying to convince herself that it was perfectly normal for her to entertain one of the men in her private room. Anyway, he was rather a special case, being the sergeant . . . but Lizzie knew that her mother would not approve if she found out.

'This is a cosy room,' he said, glancing around appreciatively. 'It's nice to see a coal fire.'

'Yes, I only light it around teatime, though, to save our coal ration. Megan and I have our midday dinner downstairs with Mother, seeing as I'm working down there. Take your jacket off, Alan . . . if you'd like to. Make yourself at home.'

'Thanks,' he said, placing his service jacket on the back of an easy chair. He sat down in one of the two armchairs. Lizzie was aware that they were a little shabby, the maroon moquette rather worn on the arms.

The dark red velveteen curtains were closely drawn over the blackout blinds. A cherry-red hearthrug stood in front of the brass fender, and on the hearth there was a brass coal scuttle and a collection of brass fire irons. At either end of the mantelpiece there was a brass candlestick. Cleaning them all was a fortnightly chore which Lizzie did not particularly enjoy but which had to be done. She was proud of her little domain and wanted it always to look bright and cheerful.

In one alcove at the side of the fireplace there was a gramophone with a horn, and in the other alcove a wireless set in a cabinet.

'It's nice to be in a real home again,' said Alan, smiling at Lizzie. 'That's the thing we miss most of all. It's a comfortable billet, of course; it couldn't be better, but it's little things, like a coal fire and a hearthrug and all these nice brass things you have.'

'A devil to clean, though!' said Lizzie.

'Well, more power to your elbow,' said Alan. 'I know a woman's work is never done.' He handed her the two books he had brought.

Lizzie sat down in the opposite chair and looked at them. 'Thanks,' she said. '*The ABC Murders*; I shall enjoy reading that. And what is this?' She glanced at the name of the author of the other book. 'I've never heard of her, or is it a man? I can't read the name; at least I can't pronounce it. Ne-ge . . . ' She shook her head.

'Ngaio Marsh,' said Alan, 'pronounced Nigh-o. She's a New Zealander; that's why it's such an odd name, to us at any rate.'

'And is this a murder mystery?'

'Yes, one of her earlier ones. Some people say they're rather more intellectual than Agatha Christie's, but they're quite easy to read and very intriguing. Anyway, read it and see what you think.'

'Yes, I will, when I have time,' said Lizzie. 'I've told you my mother's views on reading. There are far more important things to be doing! But I do try to have a life of my own; she doesn't know everything!'

'It must be lonely for you at times with your husband away. How is he getting on?'

'All right, as far as I know. He's not the world's best letter writer; but then you're not allowed to say too much in letters, are you? I know that they're censored. I suppose they're just training and marking time, aren't they, the soldiers that are still in England. Waiting till the time is right to make a move?'

'Yes, the war is being fought mainly in the air at the moment, as we know to our cost. But our lads are bombing the German cities as well.'

'Tit for tat . . . '

'Yes, you could say so.' Alan sighed. 'Ridiculous, isn't it? I don't suppose many of the Germans want this any more than we do. I often wonder what the children think about it all; kiddies like your Megan growing up in a world full of hatred. It's bound to have some effect on them. There's so much on the wireless and in the newspapers.'

'I don't suppose they think too much about it,'

said Lizzie. 'School carries on as usual, and that's where they are most of the time. I dare say the lads play war games in the playground; pretending to shoot one another, and dropping bombs, and so on. But it's always been the same, hasn't it? It used to be cowboys and Indians. And they have special efforts at school for the soldiers, sailors and airmen; raffles and jumble sales — it's all quite light-hearted. Megan certainly doesn't dwell on what's happening in the war. She misses her daddy, of course.'

'As I'm sure you do?'

'Yes, of course I do,' Lizzie answered promptly, 'but we just have to get on with the job, all of us, whatever it might be. I remember the first war — just about. Not the start of it; I was only two when it started, but I remember my dad coming back.'

'Was he over in France or Belgium?'

'Yes, he was, so I suppose it was lucky he came back at all. He had suffered, though, from the effects of poison gas. That was a dreadful thing, wasn't it?'

'Yes, indeed, and that's why we've all got these flippin' gas masks. It was only a precaution and thank God we haven't needed them. Your father died, though, didn't he, as a result of his war injuries?'

'It must have had an effect. He actually died of the Spanish flu, as so many did. He was one of the last to pass in 1920, such a way to go. That was a year after Alice was born; and soon afterwards my mother and the two of us moved to Blackpool. And the boarding house became a

98

way of life for all of us. Anyway, I'll make us a cup of tea. I have an electric kettle up here so we can have a drink and a snack. If I want to cook anything I have to go downstairs to the kitchen, but we manage, especially as there's only me and Megan now.'

She went to the large dark oak sideboard at the back of the room and took out the kettle and cups and saucers and a biscuit tin from the cupboard. There was a power point nearby, and they were soon enjoying tea and biscuits, which Lizzie placed on a small table between the two armchairs.

'You seem to do very well for us here, despite the shortages,' said Alan. 'You put on such appetizing meals.'

'We listen to 'The Kitchen Front' on the wireless in the morning while we're washing up,' said Lizzie. 'Lord Woolton has all sorts of hints to make the food go further. And we have a very good butcher and grocer. I think they all do a bit of under-the-counter business on the quiet. And we get black-market eggs now and again from a farm near Poulton,' she added in a whisper. 'But don't tell anyone! Alice rides out there on her bike on a Sunday.'

They chatted easily of this and that; about his sister's work as a Land Girl and how she was enjoying the country life after being brought up in a city. He told her about his father's garage and the older men he now employed because all the younger men were in the forces; and about his mother's work with the WVS.

The time flew by as Lizzie enjoyed the

companionship of a young man who seemed to be on her wavelength. She and Norman, after several years of marriage, had sometimes hardly spoken when they sat together in the evening. Not that the silence was loaded with tension or animosity; it was just that they had found very little to talk about any more, preferring to listen to the wireless or for Lizzie to knit while Norman hid away behind a newspaper.

Lizzie could scarcely believe that it was eleven o'clock so soon.

'Goodness! I'd better be off,' said Alan, glancing at the clock on the mantelshelf. He rose and put on his jacket. 'You need your beauty sleep, and so do I.' He laughed. 'Not that it ever improves the way I look, but you always look bright-eyed and bushy-tailed when you serve breakfast in the morning. Thank you, Lizzie; I've really enjoyed our evening together.' He took hold of her arms and leaned forward, gently kissing her cheek. 'Shall we . . . do this again?'

'I don't see why not,' said Lizzie. 'I've enjoyed it too.'

'Next Thursday then?' he asked.

'Yes, I'll look forward to it.'

'Goodnight then, Lizzie. God bless . . . ' He opened the door then closed it quietly behind him.

And that was how it started. They met on Thursday evenings through the spring of 1942 and into the summer. Lizzie read the books he lent her, when she had time, so that they could talk about them, although they never ran short of topics for conversation. Occasionally Alan arrived a little earlier, before Megan had gone to bed. The little girl and the sergeant had a good rapport. He asked her about school, though never in a condescending way. She sensed that he really was interested, and she told him that she loved reading and writing stories, but she wasn't too keen on sums. Lizzie never warned her daughter not to say anything to Grandma about Alan visiting them. That would be making too much of what was just an innocent friendship . . . at least that was how it started. But Lizzie need not have feared. Megan seemed to know instinctively that it was a secret and that it would be best if her gran did not know about it.

Occasionally when Alan was leaving Lizzie's room he had encountered Alice on the landing. He had smiled and said goodnight in a casual manner, and Alice had smiled back rather knowingly.

'Don't worry about our Alice,' Lizzie told him. 'She's too much sense to say anything to Mother. Anyway, I guess she has a few secrets of her own.'

In the early summer Alan told Lizzie that his stay in Blackpool had been extended. He was now acting as an instructor on the maintenance of engines to new recruits and would be there for several more months.

By this time their friendship had become more meaningful. Their liking for one another had developed into fondness and a desire to be together, which might well lead to a more intimate relationship. They both knew that this would be foolish, and that they must try not to let their feelings get out of control.

Alan was single and free to do as he wished, but Lizzie was married with a child. Moreover, her husband was in the army serving his country, and was deserving of her love and loyalty while he was away. Their awareness of one another grew stronger as the weeks went by, although they did not speak of it to one another.

They sat together in a companionable way one evening in late May. They had enjoyed a pleasant chat over a cup of Nescafé and an iced bun; Megan had helped her mother to bake them and insisted that Alan should try one. They were now relaxing, each of them in an easy chair listening to the evocative strains of Glenn Miller's 'Moonlight Serenade'. The air was charged with their desire for one another.

Suddenly Alan sprang to his feet and stood in front of Lizzie. He held out his hand. 'Care to dance, ma'am?' he asked in a somewhat corny American accent.

'Sure, I don't mind if I do,' she replied, standing up and taking hold of his hand. Then, in her normal voice, she added, 'I'm not much of a dancer, you know. What is this anyway? I suppose it's a foxtrot; I was never much good at that.'

'Never mind,' said Alan. 'Neither am I. But a foxtrot is just walking backwards, isn't it? It's a shame to waste this lovely tune.'

He put his arm around her, holding her close, and they moved around the room swaying gently to the rhythm, not really dancing but feeling a deep contentment in what was their first real embrace. She laid her head on his shoulder and he gently stroked her hair.

When the magic ended and the needle started to scratch they were standing still in a world of their own, not wanting to let go. Then Alan bent to kiss her lips. He had kissed her before, fleetingly, in a friendly way when they said goodnight, but this was different. Lizzie felt herself responding, her lips parting as his kiss became more ardent.

Then he released her, standing back and smiling at her. She smiled back, their eyes expressing what they had both been feeling for quite some time.

'That was what we both wanted, wasn't it?' he whispered.

'Yes,' she replied. 'But . . . oh, Alan, we shouldn't — we mustn't.'

'It was inevitable,' he said. 'You know that, Lizzie, don't you?'

'Yes, but . . . ' She drew away from him, crossing the room. She lifted the arm from the gramophone and put the record back in its cover.

She had been going to say that Norman would be very hurt if he found out.

There was a time in mid-summer when Norman came home on leave for a few days. Lizzie found that she was pleased to see him, more so than she had thought she would be, and she knew when he made love to her that she must respond and appear eager. She tried to convince herself that this was something apart from her relationship with Alan. She had never done this with Alan; they were just very loving friends expressing what they felt for one another. That was something quite separate from her marriage, and she had known all along that a time would come when she and Alan would have to part. And never once did she even wish to put an end to her marriage. She and Alan were just 'ships that pass in the night'.

Lizzie did not warn Megan not to say anything to her daddy about Alan visiting them. And just as the little girl had kept quiet and not told her grandma, neither did she mention it to her father. How much did she know, how much did she understand? Lizzie wondered. But children had a way of accepting things, not always comprehending them but knowing instinctively that they must keep it to themselves.

There was someone who had guessed what was going on, however, and that was Alice. She had always got on well with her brother-in-law and she felt that what Lizzie was doing was wrong.

'You're getting on very well with Sergeant Whittaker, aren't you?' Alice said to her one Sunday in August when they were washing up together. 'I've seen him several times coming out of your room.'

'Yes, we're quite good friends,' said Lizzie nonchalantly. 'He lends me books and we have a chat together. He gets lonely sometimes because he doesn't go out drinking and dancing like most of them do.'

'You're doing rather more than read books though, aren't you?' said Alice, raising her eyebrows.

Lizzie felt herself colouring a little, and she

knew she couldn't deny that they were a little more than friends.

'Not really,' she replied. 'Not very much . . . It just happened, Alice. We like one another, a lot. But we haven't done anything — you know — really wrong. Anyway, you've no room to talk, have you? What about you and Tony Sinclair?'

'What about it?' retorted Alice. 'The difference is that I'm not married, am I?'

Lizzie thought to herself how much Alice had changed; how assertive she had become since she started going out to work.

'Don't worry, I won't tell Mother,' Alice went on. 'And I certainly won't tell Norman. He would be heartbroken, our Lizzie.'

Lizzie knew her sister was right. 'I know,' she said. 'I don't want to hurt him but he won't ever know. And I've told you, nothing much has happened. Anyway, he'll be leaving soon . . . '

Alan left towards the end of October. He was transferred to a camp in the south of England to continue his work as an instructor. They both knew that their parting would be a final one. They would never meet again. The night before he left, however, they both knew that their feelings were too strong to be denied. Their love reached a conclusion for the first and only time.

Lizzie never saw Alan again and heard from him only once. He sent her a letter soon after they had said goodbye. She shed a few tears, then hid it away in her underwear drawer. And there it remained.

By this time Alice and the young corporal, Tony Sinclair, knew they were falling in love.

8

The thought of going out to work, especially working in a munitions factory with probably hundreds of other young women — and men — had at first frightened Alice to death. But she knew she had no choice. All young unmarried women were obliged to do war work of some kind — to join one of the women's services, to work as a Land Girl, or to work in an aircraft or munitions factory.

Her sister, Lizzie, had tried to convince her that it might not be a bad idea to get away from home for a while, mainly to cut loose from her mother's apron strings.

'Learn to stand up for yourself,' Lizzie told her. 'I don't know how you put up with it, being bossed around day after day. You're nothing but a skivvy for her, Alice, and the less you say the more she'll put on you.'

'I haven't got your spirit, Lizzie,' replied Alice. 'I daren't answer her back like you do. She's clouted me across the head before now for giving cheek, as she calls it.'

'She was the same with me before I married Norman, but she daren't do it now. Anyroad, you'll have to make up your mind, Alice, what you're going to do. You don't want to join the ATS or the WAAF, and I can't say I blame you, but what about going to work as a Land Girl? Nice countryside and fresh air, and you like animals, don't you?'

'Only cats, or dogs, if they're small ones,' said Alice. 'I don't think I'd be right keen on cows or horses. No, I shall go to work at the Vickers-Armstrongs factory over by the bus station and help to make aeroplanes. I'll be doing my bit for King and country, won't I? And there'll no doubt be some girls there that I can be friendly with.'

'That's the spirit,' said Lizzie. 'I wish it was me that was going, but I'm stuck here in the bloomin' kitchen. You make the most of your freedom, Alice.'

And after a few weeks, sure enough, Alice had come to enjoy working at the factory; not so much the work itself, which was mindless and monotonous, endlessly fastening rivets together, but she enjoyed the chatter and the comradeship of other young women, which was something she had not experienced very much before. She realized what a relief it was to get away from her home and from the constant demands of her mother.

The best thing of all was that she made some new friends. There were three of them, Freda, Doris and Winnie, who all worked at the same bench as Alice. Freda and Doris were eighteen years old, younger than Winnie and Alice who, at the time they met, were twenty-one.

Alice's new friends were surprised when she told them her age; they had assumed she was a few years younger. This did not please Alice; she did not want to be thought of as young and immature, aware that her new friends were more worldly wise and self-assured than she was. They did not tease her, though, or make fun of her in any way. They listened in amazement when she told them how she had worked in her mother's boarding house since leaving school at fourteen. They were astonished when she told them that she had never had a boyfriend.

'Well, not a proper one,' she said, trying to make it sound a bit less incredulous. 'There were some lads I was friendly with at the church youth club.'

She had gone there for a while when she was in her teens and had learned to play table tennis and to dance a little at church social evenings. But none of the lads had ever asked her to go out with them. The truth was that she was very shy and not good at making conversation. In a group she was the one who had very little to say. It was not because she was dull or unintelligent, just very lacking in confidence.

She had never been dancing at any of the places in Blackpool, and when her new friends suggested they should all go to the Tower Ballroom, Alice was scared stiff at the idea.

'I can't dance,' she protested. 'Well, not properly, and . . . it's something I've never done.'

'Then it's high time you did,' said Winnie. 'She's going with us, isn't she, girls?'

Freda and Doris agreed, and between them they persuaded Alice to go with them to the Tower Ballroom the following week.

It was Winnie who took Alice in hand and told her it was time she started living and, above all, started sticking up for herself against her tyrannical mother. Winnie thought she sounded unbelievably awful.

'She's not really so bad,' said Alice, feeling guilty at the impression she might have given. 'She can be quite nice sometimes, but she still thinks of me as her little girl.'

'Well, you're not,' said Winnie. 'You're old enough to get married without her consent; don't you realize that?'

'Fat chance of that ever happening,' said Alice.

'There you go again,' said Winnie. 'Stop running yourself down, Alice. There are lots of fellows out there, and there'll be one for you, if you give yourself a chance, you'll see. I had one or two boyfriends before I met Keith, but we both knew quite soon that we were right for each other. But he's told me to go out and enjoy myself while he's away. There's no point in staying at home and feeling miserable.'

'He knows you go out dancing, then?'

'Of course he does. And you know what they say about sailors — a girl in every port. But we trust one another, Keith and me.'

'When are you getting married then?'

'We're supposed to be waiting till the end of the war, but who knows? We might decide that's too long to wait.'

Keith was in the Merchant Navy and was away for several months at a time. Winnie wore her three-stone diamond ring with pride, not disguising the fact that she was engaged even when she went out dancing. Freda and Doris also had boyfriends who were both in the army, but Alice guessed that for both of them it was

109

quite a casual relationship.

Winnie lived not very far from Alice, not in a boarding house but in a small terraced house with her parents and young brother. Her father was a bus driver in Blackpool, and her mother had a part-time job at the Boots the Chemists store in the town.

Winnie invited Alice to go round one evening. 'I'll show you how to do your hair and make-up,' she told her, 'then you'll know what to do when we go to the Tower. You're a pretty girl, Alice, but you don't make the most of yourself. I wish I had nice blonde hair like yours.'

Alice's hair was a pale golden colour and reached almost to her shoulders. It had a slight natural wave, but she usually fastened it back with a couple of grips when it was not hidden under her turban. By contrast, Winnie's hair was dark brown and perfectly straight. Every few months she had a permanent wave which tended to make it frizz. She wore a couple of diamante slides in it when she went out in the evening. She had warm brown eyes and a winning smile, and if her hair was not her crowning glory, no one really noticed.

They sat on the bed in Winnie's bedroom, and she brushed and combed her friend's hair. 'There you are,' she said. 'It looks real nice when you have it loose, and you could coax it into a pageboy style. A few curlers in the ends and you'd look just like Betty Grable!'

'Go on with you!' said Alice. 'Don't talk daft!'

'I mean it,' said Winnie. 'A bit of powder and lipstick, and maybe a touch of eyeshadow, and

110

you'll be a real glamour girl.'

'I've never worn make-up,' said Alice. 'Mother always says that all you need for your skin is soap and water, and a dab of cold cream in the winter to stop it from getting chapped.'

'My mum's a lot younger,' said Winnie. 'She was only eighteen when I was born. My dad's quite a lot older, though. Mum's never been all that strict with me. And it's good her working at Boots. She's on the make-up counter sometimes, and she tells me when they've got some new lipsticks in. They're real scarce now, of course, but she brought one home for me the other day. Look . . . ' Winnie took a lipstick in a golden case from a tray on her dressing table. 'It's a Max Factor. See . . . it's a nice cherry red.' She tried it on her hand. 'I think it would be a bit bright for you; a pink one would be better. Would you like one?'

'Er . . . yes, I think so. It would be nice, but . . . '

'Go on, be a devil! Never mind about your mother. You could put it on when we get to the Tower, but I wouldn't bother about her, really I wouldn't.'

There was a knock at the door at that moment, then Winnie's mother came in with a laden tray.

'Supper for you, girls,' she said. There were slices of jam sponge cake, custard cream biscuits and a pot of tea. 'Hello, Alice. Nice to see you again, love.'

'Hello, Mrs Brewster,' said Alice. 'That looks lovely, have you been baking?' She smiled at the pretty, dark-haired woman who didn't look much older than Winnie.

'Yes, we deserve a treat once in a while, don't we? And there are real eggs in the cake, not that awful dried stuff. Let me know when you're going, Alice. Not that I'm rushing you — you can stay as long as you like — but George will walk you home. We don't want you stumbling about in the blackout.'

'I've got my torch, Mrs Brewster, but . . . yes thank you, that would be good. Mother worries about it as well, and she likes me to be in by half past ten.'

'Mum, do you think you could get one of those lipsticks for Alice?' asked Winnie. 'I showed her mine, but we think a pink shade would be better.'

'Yes, of course,' said Elsie Brewster. 'They're under the counter,' she added in a whisper, 'but I'll see what I can do.'

'Your mum's lovely, isn't she?' said Alice when Mrs Brewster had gone.

'Yes, I can't complain,' said Winnie. 'Come on now; tuck in, then we'll make you all glamorous.'

It was decided that Alice should go round to Winnie's home on Wednesday evening, then they would get ready together for their visit to the Tower. Alice had her new pink lipstick, and she wore a few curlers in her hair beneath her turban while she was at work that day.

'I can't believe you've never been to the Tower before,' said Winnie as they prepared for their evening out.

'I didn't say I'd never been to the Tower,'

112

replied Alice. 'I've been in the Tower building but I've never been dancing. I've seen the animals in the menagerie — I felt sorry for them — and the fish in the aquarium, and I had a peep into the ballroom but not to dance. And Mum took us to the Tower circus when we were little — well, I'd be about four. I remember I was a bit scared of the clowns, but I liked all the rest of it; the galloping horses and the acrobats and the elephants sitting on little stools.'

They put on their dresses. Alice's was her one and only 'best' dress that had been new for her twenty-first birthday. It was deep pink and made of a silky rayon material with fashionable padded shoulders, a short skirt and fitted bodice with silver buttons down the front. Winnie's dress was turquoise blue in a similar fabric, with a pleated skirt and a sweetheart neckline.

'Now, let's see to your hair,' said Winnie. She combed out Alice's silky blonde hair, deftly turning the ends under so that it framed her face. 'There, what did I tell you? You look just like a film star.'

Alice looked in the mirror and smiled, admitting to herself that she did look nice. And with her lips coloured in a shade that complemented her dress, a dusting of powder and a touch of blue eyeshadow she looked a completely different girl.

They had arranged to meet Freda and Doris outside the Tower at the promenade entrance as they lived in a different part of the town. The April evening was chilly and they needed to wear coats, which they left in the cloakroom before they went through to the ballroom.

It was already crowded with couples dancing energetically to the music of 'It's a Hap-Hap-Happy Day', while Ena Baga played with all her heart and soul on the great Wurlitzer organ.

The dance floor was dominated by air force blue, as were the streets of Blackpool day after day, but there was a touch of khaki here and there and a few naval uniforms, and the ladies' dresses added a splash of colour.

Alice gazed around at the magical scene before her; the marble pillars leading up to the gilded balconies, the red plush seating and the frescoed ceiling with its scenes of nymphs and shepherds and shepherdesses, and the ballroom floor with its tessellated design of oak, walnut and maple woods, resounding with the clatter of hundreds of dancing feet. She felt that she was in an enchanted world.

She soon came down to earth, though, as Winnie persuaded her on to the floor to dance a quickstep and she had to concentrate on her footwork. It was not unusual for girls to dance together, and the four of them did so, changing partners after each dance.

Alice wondered if someone else — a man of course — would ask her to dance, something she half dreaded and half wanted to happen, and so it did. She danced with a young airman, a soldier, and then an older man in a lounge suit, who said he thought she looked rather lonely standing there.

All in all it was a pleasant evening and Alice had a good time. Her friends persuaded her to go with them to one of the several bars in the Tower, and she enjoyed her first taste of a shandy.

This was the first of many such outings that the friends made together. They did not always go to the Tower. The Empress Ballroom in the Winter Gardens was equally magnificent, and so was the one in the Palace building, although it was rather smaller. At the Palace you could go to the cinema or to a show at the Variety Theatre, then go dancing at no extra charge, and Alice found that she enjoyed the more intimate feeling of the Palace ballroom.

In the summer of 1942 Winnie's fiancé, Keith, returned from a voyage. They decided they did not want to wait any longer and were married by special licence. When Keith returned to sea Winnie continued to live with her parents; and a few weeks later she discovered that she was pregnant.

And at the same time Alice met Tony Sinclair. It was a warm evening in July and she was at the Winter Gardens with Freda and Doris. Winnie didn't go with them now when they went dancing. She would go to the cinema or to a variety show at the Palace theatre, but she had decided, because she was a married woman, and particularly because she was pregnant, that dancing was a step too far. Apart from that, she was also tired after a day's work at the factory; she hoped to continue working there for several more months.

Alice, with Lizzie's help, had been doing a bit of 'make do and mend'. Articles were always appearing in women's magazines, showing women how to renovate their clothes to give them a new lease of life. New clothes could now only be purchased with clothing coupons, and if one wanted, for instance, a new coat, or a dress and a pair of shoes, the allocation was soon gone.

Lizzie had helped Alice to transform a summer dress she had had for a couple of years by adding a band of bright blue cotton material to lengthen the skirt, and blue buttons and a wide blue belt and a lace collar to the bodice. It was obvious that it had been re-modelled, but no one bothered as countless girls were doing the same with their old garments.

Alice was standing by a pillar at the side of the ballroom floor. Freda and Doris had gone on for a dance together, but Alice no longer worried about being a wallflower as she had at first. She enjoyed listening to the music and watching the dancers, and if someone asked her to dance she no longer feared that she would be tongue-tied or fall over her feet.

It was not long before a young RAF man approached her. 'Would you like to dance?' he asked her, and she smiled and nodded in agreement.

Then he looked at her more intently. 'I know you, don't I?' he said.

She looked at his puzzled grey eyes. He had a pleasant face with rather angular features and a wide mouth.

'I don't know,' she began, 'unless . . . might you have billeted with us? My mother has a boarding house in North Shore, and we've had the RAF with us since the start of the war.'

'Of course, that's it!' Light dawned in his eyes. 'I knew I'd seen you before. I've seen you coming home from work, but you're usually wearing a turban and overalls. I've only been at Mrs Fletcher's for a couple of weeks. She's your mother, is she?'

'Yes, that's right. I don't see much of the lads because I'm out at work at the aircraft factory. I sometimes help with the suppers, though, on a Thursday evening. I'm sorry if I didn't recognize you at first. I think I do now.'

'Well, come on then, let's dance,' he said, taking her hand and leading her on to the floor.

The band was playing 'Run Rabbit Run' and Alice followed the young man's competent lead as they danced the quickstep.

'I don't know your name,' he said, 'except that your last name's Fletcher unless . . . you're not married, are you?'

She laughed. 'No, of course not. My name's Alice.'

'Pleased to meet you, Alice,' he said. 'I'm Tony . . . Tony Sinclair, and I'm not married either.'

She did not know how to answer that. She could hardly say 'Oh good'. Instead she said, 'My sister's married. You've probably seen Lizzie. She helps my mother in the boarding house. So did I, before I had to do some sort of war work.'

'Yes, I've seen Lizzie serving the meals. Your mother made me feel very welcome. She told me she's from Yorkshire, same as I am.'

'Yes, I thought you were a Yorkshire lad. We

117

came here from Bradford, my mother and Lizzie and me, soon after the last war. My father had died, and Mother decided to try her luck as a seaside landlady.'

'And I would say she made a jolly good job of it . . . You don't remember the last war though, do you?'

'No, but my sister does, just about. I was born in 1919, and my dad died soon afterward from Spanish flu; he'd served in the war and suffered from gas poisoning. So I don't remember him.'

'That's tough. My dad came through it all right, thank the Lord. I was born in 1919, same as you.'

'And whereabouts do you live in Yorkshire?'

'In Malton; it's on the road to York.'

'I've heard of it, but I've never been there. And what did you do in 'Civvy Street', as they call it?'

'I was an electrician, same as my dad. He has his own business and I worked with him, doing maintenance of people's appliances: cookers and radios and lighting and all that. I was training to be a wireless operator. I was at a camp in the Midlands at first and now they've sent me up here to work as an instructor for a while. That's why I've been promoted.' He smiled a little self-consciously but also with a touch of pride.

'Yes, I noticed you're a corporal. Well done!'

The quickstep music came to an end and a young lady vocalist stood at the mike singing 'Somewhere Over the Rainbow'.

'I love this song,' said Alice, 'but I'm not sure I can dance to it.'

'Let's sit this one out then and just listen,' said Tony.

They sat on the red plush seats and listened to the song made popular by Judy Garland.

'I went to see 'The Wizard of Oz' with my niece, Megan,' said Alice. 'I enjoyed the film just as much as she did.'

'You like going to the cinema, then?'

'Yes, who doesn't these days? I know it's escapism, but it's good to try and forget the horrors of war now and again. And there are some great films being made nowadays. Have you seen 'Gone with the Wind'?'

'Yes, of course . . . Let's go and have a drink, shall we? Then you can tell me what else you enjoy.'

They stayed together all evening, drinking shandies, dancing occasionally and enjoying one another's company. As evening blended into night it seemed that they had known each other for an age. And, of course, they would have to walk home together.

Alice said goodnight to Freda and Doris, explaining that she had met a young man who was billeted with them and that she would see them at work the next day. Her two friends winked and raised their eyebrows, and Alice walked home with her new friend through the blacked-out streets feeling as though she was in a dream.

Normally she would have gone on a bus, not daring to walk alone in the blackout, but Tony took her arm as they walked the mile and a half back to her home and his billet.

It was still not eleven o'clock when they arrived back as the dance halls closed early. No lights shone from the windows of the houses and Alice opened the door for just a few seconds, closing it quickly behind them for fear that even the dimmest light should shine out into the darkness.

There was the sound of the piano and chatter and laughter from the room where the men congregated in the evenings, but Tony didn't feel inclined to join them.

'I'd better go and say hello to my mother and Lizzie,' said Alice. 'They'll be having a cup of tea in the kitchen.'

'I'll say goodnight then,' said Tony. He put an arm around her shoulders, where they stood at the bottom of the stairs, then very gently kissed her lips. 'It's been a lovely evening, Alice,' he said, speaking almost in a whisper. 'I'm so pleased we've got to know each other. Will you go out with me again?'

'Yes, I'd like that,' she replied. 'I've enjoyed it too. Goodnight, Tony.' She stood on tiptoe — he was a few inches taller than her — and kissed his cheek.

He went quietly up the stairs, and Alice went to talk to her mother and Lizzie. They would think it odd if she didn't, and her mother always liked to know she was home safely when she had been out for the evening. She wouldn't say anything about Tony, at least not yet. But she had a feeling that this friendship would be a lasting one.

And that was how their romance started. They

both soon realized that their friendship had developed into a love that would go on and on. But who could say for how long in those uncertain times? They had to make the most of the precious time they had together.

Sunday was the day when they both had some free time. Alice did her share of work along with Lizzie in the morning, then she spent the afternoon and evening with Tony.

It was a memorable summer for Alice; one she looked back on with joy and nostalgia, but also with acute sadness when it came to a bitter ending. They walked northwards along the cliffs, or on the beach when the tide was out. They even paddled in the shallow water as the sea ebbed, then ran together hand in hand across the stretch of golden sand.

Sometimes they took a tram in the other direction, to Squires Gate, where they walked on the sand hills. They found a cosy spot out of the breeze that was always blowing, where they could be alone and express their love for one another. Tentatively at first, but there were times when their feelings were too strong to be denied. Tony always tried to be careful and considerate with this girl he loved so much, aware that he was the first real boyfriend she had had, and that these feelings and ardent lovemaking were new to her.

They had fun together at the Pleasure Beach, on the Big Dipper and the Ghost Train and Fun House. Tony tried his skill at the rifle range and the coconut shy, winning frivolous little prizes for Alice, which she kept in a special place knowing she would always treasure them.

His stay in Blackpool was extended as they were short of instructors, to the delight of both of them. As autumn turned to winter it was harder to find places to be alone. There were isolated tram shelters and dark alleyways and corners, but this made their love seem rather furtive.

Both Lizzie and her mother knew of her blossoming friendship with Tony Sinclair and he was openly accepted as Alice's boyfriend. Ada had little idea, though, of how deeply they felt about one another. Alice kept her feelings and emotions to herself.

'She might as well enjoy it while it lasts,' Ada said to Lizzie. 'He'll move on like all of 'em do, then that'll be the last we hear of him.'

Tony went home to Yorkshire for Christmas, then at the end of January he was told he was soon to be posted to a camp in the east of England. They both knew that they must spend some precious time together. Tony slept in a room with two other men but did not like to suggest to her that he should visit her in her bedroom. It was Alice who decided to do so.

'My room is on the top floor,' she told him, knowing that he was wary of making the suggestion. She was well aware of what her mother's reaction would be were she to find out.

They spent two nights — or part of the nights — together. They both knew that there would never be anyone else, and promised, God willing, that they would be together again when it was all over. Alice did not have a ring, but she wore a brooch he had given her as a token of his love.

They exchanged letters, declaring their love for one another. He told her that he was soon to stop his work as an instructor to become a wireless operator as part of Bomber Command.

She prayed continually for his safety but kept her deeper feelings to herself. It was at the beginning of March that she realized she might be pregnant.

9

Alice was frightened and incredulous. How could this have happened? Well, she knew how, of course; she wasn't so naive. But Tony had been so careful . . . Obviously not careful enough.

She did not confide in anyone at first. Freda and Doris were both happy and carefree chatting about the new boyfriends — airmen, of course — that they had met recently at the Tower. They thought that Alice's moodiness and lack of interest in anything was because she was missing Tony.

But by mid-March Alice was frantic with worry. One evening she went round to visit Winnie, who had now finished work and was at home with her parents, awaiting the arrival of her baby in a few weeks' time. When Winnie opened the door Alice thought how radiant and happy she looked. She flung her arms around Alice.

'How lovely to see you! Come and sit by the fire and we'll have a chat. Mum and Dad have gone to the pictures, so we'll be on our own.'

She led the way into the small living room where a cosy fire was burning. 'Take your coat off and make yourself at home . . . ' Then Winnie looked more closely at Alice. 'What's the matter, love?' she asked. 'Is it Tony? Not . . . bad news?'

Alice flopped down on the settee. She shook her head. 'No . . . no, it's not Tony. Well, I suppose it is in a way. Oh, Winnie . . . I'm pregnant!'

Winnie gasped, then realized she must not appear shocked. After all, it could happen to anyone; it might have happened to Winnie herself before it should have done! She must try to help her friend, if that were possible. She sat next to her and put an arm round her.

'Now, are you sure?' she asked.

'Yes; I've just missed a second period, and I've been sick in the morning.'

'So have you written to tell Tony? It's not as if he was a casual boyfriend. You really loved one another, didn't you?'

'No, I haven't told him. I can't worry him with all that. He's on active service, you know, flying over Germany. He needs all his wits about him.'

'And . . . have you told your mother?' asked Winnie, well aware that this was a silly question. Of course she hadn't. 'Or your sister?'

'Goodness me, no!' replied Alice, almost screaming. 'She'll kill me if she finds out. And I've not told our Lizzie, neither. She's been a bit funny with me lately. I suspected she'd got too friendly with that sergeant we had billeted with us. I said she wasn't being fair to Norman, and we had words about it.'

Winnie nodded. 'Yes . . . I see. But you really must tell your mother, Alice. She won't kill you, and I know you didn't really mean that. She'll probably be very shocked, but I'm sure she'll want to help you and support you, won't she? That's what mothers do. I know that mine would.'

'Yes, I know that. Your mum's lovely. But my

mother is a different kettle of fish. OK, she won't kill me — that's just a figure of speech — but she'll disown me; most likely show me the door.'

Winnie squeezed her hand. She knew that Alice's mother was rather a battle-axe; she was glad her own mother was not like that.

'I'll go and make us a cup of tea,' she said, making her way to the kitchen.

Alice reflected how a cup of tea was a panacea for all ills. But it would do little to solve this crisis.

Alice felt slightly better after her evening with Winnie. She tried to put her worries to one side as they talked about work and mutual friends, and about Winnie's baby that would soon be here. They hoped that Keith would get compassionate leave, and Winnie admitted that she would really like a little girl, although she wouldn't mind so long as the baby was healthy. And she asked Alice in advance if she would be godmother to the child.

Alice's eyes filled up with tears again. 'Thank you; I'd love to,' she replied, 'but I'll have to wait and see what happens, won't I?'

'Take care of yourself and try not to worry too much,' said Winnie as Alice was leaving. She put her arms round her friend again. 'It'll be all right, you'll see.'

But deep down Winnie was very concerned for her friend.

Lizzie poked her head round the kitchen door when she heard Alice come in.

'Is that you, our Alice?'

'Yes, I'm tired so I'm going straight to bed.

126

See you in the morning.'

'OK. Goodnight then . . . '

'Goodnight . . . ' Alice knew she was unable to talk any more that evening.

It was two days later, on Sunday, when they had washed the breakfast pots, that her mother tackled her.

'Get yerself into the kitchen an' sit down,' she said. 'I want to talk to you.'

Alice felt sick again. She had been sick already this morning, but this time it was with fear. Her mother already knew . . .

'Now, have you got summat to tell me?' Ada sat down in a chair opposite with Lizzie hovering in the background.

'No . . . no . . . ' Alice stammered, at a loss for words. 'What do you mean?'

'Don't you play silly beggars with me, young madam, pretending you don't know what I mean. You're pregnant, aren't you?'

'No!' shouted Alice, without really thinking. Then, 'Well . . . I don't know, I might be . . . '

'Of course you know, you little hussy! Our Lizzie's heard you throwing up in the morning. Anyroad, I can tell. It's as plain as the nose on your face. You're having a baby, God help us!' Ada shuddered. 'To think that a daughter of mine should do this to us! It's a good job that young feller isn't here or else I'd tear him limb from limb.'

Alice burst into tears. 'We didn't mean it to happen. We love one another. I love Tony and . . . and when all this is over we're going to be together. He loves me . . . '

'Over my dead body!' yelled Ada. 'There'll be no baby, at least not one that comes here. I'm ashamed of you, our Alice. I thought I'd brought you up to know what's right and what's wrong. I'll not have folks pointing their fingers at us because of your bad behaviour. The less anyone knows, the better. You haven't told anyone, have you?'

'I've . . . I've told Winnie,' said Alice in a whisper. Then, feeling angry now as well as frightened, she said, defiantly, 'I'm not ashamed, you know. I've told you, me and Tony love one another and . . . and I'm twenty-three years old now, Mother. You can't tell me what to do.'

'Don't you speak to me like that, you little madam!' Ada's face was as red as a beetroot and she was almost foaming at the mouth. 'So long as you live under my roof you'll do as I say, but you won't be here much longer. You'll go away and have that baby, then you'll come back here without it. I'm having no bastard kids in my house.'

'What do you mean?' cried Alice. 'You can't do that! Anyway, where do you think I can go?'

'You can go and stay with Maggie, my sister in Yorkshire. I could send you to one of them homes for naughty girls who've got themselves into trouble, like you've done, but it's best kept in the family. I know I've not seen Maggie for ages, but we've never fallen out, and she's the closest family I've got. But before that you'll go to the doctor and find out when this baby's due.'

'I don't want to go to Aunt Maggie's. I hardly know her. No . . . no, I don't see why I should . . . ' Alice was starting to realize, though, that her mother would have the last word, as always, and she could offer no defence.

'You'll damn well do as you're told! I'll write to our Maggie; she's still at that place in Baildon as far as I know; she'd have let me know if she wasn't. You can go and stay there till it's all over, then the child can be adopted and nobody'll be any the wiser.'

'No . . . no!' Alice burst into tears again. 'I won't give up my baby, and I've not done anything wrong.'

Ada sighed, then she was quiet for a moment. When she spoke again it was in a softer tone. 'Come on, Alice; it's not the end of the world, and I know you're not the only one that it's happened to. But it's the best way, the only way. We're in the middle of a war, and God knows what might happen to that young feller.'

'Don't say that, Mother!' shouted Alice.

'But it's true. God knows what's going to happen to any of us. Aye, I know they say it's getting better now those Yanks are in it, but we've all got our own little problems to solve. Come on now; pull yourself together. Make her a cup of tea, Lizzie, then the pair of you can get on with the washing-up.'

Lizzie had kept very quiet in the background, and Alice tackled her as they sat drinking their tea.

'Why didn't you stick up for me? You let her rant and rave at me and you never said a word. I've not committed a crime, Lizzie. I know it shouldn't have happened, but it did, and I'm prepared to go through with it and have the baby and keep it an' all. Why shouldn't I?'

'Because, like Mother says, it's bringing disgrace to the family. At least that's what she thinks, and I've got to go along with her. You should have been more careful.'

'You've no room to talk! What about you and that sergeant, that Alan Whittaker? Don't tell me that you didn't do the same thing. Supposing I tell Mother about that?'

Lizzie's cheeks turned red. 'Don't you dare say anything! Anyway, we didn't . . . do that.' She crossed her fingers tightly, knowing that she was telling a lie. 'We were fond of one another, but he's gone now and I've had to forget him. I love my husband,' she added somewhat piously. 'You'd better do as she says. There's no way she'll change her mind.'

'But what about my job at the factory?' Alice asked.

'We'll have to say that you've been taken ill and you've gone away to recover, or something of the sort. Anyway, go to the doctor and see what he says.' Lizzie smiled. 'Maybe there's a chance you're not pregnant.'

'Pigs might fly!' said Alice glumly.

In a day or two the doctor confirmed that Alice, indeed, was pregnant, and the baby was due at the beginning of September, as far as he could tell.

'Is there a problem, my dear?' he asked kindly. He had known the family and Alice since she was a little girl, and knew, of course, that she was not married.

'My boyfriend is in the RAF,' she told him. 'He's part of an aircrew, a wireless operator. I haven't told him because I don't want to worry him.'

'And . . . do you intend to get married?'

'Yes, evidently . . . '

She'd had a letter from Tony the previous day saying how much he loved her and that one day they would be together for always. But who could tell how long that might be?

'But my mother insists I must have the child adopted. She says I have to go and stay with my aunt in Yorkshire until . . . it's all over.'

'I see . . . ' Dr Entwistle looked thoughtful and a little perturbed. He knew Ada Fletcher of old, and there was no way he would argue with that formidable lady.

'Well, you're a healthy young woman,' he told her, 'and I don't foresee any problems with your pregnancy. It must be a worry for you, my dear, but believe me, you're not the only one. I've seen dozens of girls in the same situation.' He smiled at her in a fatherly way.

'Come and see me again before you go away and try not to worry too much. Sometimes things turn out to be for the best. Goodbye, Alice. Take care now . . . '

Ada wrote to her sister and received a reply a few days later. She told Alice one evening when she arrived home from work.

'Well, you're a lucky girl. Your Aunt Maggie has agreed you can go and stay there. You can help out there in exchange for your bed and board, though I shall have to pay her summat

131

else as well. I don't like to be beholden to anyone.'

'Very well, Mother . . . Thank you,' she muttered, knowing that a word of gratitude was expected from her.

She would hardly call herself a lucky girl, but she knew she would be jolly glad to get away from her mother for a while. Admittedly Ada had not gone on at her since the first outburst of anger, but the sense of disapproval was still there.

Aunt Maggie was her mother's sister, about four years younger than Ada, and she was married to Fred Turnbull who had a farm just outside the village of Baildon, near Bradford. It was more of a smallholding than a farm but they had always seemed to make a good living from it. They kept chickens and ducks and a few pigs. Many people in the country now kept a pig to provide them with meat over and above the weekly ration. They grew vegetables, too, and had a small orchard of apple and pear trees. The fruit and vegetables were delivered to shops in the area around Bradford, and Maggie had a market stall three times a week where she sold their produce, along with freshly laid eggs and homemade jams and chutney.

Alice had not seen her aunt and uncle for many years but she remembered visiting them when she was a little girl. She remembered her aunt was a kindly woman, and her Uncle Fred was fat and jolly, always puffing away on his pipe.

Alice found she was not worried about the

132

idea of spending time with them — in fact she was looking forward to it, despite the circumstances. No doubt Maggie would have been given her instructions about the forthcoming baby, that it was to be adopted and then never spoken of again. But maybe Ma would be more understanding, less rigid in her principles. Maybe — just maybe — Maggie might be able to persuade her sister to let Alice keep the baby, even though it would mean making her home in Yorkshire and never returning to Blackpool. And then there was Tony, of course. Her mother never spoke of him and she expected Alice to forget about him. These thoughts raced around in her mind as she went to work each day, and as she lay in bed at night, sleep often eluding her until the early hours of the morning.

Ada decided that Alice must go to Yorkshire quite soon before she was 'showing'. She intended to write to the person in charge of the munitions factory, saying that her daughter had been taken ill and had gone away to stay with relations until she had recovered.

Alice knew she must go along with her mother's plans, but once she got away perhaps she might find a way to change the outcome. When the time came, how could she possibly give up her child, a child that was the result of the love that she and Tony had felt for one another? Tony had given her his home address in Yorkshire, although she was not sure what use she could make of it. She intended to write and tell him when she moved so that he could write to her new address. She would have to tell him the same lie — that she was ill and was recovering in the country air.

These thoughts were making it hard for her to concentrate on her work. Freda and Doris were concerned about her, and although Alice knew her mother would be angry if she knew, she decided to confide in them. It was good to have sympathetic friends, and they swore they would say nothing when she disappeared from the factory. If others who worked along with her guessed at the truth they would not hear it from her two friends.

Alice made the journey to Yorkshire on her own towards the end of April. Lizzie went with her on the bus to North Station, with as many of her belongings as she could carry in a large suitcase. Her mother gave her a quick kiss on her cheek, telling her to take care of herself, and if there was a glimmer of a tear in her eyes behind her thick glasses she soon blinked it away.

Relations between the two sisters had continued to be strained, but Lizzie seemed to relent as she saw Alice on to the train, lugging her suitcase on to the rack above and settling her into a seat by the window. She put her arms round her and kissed her on both cheeks.

'Take care, Alice, love,' she said, adding in a whisper, 'I do understand, but you know what Mother's like. Write to us, won't you? And try not to worry. It'll work out all right, you'll see.'

Alice nodded, not knowing what her sister meant. Probably Lizzie didn't know either, but words of farewell were always difficult.

'I'd better get off,' said Lizzie with a laugh, as

the guard with a green flag walked up and down the platform, 'or else I'll be coming with yer. Ta-ra, Alice; keep yer chin up.'

Then she was gone. The guard blew his whistle and waved his flag, and they were off with a squeal of brakes and a cloud of grey smoke.

Alice settled down in her seat, pleased that she had managed to find a space. Trains were always crowded now, mainly with servicemen and women. There were civilians, too, like Alice, who needed to travel for one reason or another but the general public were constantly aware of the posters on walls and hoardings asking them: *Is your journey really necessary?*

This one really was, and she would be glad when she reached her destination. She quietly buried her head in her *Woman's Own* magazine, not feeling inclined to chat with her fellow passengers. She idly turned the pages, looking at the pictures rather than reading the articles and stories. She could not concentrate on other people's problems with her own always on her mind.

The occupants of the carriage frequently changed, people boarding or departing at Preston, Chorley, Blackburn, then onwards into Yorkshire. The names of the stations had been removed at the start of the war, to confuse the enemy, so you needed to know exactly where you were going. Soon they were heading across the Pennines. Alice took out her packet of potted-meat sandwiches that her mother had made for her, eating them somewhat furtively as she looked out at the changing scenery.

The drab, smoky towns of inland Lancashire were left behind as the train travelled through the foothills of the Pennines. There were vast stretches of lonely moorland where there was little sign of habitation, only sheep grazing on the hillsides and a swirl of smoke from a lonely farmstead. Yorkshire had its share of smoking mill chimneys, too, as the train passed through Todmorden, Sowerby Bridge and Halifax, and now the houses were of grey stone rather than the red Accrington brick of Lancashire.

Then they arrived at Bradford, and Alice knew that her Uncle Fred would be waiting for her. A helpful young soldier lifted her case off the rack and humped it on to the platform. She thanked him, then stood for a moment, staring around feeling a little lost and bewildered. Then she saw her Uncle Fred hurrying towards her, a pork pie hat on his head and a beaming smile on his face. She hadn't seen him for several years but she knew him at once, just as he knew her. He put his arms round her and kissed her cheek.

'Welcome to Yorkshire, Alice, love. It's grand to see you. Now you mustn't worry about a thing. We'll take good care of you.'

'Thank you,' said Alice, feeling a tear come to her eye. 'It's very good of you to have me.'

'Say no more, lass. I've got the old jalopy outside. She's not a Rolls-Royce but she can still go when we get the petrol.'

He picked up her case as though it was as light as a feather, and she followed him out of the station to where an old and somewhat battered

Ford car was parked at the roadside. They soon left the busy streets and the soot-blackened buildings of Bradford behind and were on the moorland road leading to Baildon. There was one main street of shops, then Fred turned into a side road leading to the valley at the bottom of which was Turnbull's farm.

The farmhouse was not old compared with many in the area, which were hundreds of years old. This one was built in the Edwardian era, some thirty-odd years ago. It was a fair-sized, squarish building of grey stone with a small garden at the front: a strip of grass that could hardly be called a lawn with daffodils in full bloom surrounding it and a short path leading to the green painted front door.

Fred drove the car down a path leading to the back of the house where there was a paved yard and beyond that the hen coops and pigsties, the vegetable garden and the orchard. A few hens were pecking in the yard, and a black and white collie dog ran towards Fred, barking excitedly.

'Hello, Benjy, old chap,' said Fred, ruffling the dog's head. 'Pleased to see us, are you? Down, boy!' he shouted as the dog sniffed at Alice then jumped up, pawing at her and wagging his tail. 'Alice might not be used to dogs.'

'No, I'm not really,' she replied, tentatively patting Benjy's head. 'But I dare say I'll soon get used to him . . . Hello, Benjy,' she said, rather timidly.

And then her Aunt Maggie appeared at the back door wearing a floral apron and with her hair in a turban. She hurried towards her with her arms outstretched. Alice saw a rather younger version of her mother, plumpish and not very tall with a pleasant open face and a welcoming smile which lit up her kind brown eyes, the sort of expression that Alice had not seen on her mother's face for a long while.

Maggie flung her arms round her niece, kissing her on both cheeks. 'It's good to see you again, Alice,' she said, 'And never mind why you're here,' she added quietly. 'You're very welcome, and we'll do all we can for you, Fred and me.'

Alice felt tears in her eyes again at the unrestrained welcome. She sniffed and blinked them away. 'It's good of you to have me, and I can't tell you how glad I am to be here, believe me.'

'Aye, I can imagine it's not been easy for you at home, but you won't get any grief from Fred and me. We just want to help as best we can . . . Our Sally had to get married in a hurry, as you might say,' she added confidingly. 'She's got a grand little lad, four years old now. We wouldn't be without him. And a little girl an' all.'

Alice nodded, muttering, 'That's nice,' but reflecting that there would be no such happy ending for her. She hadn't had a letter from Tony for a few weeks but she knew the post was erratic. He had her new address and she hoped she would hear from him soon.

Maggie had led her into the kitchen; a typical farm kitchen with a flagged floor and a large pine table in the centre. There was a large, quite modern gas cooker rather than the open range found in many farmhouses, plentiful cupboards and a dresser holding willow pattern crockery and a few plates depicting flowers and rural scenes, as well as the pots that were in daily use.

'Sit yerself down,' said Maggie, 'and we'll have a cup of tea, then I'll show you your room and you can unpack and make yourself at home.'

'It's really kind of you to have me here,' Alice said again as they drank their tea. 'Mother couldn't wait to see the back of me, before anyone noticed I was pregnant. She's so ashamed of me . . . ' She shook her head. 'We didn't mean it to happen. We did love one another, Tony and me. Well, we still do, but I don't know . . . ' She could not put the rest of her thoughts into words.

Maggie smiled sympathetically. 'Ada didn't tell me anything about your boyfriend . . . You can tell me, if you would like to?'

And so Alice told her about Tony and how they had met. 'Mother liked him well enough when he was billeted with us, but now she won't even have his name mentioned. He doesn't know . . . about the baby. And I don't know what's going to happen. I haven't heard from him for quite a while.'

Maggie nodded understandingly. 'I know. The waiting and worrying is dreadful. But you're among friends here and we'll keep you busy, helping Fred and me. That's the best thing to do, to keep yourself busy. Come along, love. I'll show you your room.'

When her aunt had gone Alice stood at the window staring out into the far distance; to the range of hills where sheep were grazing, their white fleeces hardly distinguishable from the outcrops of rock dotted here and there on the moorland. In the nearer distance were the trees of the orchard now beginning to show the new green of springtime, the farm sheds, the pigsties and hen coops, and Benjy yapping at Uncle Fred's heels. The sky was blue, with fleecy clouds, and despite the turmoil and anguish that was always at the back of her mind, Alice gave a sigh of relief at the peaceful rural scene. She knew, for the moment, that this was the best place for her, and she would try to be happy, or at least content.

10

Alice settled down with her aunt and uncle and was as contented as it was possible to be under the circumstances. She made up her mind that she would work hard and, as her mother had said, earn her bed and board and not be a burden to her relatives. Working hard was nothing new to Alice, neither did the long hours bother her. She was used to rising early, before seven o'clock, when she worked at the boarding house, and later at the munitions factory.

She did all sorts of different jobs, assisting both her aunt and her uncle. She mucked out the pigsties, she fed the hens and ducks and collected the eggs, helped to gather and package the vegetables, and assisted Maggie with the making of jam and chutney.

She met up again with her cousin, Sally, who was almost the same age as herself and whom she had not seen for many years. Sally lived not very far from her parents, in the village of Baildon. She had two children — a four-year-old boy, Charlie, and two-year-old Susan. Sally was on her own now as her husband, Kenneth, was in the army at a camp in the south of England. The two young women found they had much in common and became good friends.

Alice wrote home to her mother and sister, mainly as a duty, and she received stilted letters in return, Lizzie's being rather more sympathetic.

The days passed by, spring giving way to early summer, a time of great beauty in the countryside with blossom in full bloom in the hedgerows, sunshine lighting up the hills and a chorus of birds singing in the trees.

Alice's figure began to change and it was obvious now that she was expecting a child. It was a time of joy, but also of heartache when she felt the child quicken in her womb. She had paid regular visits to the doctor who assured her that all was well, and she was booked into the nearest hospital for the birth in early September.

Alice sometimes tried to convince herself that all would be well, that her mother would relent and allow her to keep the baby and that, eventually, she and Tony would be together. But it was now several weeks since she had received a letter from him. There had been only one since she moved to Yorkshire, in which he had expressed concern that she was not well, assuming, as she had hinted, that it was due to tiredness and overwork.

She knew, deep down, that there must be something amiss to explain the cessation of the letters. She discussed it with Sally one evening in July. She sometimes walked up to the village in the evening to visit her cousin in her little house just off the main street.

'Tony gave me his home address in Malton,' she told Sally. 'Do you think I should write — to his parents, I suppose — to see if they have heard anything about . . . well . . . about what has happened to him?' she added in a whisper.

Sally's brown eyes, just like Aunt Maggie's,

were full of concern. 'I really think you should,' she said. 'That is probably why he gave you the address, although he probably didn't want to make too much of an issue of it. Tony's parents are his next of kin, you see. If you and Tony had been married — as I'm sure you would have been, as soon as possible — then you would be next of kin. You must write to them, Alice. You can't go on like this, waiting and worrying. It would be better to know for sure, even if . . . '

'Even if he's been killed, you mean?' said Alice. 'I think I already know, Sally — in here.' She placed her hand over her heart. 'I feel that . . . something has happened to him.'

Alice wrote to the address in Malton, to Mr and Mrs Sinclair. She said that she and Tony had met when he was billeted with them in Blackpool and that they had become very fond of one another. She did not say, of course, that she was expecting his child, only hinted that they had hoped to be together 'when it was all over'. She added that she was now working at her uncle's farm, and if they assumed she was a Land Girl then that was not far from the truth.

It was ten days before Alice received a reply. Maggie handed her the letter one morning, soon after she had started working in the vegetable garden with Fred.

'This arrived a few minutes ago,' her aunt said. 'Come in and wash your hands, then you can read it in peace. I'll make you a cup of tea.' She smiled at her niece in what she hoped was a reassuring way, but she knew that Alice was worried about what the letter might reveal.

'Yes . . . thank you,' said Alice, following her aunt back into the house. She looked at the blue envelope in her hand. The writing was unfamiliar but the postmark was York.

Alice sat down in a comfy armchair in the small living room. She held the flimsy envelope in her hands for several minutes. They were trembling a little and there was a hollow, sick feeling in her stomach.

Maggie put a cup of tea on a little table at her side, noticing that she had still not opened the letter. 'I'll be in the kitchen if you need me,' she said quietly, leaving her niece alone again.

Alice knew she could put the moment off no longer. She tore open the envelope and took out the two sheets of paper. A brief glance told her that it was what she had dreaded, yet expected, to hear.

Dear Alice,

I'm sorry to have to tell you that our dear son, Tony, was killed in a bombing raid over Germany at the beginning of June. We have another son who, thank God, is not old enough to be in the war, and a daughter, but that does not make the loss any easier to bear. Tony was our first born and a wonderful son.

We had heard about you, my dear. Tony told us that he had met a lovely girl called Alice and he hoped that we would meet you one day. He didn't tell us much; he was a rather private sort of lad, but we know that you made him happy.

144

My husband, George, joins me in sending you our love and sympathy because we know you will be feeling sad as we are and unable to understand this dreadful war.
Yours sincerely
Hannah Sinclair.

When Maggie came back into the room some ten minutes later, having heard not a murmur from Alice, she found her niece staring into space, the letter clutched tightly in her hands.

'Alice . . . what is it?' Maggie knelt by her side and took hold of her hands. 'Do you want to tell me?'

Alice passed the letter to her. 'Read it,' she said. 'It's a nice letter, but it's what I was expecting.'

Maggie scanned the pages. 'Yes, it was a lovely letter.' Alice seemed calm, too calm, but she would be in shock. She put her arms round her. 'I am so sorry, my love.'

And then Alice burst into tears. She sobbed for a while, but quietly, scarcely making a sound.

'I knew,' she said after a while. 'I've known for a while that he'd . . . gone.'

'This dreadful war,' said Maggie, repeating the words in the letter. What else was there to say? 'Your tea has gone cold. I'll make you another cup, and I'll have one with you.' She didn't want to leave her niece on her own.

They sat quietly for a while drinking their cups of tea. Alice had calmed down, and her look showed resignation now, as well as sadness. She shook her head, muttering, 'I knew something had happened to Tony. I just . . . '

When she looked at her aunt again there was a look of determination on her face. 'This makes no difference,' she said. 'I still want to keep the baby, even though Tony . . . won't be with me. I won't bother about the shame of being an unmarried mother. I'm not ashamed; we loved one another, Tony and me, and the baby will be a part of him. I shall tell him — or her — about Tony and what a brave man he was. They are all brave, aren't they, those lads in the bomber crews. I did pray for him, you know, that he would be safe, but it was not to be.'

'Yes, I'm sure you did,' replied Maggie. 'We are all praying for our loved ones. We must keep on praying that it won't go on much longer.'

Maggie did not comment on her niece's remark about keeping the baby. She had had similar conversations with her before but had made no promises that she would try to persuade her sister to change her mind. She knew how adamant Ada was, and could see there was no way that she would change her mind, especially now.

Maggie felt that she must be the one, rather than Alice, to write to Ada and Lizzie and tell them what had happened. She did not think for one moment that her sister would be pleased at the news. Ada did have a softer side although it was not always easy to find. But maybe Ada would think that this would help Alice to see that she must put all this behind her and make a fresh start.

And, in her heart, that was what Maggie

hoped as well. She could imagine the sort of life Alice must have had, working for her mother ever since she left school. She had been a timid girl, not one to stick up for herself or to rebel against her mother's rigid discipline.

She doubted that Alice had had any boyfriends until she met Tony and had never spent much time in the company of the opposite sex. It was hardly surprising, then, that she had fallen in love with the young man who had found her attractive and had shown her what it was like to be in love, for she was sure that it had not been one-sided, and that Tony had loved Alice just as much as she had loved him.

But it was, after all was said and done, Alice's first love affair and it had ended in heartache. It would be far better for Alice if she was able to put it all behind her and to start afresh. Not to forget Tony; she would never do that, but maybe in time she might be able to make a new life for herself with someone else? Who could tell what the future might hold? But Maggie hoped so much that Alice would find happiness again.

As the weeks went by and the baby's due date drew nearer, Alice, to her aunt's surprise, did seem more resigned to what she knew would be the outcome. Maggie did not know what had happened to change her mind. She had become quiet and withdrawn, resigned rather than determined, and she no longer talked about her wish to keep the baby.

Alice felt at first as though life was meaningless, and the only way she would be able to carry on would be if she could keep her baby, a lifelong reminder of Tony. She felt that she would never love anyone else.

She was able to continue with her work, although she'd spent most of the time with her aunt, helping with the work in the kitchen and preparing the produce for market. She tried to put on a brave face and to be cheerful with her aunt and uncle and the older men who came to help with the farm work.

But she had her quiet, reflective moments, in her own room, when she remembered Tony. She took out her box of keep-sakes, looking at postcards of favourite places they had visited in Blackpool. She reread his letters and the poems in the little book of love poetry that he had given her.

'How do I love thee? Let me count the ways . . . ' by Elizabeth Barrett Browning. The famous words of Robbie Burns, 'Oh, my love is like a red, red rose . . . '

But there was one in particular that seemed to speak to her, the one called, simply, 'Remember' by Christina Rossetti telling of the loss of a loved one, whether by death or by absence was not entirely clear to her. She kept returning to the last line:

Better by far you should forget and smile,
Than that you should remember and be sad.

She would never forget Tony, but maybe in time the heartache would ease, little by little, and she would be able to smile as she remembered the times they had spent together.

She confided in her cousin, Sally, who tried to persuade her that it might be better to agree to the plan for adoption.

'I understand your feelings,' Sally told her, 'probably more than most people might. When I discovered I was pregnant I was panic-stricken at first. We'd been going together for a few months, Ken and me, but we weren't engaged, and he hadn't mentioned getting married. I knew it shouldn't have happened, but it did, and it was my fault just as much as his. I was scared to death that he wouldn't want to know, but he said straight away, 'Let's get married'. And we did, as soon as we could. He said he'd wanted to save up a bit before he asked me to marry him, but we managed all right. We got this little house to rent, and it's worked out just fine.'

'Your parents were supportive, though, weren't they? Would you have wanted to keep the baby — Charlie, I mean — if you'd had to manage on your own?'

Sally was thoughtful for a moment. Then, 'D'you know, I don't think I would,' she replied. 'I was only eighteen. I imagined myself at home with a baby and no husband and being dependent on my parents. I thought how awful it would be, and then, what a relief it was when Ken told me not to be silly; of course we'd get married.'

Alice nodded. 'Yes, I'm pleased it worked out well for you. But there'll be no such happy ending for me. I suppose I could refuse to have the baby adopted. I'm nearly twenty-four; a few years older than you were. But I couldn't go

149

home. My mother has made that quite clear, and I know I can't depend on your parents forever. They've been wonderful to me, Aunt Maggie and Uncle Fred. You're lucky to have them. But I know now what I have to do. It'll be hard, but I can see that I have no choice.'

Sally put her arms round her cousin. 'You're being very brave, Alice, but you'll get through it. And you're not on your own. You've become one of our family since you've been here. We were relations, but we didn't know you very well before. We must keep in touch . . . afterwards.'

Maggie was relieved, too, when Alice told her she had decided she would agree to the plan for adoption. 'It's not what I really want,' she said, 'but I can see all sorts of problems ahead if I insist on keeping the baby. I would have no husband and no home either . . . I don't want there to be a rift between my mother and me, and Lizzie.'

'You're a brave girl,' said Maggie, just as Sally had said, 'and we're all here for you, me and Fred and Sally. You don't need to go home until you're quite ready.'

Maggie was surprised, and a little concerned about how calm Alice seemed to be over the next few weeks.

'There's one thing that worries me,' Alice said to her aunt. 'I want the baby to go to a good home, to people who will really love him . . . or her. I realize I have no say in what happens, but . . . '

'I'm sure you don't need to worry about that,' said Maggie. 'When a couple adopt a child it's usually because they're not able to have one of their own. An adopted child is always loved because it's been chosen. Some babies born to married couples are not really planned for and can be . . . well . . . they are sometimes regarded as a mistake. Your baby will go to people who really care, Alice. You can be sure of that.'

Maggie was more certain of this than she could admit to Alice, if everything went according to plan. She and Fred knew of a young couple who wanted to adopt a child. The parents of the young man concerned, who owned a farm a couple of miles away, had long been friends of Fred and Maggie. Their son, Ted, and his wife, Mary, had been married for four years and there was no sign of the child they both longed for. Maggie said nothing of this to Alice, but during the final weeks of her pregnancy plans were being made for the adoption to go ahead. It was all legal and above board, and with just a little inside information the powers that be were persuaded to agree to the decision.

Alice gave birth to a baby boy during the first week of September. The birth was comparatively easy, and Alice went through it all with as much fortitude as she could muster. The nurses were very kind, being aware of the circumstances, and they admired the young woman for being so brave.

'He's a strong lad, seven and a half pounds,' the midwife told her. 'Would you like to hold him, my dear, just for a moment? And then . . . I think it would be best if we took care of him.'

Alice looked down at the tiny child, wrapped

151

in a blue blanket. He was beautiful; pale, slightly mottled skin, a covering of brownish hair clinging wetly to his scalp, the tiniest little fingers and a button of a nose. His eyes were a bluey-grey and seemed to be looking up at her, but she knew he was unable to focus yet. She stroked his cheek gently with one finger.

'Hello, little man,' she said softly, knowing that it was also goodbye. She held him for a few moments, then looked at the midwife. 'It's best if you take him now,' she said.

She turned her head away, unable to stop the tears from falling. But she had made up her mind and there was no going back.

11

After a couple of months had gone by Helen found she was getting used to life in the village and in the small country town where she worked. It was vastly different from the busy town of Blackpool, which became even busier in the summer with the arrival of the holiday-makers.

There were visitors in Thornbeck and Pickering as well, usually day-trippers or hikers and those who wanted a few quiet days in the country. They were far removed from the people who visited Blackpool who wanted the sea and sand and sunshine (if they were lucky) and enjoyment in the evenings in the bars, dance halls and cinemas.

Helen found it to be a pleasant and, on the whole, friendly community in Thornbeck. Some who had lived there all their lives were inclined to be suspicious of newcomers, but there were younger folk as well, many of whom worked outside of the village as Helen did. And there was social life and entertainment to be found in the village without having to travel far in the evening.

There were a few pubs and inns in the village and some a few miles away. Many of the activities centred around the church and the village hall, sometimes called the community centre. That was where the Women's Institute — the WI — was held each week, but Helen felt she was not of an age just yet to join their ranks.

She had kept her promise to herself that she would attend St Michael's Church on a regular basis. She discovered there were youngish people of her own age as well as the elderly ones, although many of them were married couples with children.

It soon reached the ears of the organist and choir master, Cyril Chadwick, that she had a tuneful voice, and she was invited to join the church choir. She sang second — or mezzo-soprano — along with two other ladies, and joined an amateur operatic society in the village, the Thornbeck and District Light Opera Company, which met each Wednesday evening in the community centre, and Helen was pleased to be a member of such a lively and friendly group of people. She was made very welcome, especially so when they found out she played the piano and was willing to help out as an accompanist when required. They presented Gilbert and Sullivan operas occasionally, and Helen was delighted that they were now rehearsing *Iolanthe* to be presented towards the end of the year. This was one of Helen's favourites, and she agreed to be one of the chorus of fairies.

It was Robert and Pamela Kershaw who had told Helen about the group. Her friendship with the couple had grown as she heard more from them about their long association with her Aunt Alice. In fact, Helen was starting to wonder if

154

there might have been more to the friendship than met the eye, but as yet she did not feel ready to ask them. She might be letting her imagination run away with her and be barking up the wrong tree altogether.

There had been a great deal of sorting to do with her aunt's possessions, and she came across a few items that seemed to be significant. She found a photograph album among the books on the shelf in what had been Alice's room, containing old snapshots and some more formal photographs from long ago — ones of Lizzie and Alice as children, and as young women; the wedding of Helen's parents and some of Helen herself as a little girl.

But the more recent photos were of more significance to Helen. There were several of Jennifer and James Kershaw with captions below them: Jennifer, five years old; James, his first school photo; Jennifer and James on holiday in Filey . . .

Helen's mind started to go into overdrive. But was she, perhaps, guilty of putting two and two together and making five, or a good deal more? After all, Alice had been a babysitter for the children and would, therefore, have appreciated a few photos of them.

Helen turned also to the little book of Romantic poetry which had been in the box of mementoes of Alice's love affair with the RAF corporal, Tony Sinclair. Reading one particular poem made Helen feel more and more certain that the young man had gone on a bombing raid and had never returned.

155

Remember me when I am gone away,
Gone far away into the silent land . . .

She read the words telling of a loved one's departure. Tony could not have known he would not return, but the words seemed to speak to her, especially the last lines:

Better by far you should forget and smile
Than that you should remember and be
sad.

Her mother came occasionally at the weekend to help Helen sort Alice's belongings. Helen's job at the estate agency, which she was enjoying very much, and her increasing social commitments meant that she had little spare time.

One Saturday afternoon as they were sorting out a kitchen cupboard Helen decided to find out if her mother knew any more about Alice than she had, so far, divulged.

'Mum,' she began, 'who did Aunt Alice stay with when she came to Yorkshire? I mean the first time, when she had the baby.'

'Oh, Helen, you're not still worrying about all that, are you?' said her mother. 'Surely it's best to try and forget about it? Aunt Alice had a love affair and she gave birth to a baby. We know all that, but it's in the past. Isn't it time we just let the past go?'

'I'm not worrying about it, Mum, but I'm interested. I'm discovering a whole lot of things about Aunt Alice that I didn't know, and I really feel that there are things she would like me to find out for myself.'

'But surely, if she'd wanted you to know her story she would have told you about it? She was very fond of you, and you were closer to her than the rest of us were. That was why she left you her house, and you deserved it, love. You were very good to her.'

'I liked her, Mum. I loved her, but she was a very private sort of person, and maybe she didn't want to admit about the baby and everything. You told me what a disgrace it was in those days, but I feel she's trying to tell me something now.'

Helen hadn't told her mother about the photos of Jennifer and James and what she thought they might mean. She could be entirely wrong. But she had shown her the book of poems and how the page fell open at the one called 'Remember Me', as though it had had a special meaning for Alice.

Megan smiled. 'I'm sure you'll go ferreting away until you find something out, but it'll be amazing if you do. Are you thinking you might find out who the baby was, and where he or she is? But does it really matter now, after all this time, especially now Alice is no longer with us?'

'I just feel it would be right to find out, if we can. She stayed with a relation, didn't she? One of Great-Grandma Ada's sisters, wasn't it?'

'Ada was my grandmother, and she's long gone. It was her sister, Maggie, I believe, but she died a long time ago. She had a daughter; she was called Sally, and I think she was about the same age as Alice, so she could still be around. After all, your gran's still hale and hearty at seventy-eight. That's why it was such a shock when Aunt Alice died.'

'Sally — she would be Alice's cousin then, and Gran's cousin as well. So she's your second cousin, Mum? Or cousin once removed, is that what it's called?'

Megan laughed. 'Goodness me, Helen! I don't know. We've lost touch with them all, but I have Sally's address somewhere, if she's still at the same place. She lived in Baildon, near Bradford.'

Relationships within families had always fascinated Helen. What relation was so-and-so to so-and-so? Cousin by marriage, or step-cousin, or what?

'I think it's a pity we've lost touch,' she said. 'I might have a whole lot of relations that I know nothing about. And I'm living in Yorkshire now, aren't I? Maybe it's time to do something about it.'

Megan laughed. 'I know you won't be satisfied until you've done some detective work. Proper little Miss Marple, you are! I'll find Sally's address when I get home. Sally Townsend, that was her name after she got married. I can't remember what her husband was called. They had two children, a boy and a girl, then another boy a long time later, if I remember rightly.

'Alice went back to live in Yorkshire in the early fifties, before you were born. It was all very mysterious. She lived in a couple of places before she settled in Thornbeck.'

'Do you think she might have found something out about her child, Mum?'

Megan shook her head. 'I have no idea, Helen.

It was never talked about. My grandma, Ada, must have forgiven her to a certain extent, because we all used to go and visit her in Thornbeck. Well, you remember that, of course, don't you? But it was a closed chapter until you decided to open it all up again.'

'I'm only doing what I feel is right, Mum,' said Helen, a trifle sharply.

'Yes, I know that. But be careful, love. You never know what skeletons may lurk in cupboards. I shan't tell your gran, of course, but I'll let you have Sally's address, and then it's up to you.'

Megan didn't really approve, but she sent her daughter the address in Baildon as she had promised. Helen wrote the letter, addressing the envelope to Mrs Sally Townsend. She was not sure what to call the lady, but she decided to be informal, so she started the letter:

Dear Sally,

You may not remember me. My name is Helen Burnside, and I am a distant relation of yours, third cousin or something, I'm not sure. But you will certainly remember Alice Fletcher who was my great-aunt and your cousin, I believe? I am sorry to tell you that Alice died earlier this year from a sudden heart attack, which was a great shock to us all.

Aunt Alice left her cottage in Thornbeck to me. We had become very close when I looked after her following her hip operation, but it was a great surprise to me when I found out. I am living in the cottage now because I decided to leave Blackpool and make a new start in Yorkshire. But I still see my parents and my grandma, your cousin Lizzie, quite often. I work at an estate agency in Pickering but I am free at the weekends.

I wonder if I could come over and see you one Saturday or Sunday, if it is convenient and agreeable to you? I said to Mum that it was a pity we had lost touch, and it is nice for me to think I have relations in Yorkshire, not too far away.

Hope to see you soon.

With best wishes,

Helen

She felt it was not appropriate to send love to this scarcely known aunt or cousin or whatever she was.

She did not know, of course, whether Sally was still at the same address, or even if she was still living. When ten days had passed and there had been no reply she was beginning to think that it might be a wild goose chase. Then, the next day there was an envelope with unfamiliar writing waiting on the doormat as she returned from work. She guessed, and hoped, that it might be from her relation, but she decided that she must wait a few minutes while she made a cup of tea first, as she always did, and opened a tin of meat for Trixie. The cat had followed her in and was rubbing round her legs, glad to see her home again.

A little while later she kicked off her shoes and sat down to read the letter, which was, as she had guessed, from Sally.

Dear Helen,

I was pleased to hear from you but sad to hear that Alice had passed away. We did keep in touch but not as much as we used to do. We were both getting older and neither of us was able to drive a car. Well, I did years ago, but I don't see too well now.

I'm sorry I lost touch with my relations in Blackpool, so it's nice to hear from you now. I have been away on a coach tour to Torquay with a friend so that is why I have only just replied to your letter.

Of course I would be delighted to see you. I remember you as a little girl but that was a long time ago. My husband died a few years ago and I live on my own now. No, I tell a lie, as they say. My younger son, Matthew, is staying with me at the moment while he looks for a place of his own. My other son and my daughter have married and have moved away so I don't see them very often. I am on the phone, Matthew persuaded me that I should have one so you will be able to ring me which will be quicker than writing. I am getting used to it now but it seemed odd at first.

I will look forward to hearing from you and seeing you, very soon I hope.

With love and best wishes from Sally.

No time like the present, thought Helen when she had warmed up and eaten the meat and potato pie she had bought from the bakery in Pickering, and finished her meal with a banana. She rinsed the plate and cutlery, then rang the number at the top of the letter.

'Hello,' replied a rather anxious little voice. 'Sally Townsend here.'

'Hello, Sally,' said Helen. 'I hope you don't mind me calling you Sally. It's Helen . . . I've just got your letter, and I'm so pleased to hear from you.'

'So am I, love,' said Sally in the broad Yorkshire accent that Helen was now so used to hearing, especially from the older people. 'What a lovely surprise it was to get your letter. And of course you must call me Sally. You were a little girl the last time I saw you. Let's see, how old are you now, Helen?'

'I'm thirty-three, still single, or 'on the shelf' as my gran might say.' She laughed. 'I'm very happy as I am, and I love living here in Yorkshire.'

'Aye, it's best to wait till Mister Right comes along. Your gran, that's my cousin Lizzie, Alice's older sister.'

'Yes, Gran doesn't know I've got in touch with you, but my mum does. My mum is Megan, you know, and she's married to Arthur.'

'Yes, of course I know. My goodness, it's a long time ago . . . So when are you going to come and see me, love?'

They decided that Saturday would be the best day. Helen said that she sang in the church choir, and Sally said that she liked to attend morning service at her local church on Sunday morning. And so they agreed on the Saturday after next, which would be the second Saturday in the month of August.

'Would you like to come for dinner?' asked Sally, and Helen guessed she meant for the midday meal.

But Helen didn't want to cause Sally a lot of work, not for a first visit. 'No, thanks,' she said. 'We don't want to spend a lot of time washing up, do we? I'll come early afternoon, it that's OK, and have tea with you. I'm sure you're a good cake-maker like my mum and my gran, aren't you?'

'Aye, I still make all my own cakes and pastries. So you'll come around two o'clock, will you? Then we can have a good chat.'

'Yes, that'll be lovely. And it's still quite light in the evenings, so I won't need to rush back.'

'Now mind you take care on them roads. It might be busy on a Saturday.'

'Yes, I will; don't worry. See you a week on Saturday then, Sally. Bye for now . . . '

Helen guessed it would take her two hours or so to reach Baildon. She was not very sure of the route but she had a good map, so on the appointed day, after a quick snack lunch she set off around midday. She was a competent driver, not afraid of going at a good speed if the roads were clear. She took her usual route, as she did each day, to Pickering, then across to Helmsley and Thirsk, and over the moors to what was once known as the West Riding but was now called West Yorkshire.

She didn't remember the village of Baildon although she knew she might have been there before, a long time ago. Sally had given her clear instructions and she soon found the terraced house, just off the main street.

She could tell at a glance that Sally was house proud. The window frames and the door were a glossy green as though they were recently painted, the curtains were a dazzling white and the small patch of grass and the rose bushes were well-tended. Helen parked her car and walked up the short path. The door opened before she had time to knock, and she guessed that Sally had been looking out for her.

She did not appear to be an elderly lady despite her seventy-odd years. Helen could see a certain family resemblance to her gran, Lizzie, in the shrewd blue-grey eyes behind her spectacles and her plumpish cheeks, but she seemed to be much more modern in appearance than Lizzie. Her dark hair showed only a hint of grey and was nicely permed, and she was dressed in casual trousers and a flowered top. She put her arms round Helen and kissed her upon both cheeks.

'How nice to see you again, Helen, love. I can't say I would have recognized you, it's been so long, but I can see a likeness to your mum, what I remember of her. Did you have a good journey?'

'Yes, no problems. I found my way without any trouble and the roads were not too busy.'

'Well, come in and I'll make us a cup of tea.'

How often Helen had heard those words, the usual northern welcome. She followed Sally along the short hallway to the room at the back of the house, which was deceptively large. This was obviously the living room, and Helen supposed there would be a smaller room at the front — a lounge or sitting room.

'Now then, sit down and make yerself at home,' said Sally. 'It's a lovely day, isn't it?'

'Not too hot, though. Just right for driving.' Helen took off her cardigan and sat down in one of the two easy chairs at the fireside, although there was, of course, no fire.

'Now, I'll just mash the tea. No, I can manage on my own,' said Sally as Helen made a move to stand up. 'To be honest there's hardly room for more than one in my poky little kitchen.'

Helen looked round the cosy room as Sally disappeared, and noticed that the house was centrally heated. She had the impression that Sally was quite 'comfortably off' as her gran might say. There was a drop-leaf dining table covered with a red chenille cloth beneath the window, and two dining chairs stood nearby. The large mirror-backed dark oak sideboard held the usual family paraphernalia: a fruit bowl, framed photographs, a bulging letter rack, a couple of library books, a dish holding keys and loose change, and a figurine of a lady in a crinoline.

Sally returned with two mugs of tea, a sugar basin and a plate of biscuits.

'You don't mind mugs, do you?' she said. 'Saves washing up. We'll have the best china at teatime. You'll be able to meet Matthew then. It's cricket season and he's gone off to Leeds, but he said he'd be back for tea. He's looking forward to meeting a relation he knew nothing about.'

Helen laughed. 'I hope he won't be disappointed then.' She also knew nothing about this distant cousin.

'No, love, he'll be pleased to see you, I'm sure of that . . . Now, tell me all the news from Blackpool.' Sally leaned forward in her chair.

'It's a real shame we've all lost touch like we have, but there it is. We've been busy getting on with our own lives.'

Helen told her that her gran, Lizzie, was quite fit and well, and didn't seem to mind living on her own. Her mum, Megan, was busy at her market stall, and her dad, Arthur, was still contented teaching at a local secondary school.

'And you had a brother, didn't you?'

'Yes, Peter, he works at a bank in Skipton, so I'm nearer to him now. They have two children . . . '

'It was a shock to hear about Alice,' Sally said after a while. 'I was really upset about that, though, like I said, we'd not been in touch for ages.'

'Yes, it was a tremendous shock to us as well,' said Helen. 'We had no idea she had a bad heart; there had been no sign of it. I think I may have felt it more than my mum and gran because I'd been very close to Aunt Alice. She had a hip replacement a couple of years ago, and I went to stay with her while she recuperated. I came to know her quite well, and since she died . . . I've learned a great deal more about her.'

Helen knew she must tread carefully now. She did not want Sally to think she had looked her up just so that she could find out more about Alice's stay in Baildon, but she was pleased that Alice had been brought into the conversation.

Sally nodded thoughtfully. 'Yes, I got to know her quite well when she came to stay with my mam and dad during the war . . . ' She hesitated. 'You know about that, I suppose?'

'Yes, I do now,' said Helen, 'but it's only since she died that I've been told about it. My mum has told me something of what she remembers, but she was only a child at the time and my gran is still very tight-lipped about it all.'

'Yes, I felt sorry for poor Alice,' said Sally. 'Her mother had more or less disowned her and packed her off to Yorkshire until it was all over. My parents were very kind to her and we became good friends, Alice and me. I'd been in the same boat meself, you see.' Sally gave a little laugh. 'Our Charlie came on the scene a bit too early, but then, of course, we got married. No such happy ending for poor Alice. It was while she was living with me mam and dad, not long before the baby was born, that she found out the young man was dead.'

'Oh . . . how awful! How did she find out?'

'She had his parents' address; he lived in Malton, so she wrote to find out why she hadn't heard from him for quite a while. She didn't say she was pregnant, y'know, just that she'd been friendly with Tony . . . I remember he was called Tony. Anyroad, his mother wrote her a nice letter and it was what Alice had thought all along. He'd gone on a bombing raid and never returned.'

'Yes . . . I guessed so,' said Helen quietly. 'I found a box of mementoes in her bottom drawer; letters and souvenirs and a photo of the young man. So I put two and two together and I asked Mum about it. She told me what she knew, which wasn't very much, and it was all very hush hush, I believe.'

'Aye, it was in them days. It's different now. Poor Alice! She really did love him, you know.'

'Yes, I'm sure she did, but she never mentioned it; not a word or a hint. I knew very little about her when I was a child. She'd gone back to live in Yorkshire before I was born. I don't know where she lived at first, but I seem to remember that she moved to Thornbeck when I was in my teens; fifteen or sixteen, I think. By that time my great-grandma Ada had died and I suppose Alice was no longer regarded as the black sheep of the family. I'd gathered — by eavesdropping on the conversations of the grown-ups — that Ada had done what was right in the end and left her money to be shared equally between her two daughters, my grandma Lizzie and Aunt Alice.'

'Aye, I dare say that was what made it possible for Alice to buy that little cottage in Thornbeck. I never went to see her there, more's the pity. I wish I had done now. I knew she'd moved. We sent Christmas cards and the odd letter. What a shame it all was! I do hope she was happy and that she found what she was looking for.'

Helen's senses were alerted, wondering if Sally meant that Alice had tried to find her baby. But she didn't ask straight away.

'I'm sure she was happy,' she said. 'She was very contented. She had lots of friends in the village. She was a pillar of the church, as they say; she helped with the flower arranging and she sang in the choir. There was one family in particular that seemed to mean a lot to her: they're called Kershaw, Robert and Pamela, and they have two children at college. I wondered if there might be some significance in that friendship. The ages seem to fit . . . but I'm probably letting my imagination run away with me. I wondered if she might have found the baby she gave up but never let on about it to anyone?'

Sally shook her head sadly. 'Aye, poor lass! She was so brave, and in the end she decided it was what she had to do. She'd been insisting she wanted to keep it; she wasn't bothered about the shame or what folks might say, but then she knew she had to let it go. I shouldn't say 'it' should I? She had a little boy.'

'I didn't even know that,' said Helen. 'Maybe Gran knew but she didn't say.'

Sally was staring into space as though recalling those bygone days. 'She knew she'd had a boy. They let her hold him for a little while then they took him away. She said she wanted him to go to a good home where he'd be loved . . . and that was what happened, I'm glad to say.'

'You knew that?'

'Oh, yes, we knew where the child had gone — at least my parents knew, and they told me later — but we couldn't let on to Alice that we knew . . . not till several years later,' she added quietly, 'but that's another story.'

'You mean . . . Alice did find out where the baby had gone?'

'Eventually she did. That's why she came back here, to see if she could find out. The baby had been adopted by a young couple that my parents knew about. The lad's parents were farmers, and they were friendly with my mam and dad. So it was all done privately, like, without a lot of rigmarole. The young couple were called Fielding, Ted and Mary Fielding, and they called the baby Jonathan.'

Well, that's put an end to my crazy theory, thought Helen. *The name is wrong, so that's that.* She was quiet for a few moments, disappointed that her idea had come to nothing. She had been naive and foolish, she thought now, believing that Robert Kershaw might be Alice's long-lost son. When she thought about it there was no sort of family resemblance, but children did not always look like their parents.

Sally assumed her silence was because of the sadness surrounding the story. 'Aye, it's a sad tale, isn't it?' she said, smiling sympathetically at Helen.

Helen nodded. 'Yes, it is, but thank you for sharing it with me. I'll just pop upstairs and make use of your facilities, if I may?'

'Of course you can, love. Just at the top of the stairs . . . '

12

When Helen came downstairs Sally was ready to go on chatting. 'Now, tell me about yourself, love,' she said. 'You've settled down in Thornbeck, have you? Made some nice new friends?'

'Yes, they're a friendly lot of people on the whole. Maybe the older ones are a bit suspicious of newcomers, but several of them already knew me from when I stayed with Aunt Alice, and it's helped with me becoming a member of the church. I didn't attend church regularly before, but I sing in the choir now. And I've joined the local operatic group. That's not connected to the church, but a lot of the same people are members.'

'My son, Matthew, is musical. He plays the trombone in the local brass band. He learned to play when he was at school, and he's jolly good. I suppose I'm a bit biased, like, but he's a clever lad. Anyroad, you'll be meeting him soon.'

'He hasn't been living with you very long, has he?' asked Helen, rather curious about this Matthew, a relation she had never met, at least not that she could remember. It sounded as though he was the apple of his mother's eye, but she hoped he did not turn out to be a Mummy's boy.

'Oh, no, only a few weeks. He had his own little house in Bradford. That's where he works;

he's a solicitor in a large practice there, but he's got a new job in Scarborough, and he'll be starting there next month.'

'Scarborough!' said Helen. 'That's a long way from here, isn't it?'

'Aye, I suppose it is, but he wanted a real change of scene and everything. He was married, you see, but it broke up, ended in divorce; that's why he moved in with me, but it's only temporary, like.'

'Oh dear! I'm sorry to hear that; about the divorce, I mean.'

'There were no children, thank goodness. Although he'd have liked a family, our Matthew, but she wasn't too keen on the idea. She was always a bit of a flighty piece, was Yvonne. I never really took to her, but it wasn't up to me to interfere. He'd waited long enough and he'd had a few girlfriends before he made up his mind to get married, so I supposed he knew what he was doing. They'd been married for four years, then he found out she was cheating on him. She admitted it, and she's living with this other chap now. Of course, they don't consider who's right and who's wrong; it's more a matter of selling the house and dividing the money. So that's why he's been living with me.'

'And has he found somewhere to live in Scarborough?'

'No, not yet. He's thinking of staying at a bed and breakfast place for a while until he finds somewhere to live, or maybe some of his colleagues at the office might be able to help.'

Helen thought to herself that Scarborough was

not too far from Thornbeck, but she didn't mention that to Sally. 'How old is Matthew?' she asked. 'Quite a bit younger than your other two, I should imagine?'

'You're right; our Matthew was a little afterthought. Well, to be honest we hadn't thought about it at all. He came as a big surprise, but none the less welcome for that. We were delighted when we found out. He was born in 1954. The other two were in their teens by then, but they didn't resent him, not at all. They were thrilled to bits with him, and he could have been spoiled rotten, but we tried to see that that didn't happen.

'He had more chances than they had, mind you, but that was because he was a clever lad. He was the only one of ours to get to the grammar school; then he went into the sixth form and studied at night school to pass all the exams he needed to get this good job he's doing.'

'You'll miss him when he moves away?'

'Aye, I suppose I will, but you've got to let them go — I learned that with our Charlie and Susan. They've got their own lives to live. And your parents will be missing you, won't they, love?'

'Yes, but it's not all that far, and most people drive now, don't they? It's not like it used to be, depending on trains and buses . . . You were saying earlier, Sally, about Aunt Alice coming back to Yorkshire. When was it? Do you remember? I know it was before I was born.'

'Yes, it was in 1953, the year before Matthew was born. The queen's Coronation year. I remember because we bought the telly so that we could watch it, and it was soon after that when Alice came. She stayed with us for a little while. I gathered that things were not too good at home with her mother and Lizzie, and she wanted a change. It was very brave of her, making a fresh start on her own. But it was more than that. She'd got it into her head that she wanted to find her baby boy. To tell you the truth, we nearly fell out about it, Alice and me. I didn't think it was a good idea. But she pestered me so much that I felt I had to tell her what I knew, and then it was up to her. I couldn't help her any further.

'The little lad would have been ten years old by then and, anyway, they'd moved away from Baildon. I thought she might be playing with fire, stirring up all sorts of trouble, but she was like a dog with a bone. I felt sorry for her, mind you. She'd lost weight, and there'd never been very much of her to start with. So, just to satisfy her I told her that the family had moved away and started a little farm of their own near Bingley. I never really knew them; I only heard news of them from my mam and dad. Like I said, the young couple that adopted the baby were called Ted and Mary Fielding, and they called the little lad Jonathan.

'And then, would you believe it, a couple of years later they had a child of their own! They'd given up hope, thought it would never happen; that's why they adopted Jonathan. Anyway, they had a little girl, and they called her Pamela . . . '

Helen's ears pricked up at the name Pamela — that was the name of Robert Kershaw's wife.

Don't be ridiculous, she told herself. *It's a common enough name; there can be no connection.* She listened again to what Sally was saying.

'I never heard anything of them after that. They moved to Bingley when the children were small. I think Ted's parents had helped them to start the business; it was more of a market garden than a farm. I didn't even know if they were still there, but Alice had got this bee in her bonnet, and she was determined to find out.'

'And did she find out? Did she find her child?'

'I don't know. She never told me. Like I said, we nearly fell out about it, so I never knew what happened. We kept in touch, but things were never really the same between us. That's why I'm so glad I've met you, Helen, love, and found out more about Alice. She was a brave lass, and from what you say she had a happy life whether she found what she was looking for or not.'

'Did she go and live in Bingley then?'

'Yes, she did. She found lodgings, then she had a rented cottage. Then she moved to Thornbeck; that would be in the late sixties, I think.'

'Yes,' agreed Helen. 'That was when we started visiting her. Thanks for telling me about it all. It's an interesting story.' *But I'd love to know what really happened,* Helen thought to herself.

'Well, we've had a good chat,' said Sally, 'and I reckon it's time I started to get the tea ready.' She stood up and so did Helen.

'Let me help you,' she said.

'It's nearly all prepared. I did it before you

came, but you can come and chat to me if you like.'

Helen followed Sally into the kitchen which was, as Sally had said, very small but compact and the best use had been made of the available space. Helen smiled to herself listening to Sally chatting, going from one subject to another as she bustled about in the kitchen, taking the roast ham and salad she had prepared earlier out of the fridge and the bread from the large enamel bread bin. There was also a Yorkshire curd tart and Sally's speciality — a lavish coffee and walnut cake. Helen loved hearing her Yorkshire voice, which was pleasant and homely and easy on the ear. She felt very much at home there already, as though she had known Sally for ages rather than just for an hour or two.

Almost as soon as they sat down again there was the sound of the door opening, and Matthew appeared in the living room. Helen had not known what to expect. Clearly his mother thought that the sun shone out of him, and Helen's first glimpse of him was very pleasing. His fairish hair was a trifle long, but not too much so, waving gently over the collar of his sports jacket and open-necked blue shirt. His eyes were brown and shone with friendliness as he greeted her.

'Hello there! So you are our long-lost relative. I've been looking forward to meeting you, Helen.'

She stood to greet him. He was a few inches taller than herself, of a slim build and with rather angular features. Not what you might call handsome but very pleasing to the eye.

'Very pleased to meet you,' she said, not sure whether that was the correct thing to say, but it was certainly true. 'I've been hearing quite a lot about you.'

His eyes twinkled. 'Don't take too much notice of Mum, her tongue runs away with her.'

'Less of your cheek!' said Sally, grinning at him affectionately. 'Tea's ready, so we can chat during the meal. I'll just fill the teapot while you sort yourself out, then we'll make a start.'

It was a convivial meal and the conversation flowed easily. Helen was delighted she had found these relations, and she knew that her parents would be happy to be reacquainted with them too. If she had not come to live in Yorkshire this would never have happened.

'When you come again you must meet my other son, Charlie, and his wife,' said Sally. 'I thought it might be a bit too much today; I wanted to get to know you first, but Charlie and Brenda were interested to hear you were looking us up.'

'They live locally, do they?' asked Helen.

'A few streets away, that's all. He's a plumber, our Charlie, same as his dad was. That was how he learned his trade. He's got a good business going. Folk always need plumbers, don't they? Their children are all grown up and married, of course. And my first great-grandchild will be arriving soon. What about that, eh!'

Even more unknown relations! Helen thought.

'Susan doesn't live up here now,' Sally continued. 'She was a shop assistant in Baildon: stationery and fancy goods an' all that. She got friendly with one of the commercial travellers — well, sales reps they call 'em now. And they got married and went to live in the Midlands.'

'I believe you're making a move soon, aren't you?' Helen said to Matthew.

'Yes, Scarborough; I start my new job there at the beginning of September.'

'Have you been there before? Do you know the place?'

'Yes, quite well. We had a few family holidays there, didn't we, Mum? And we really loved the town. I was looking for a new position, and when I saw this one advertised I thought, why not! I wanted a complete change, and somewhere different to live, and Scarborough seemed to fit the bill. A nice bracing seaside town rather than a busy city. And I was fortunate to get the post, so that's where I shall be going.'

'You can't get anywhere more bracing than Scarborough,' said Helen. 'Apart from Blackpool, of course!'

'I've never been to Blackpool,' said Matthew.

'What!' said Helen in mock disbelief. 'You've never been to Blackpool? You haven't lived!'

He laughed. 'We have our own seaside resorts: Scarborough, Whitby, Filey. Why do we need Blackpool? Anyway, you've moved over here, haven't you?'

'Touché,' said Helen. 'Like you, I wanted a change, and when Aunt Alice left me her cottage it seemed to me that it was what I had to do.'

'And we're very pleased you did.' He smiled at her, his eyes meeting with hers for a moment before turning to his mother. 'Aren't we, Mum?'

'I'll say we are! We've been going down Memory Lane this afternoon, Helen and me. You remember I told you about my cousin Alice from Blackpool? She stayed with my mam and dad during the war. She'd got herself into a bit of trouble, and her mother — my aunt Ada — showed her the door, poor lass!'

'Yes, she had a baby, didn't she? But it's all water under the bridge now, isn't it, Mum?'

'Yes, we thought it was, but Helen's got an idea that her aunt — great-aunt, actually — might have found the baby that was adopted.'

'And I want to see if I can find out about it,' said Helen, taking up the story. 'Aunt Alice left a few clues.'

'Oh, jolly good!' said Matthew. 'Fancy yourself as a Miss Marple, do you? Why not! I love a mystery.'

Helen smiled. 'But the clues seem to be red herrings. I may be on the wrong track altogether. But it doesn't matter. I've found some relations that I didn't know about, so that's something good that has happened.'

'I've tried to help,' said Sally. 'I remember that Alice went to live in Bingley because I told her the family with the baby had gone there, but like I was telling Helen, things were never the same between Alice and me because I didn't approve of what she was doing. But Fate has stepped in, you might say, and we've met Helen at last!'

'Yes, indeed,' agreed Matthew. 'God moves in mysterious ways.' He smiled at his mother and at Helen, and she could tell he was not being flippant.

There was very little left on the table when they had finished their meal.

'That was delicious,' said Helen. 'Now you must let me help you to clear away and wash up.'

'I won't hear of it,' said Sally. 'You chat to Matthew and I'll soon shift this lot. There's only a few plates and cups and saucers; nowt messy.' She donned her apron and set to work.

'Do you mind if I take Helen out for a drink, Mum?' asked Matthew. 'If you'd like to, Helen? There's a nice little pub not far away, and it'll be quiet at this time in the evening.'

'Yes, that would be very nice, thank you, Matthew,' she replied. 'But just remember I've to drive back home.'

'Of course it's all right with me,' said Sally. 'But you watch what you're drinking an' all. And don't drive too fast in that car; I'm always telling you.'

'So you are, Mum,' he said, laughing. 'Don't worry; I'll take good care of Helen. We'll only have one drink, then she can drive back before it gets dark.'

'Gosh, that's a snazzy-looking car!' she said when she saw Matthew's red MG sports car parked outside the house.

'Thanks,' he said. 'I must admit I'm quite pleased with it. It's by no means new but it goes like a dream. It's only a two-seater, but that's what I wanted now I'm on my own. I expect Mum told you, didn't she?'

'Er . . . yes. She did mention it.'

Matthew grinned. 'It's no secret; it's just one of those things that happen. I'd never have bought it when I was with Yvonne, and Mum's not keen on it either. It was a bit of bravado, you might say. Anyway, hop in and we'll set off.'

'That's your car, I take it?' he said, driving past her red Volkswagen.

'Yes, it suits me; gets me from A to B and that's all I need.'

The pub was on the corner of the main street, a late Victorian building, modernized inside and comfortable, but still with a touch of olde worlde ambience. There were sepia prints of old Yorkshire scenes on the walls, and a huge stone fireplace, the grate filled with an arrangement of ferns and plants rather than a fire. A black and white cat lay sleeping on a cushion on a Windsor chair.

Helen stroked it gently. 'He reminds me of my Trixie,' she said. 'She's black and white like this one, but smaller. I assume this is a boy; he's rather large, isn't he?'

'I can see you're a cat lover,' said Matthew.

'Yes, so I am. I acquired Trixie from Aunt Alice and she's settled down well with me. You either like them or you don't, and they know it. What about you, Matthew? Are you a cat person?'

'Yes, definitely. We had a cat but she stayed with Yvonne . . . ' He quickly changed the subject. 'You can call me Matt, if you like; everyone else does. It's only Mum that calls me Matthew. Now . . . what are you having? Gin and tonic, Martini, port and lemon?'

'No, nothing like that. I'll just stick to a shandy, a small one, please . . . Matt. Remember what your mother said; I have to drive home.'

181

'Oh, she always warns me not to drink too much or to drive too fast! But I don't; better to be safe than sorry. A packet of crisps as well?'

'Goodness me, no! Not after that huge meal.'

'Okay-doke. Won't be a jiffy.'

He was very soon back at the corner table where Helen was sitting, with a pint of bitter for himself and Helen's shandy. He sat down next to her on the red plush seat.

'Cheers,' he said, lifting his glass. 'Here's to . . . what shall we say? Family friendships.'

'Yes, cheers,' she replied. 'I'm very pleased to have met you.'

'Let me see; what relation are we to one another?' he said. 'Your mother and my mother are . . . cousins?'

'No; it's my gran, Lizzie, and your mother who are cousins. And my aunt — well great-aunt Alice and your mother were cousins as well.'

'What does that make us then?' He looked puzzled. 'Second cousins, third cousins, cousins twice removed?' He laughed. 'Perhaps I'm a sort of uncle to you, do you think?'

'You're as bad as me,' said Helen. 'My mum says I've always worried about relationships; what relation so-and-so is to so-and-so. But does it really matter?'

'Not a bit.' Matthew smiled at her in such a way that her heart turned a somersault. 'It doesn't matter at all. We have met, and that's thanks to your Aunt Alice. Am I right?'

'Yes, that was the start of it, Aunt Alice dying so suddenly. It was a great shock to us all, especially to me . . . ' She told him how her friendship with her great-aunt had developed over the last few years and that she had left her the cottage.

'I've been curious about her life,' she went on. 'It's a sad story . . . '

She told him about the box of mementoes she had found and the photograph albums, and how she suspected that a family in Thornbeck might be connected in some way to Alice.

'The trail seems to have petered out,' she said. 'But the name is wrong anyway . . . It was a wartime romance that didn't have a happy ending. There must have been hundreds, possibly thousands of them. Aunt Alice never breathed a word about it, but I feel, somehow, that she would like me to know about it now that I'm living in Thornbeck.'

'And you like living there, do you?'

'Yes, very much so. It's a big change for me after living in Blackpool. But it seems as though it had to be.'

'Fate . . . Kismet . . . ?'

'Yes, something like that.'

'Thornbeck is on the road to Scarborough, isn't it? I've never been there, but I've seen it on the map.'

'Yes, about half an hour's drive away. Scarborough's one place I haven't visited yet, but I intend to before long.'

'And I'll be there to show you around,' said Matthew, smiling at her.

Helen felt a little embarrassed. She had said it without thinking about him being there. 'Yes . . . yes, maybe you will,' she replied.

'And do you work in Thornbeck, or nearby?' he asked. He guessed she would have a responsible sort of job. She was an intelligent young woman and he found her very interesting to talk to. 'I don't think you've mentioned it.'

'I work in an estate agency,' she replied. 'I've done that ever since I left school; worked my way up the ladder, of course; and I was fortunate to find a post in Pickering. It was supposed to be temporary but the girl who is on maternity leave seems to be changing her mind about coming back, and the boss has promised me the job if that happens.'

'Jolly good. It's not far for you to drive, then?'

'No, only twenty minutes or so; no problem. And what about your new post in Scarborough, Matthew? Is that a promotion?'

'Yes, it is really. I worked for a large firm in Bradford, dealing in all kinds of things. I was a little fish in a big pond at first, very much so, but I worked my way up to being a middle-sized fish! But it's a small firm in Scarborough and I shall be the under-manager. The father of the firm is retiring and his son is taking over, so I shall be the second in command. A bigger fish in a small pond, you might say.'

'So you'll be buying a house there eventually? Or a flat?'

'Like I said, I'll stay in a B and B while I look around, or maybe share a flat. I shall go there a week before I start work and do some house hunting. You would be good at that. You know just what to look for. What about giving me a hand?'

Helen was not sure whether he meant it or was joking. 'I shall be working,' she replied casually, 'except at the weekend. But I'm sure you will have a good idea what you are looking for, won't you?'

'Yes, we do quite a lot of conveyancing, and deal with disputes about property; insurance claims and wills and all sorts of problems that arise from time to time. And divorce, of course, but I went to another firm to sort mine out.'

'Yes . . . I was sorry to hear about that,' she said.

He gave a slight shrug. 'It was unpleasant, but unavoidable in the end. Yvonne had met somebody else and that was that. And I realized I didn't care all that much, certainly not enough to make a fuss about it, which made me wonder if I'd loved her enough at all.'

'Had you known her for a long time?'

'No, not really. We met through mutual friends, a sort of blind date, and we seemed to hit it off straight away. She was pretty, lively and lots of fun and . . . well . . . it seemed like a good idea at the time.' He smiled ruefully.

'But it wasn't?'

'No, as it turned out. We were married a few months after we met. I suppose I thought it was time I settled down. I was getting on for thirty then, and I'd had a few girlfriends. Most of my friends were married, and my mother was anxious for me to settle down with a nice girl, as she said. So I went ahead and took the plunge. It lasted four years, but I could see the cracks appearing quite early. I assumed she would want

185

a family; most girls do, but she just wanted a good time.'

'What was her job?'

'She was a supervisor in a department store in Bradford. Quite a responsible job, and she met a lot of people. She was very friendly and vivacious.'

Obviously a bit too much, thought Helen.

'We had a nice little house and a comfortable lifestyle. On the surface we appeared to be happy, but clearly it was not enough for her . . . ' He paused for a moment, before turning to Helen. 'What about you, Helen, if you don't mind me asking? Is there anyone special in your life?'

'Not at the moment,' she replied. She grinned at him. 'Friends keep hinting to me that it's time I made up my mind. There have been one or two; the last one ended just before Aunt Alice died. And since I moved here I've been busy settling in, finding my feet.'

'You're a little younger than me, aren't you?' he asked.

Helen laughed. 'That's a tactful way to ask how old I am! Yes, I'm thirty-three. Turning thirty is a milestone, isn't it? But I don't feel any different, and it doesn't bother me.'

'You are as young as you feel,' said Matthew. 'That's one of my mother's sayings. She's full of these little clichés. Another one is 'What will be, will be'.' He smiled at Helen, a serious rather than a jocular smile. 'I think we had better be heading back now,' he said. 'You'll want to spend a little more time with my mum before you set off for home.'

He held out his hand and she took hold of it as they walked back to the car in a companionable silence.

Sally was anxious that Helen must get back before it was dark. 'It's been lovely getting to know you again,' she said, 'and I know Matthew's pleased an' all.' She smiled knowingly at her son. 'We mustn't lose touch now we've met — and your mum and gran, we must meet up with them sometime soon.'

She embraced Helen warmly as they said goodbye, then she stood at the door, allowing Matthew to walk with her to her car. He kissed her cheek and gave her hand a squeeze. 'I've got your phone number,' he said, 'and I'll let you know just when I will be going to Scarborough. I could break my journey at Thornbeck and spend a little time with you . . . that is if you think it's a good idea?'

'A great idea,' she replied. 'I'll look forward to seeing you again.'

'Me too.' He looked at her fondly as she settled herself at the wheel. 'Drive carefully, won't you? Bye for now, and I'll see you soon.'

'Yes, see you, Matt. It's been lovely meeting you. Bye for now.'

She drove away feeling on top of the world. It had been a surprise to meet Matthew as well as Sally, an unexpected pleasure.

Matthew gave a contented sigh as he watched her drive away. He was smiling as he went back into the house.

'You look like the cat that's got the cream,' said Sally. 'I wonder why?'

'Do you know, Mum, I have a feeling that she might be 'the one'. And I think that she feels it too.'

Sally nodded. 'I hope so, son. She's a lovely lass. But whatever will be, will be, and remember, it's early days yet.'

13

Helen felt happy and carefree, singing to herself as she went about her work in the cottage. Not that there was much work to do. She was by nature a tidy person and did not let anything get too messy; no pots left unwashed or clothes unironed.

She knew, however, that she must not get carried away. She had only just met Matthew — Matt, as he said she should call him — and it was far too soon to fancy that she was in love. Or was it? She was sure there was something in the way they had looked at one another and the way they had talked together so easily. It was as though they had known each other for ages instead of being, as they were, comparative strangers. She was looking forward to seeing him again but she knew she must contain herself and not make the first move.

He had said he would phone when he had decided which day he would be going to Scarborough and would stop at Thornbeck to spend some time with her, so she must curb her impatience and wait until he rang.

It was incredible just how much her life had changed in the last few months. Aunt Alice's death had been a dreadful shock, and Helen had felt so sad and almost unable to believe that she would never see her again. But then so many lovely things had happened since.

How could she ever have imagined that she would be living in Aunt Alice's dear little cottage? And, moreover, that it belonged to her completely with no mortgage and no repayments to worry about, and the money she had been saving while living in her rented flat was being put to good use in modernizing the kitchen and bathroom.

She had decided, though, to leave much of the cottage as it was, to remind her of her aunt, who had not been too old-fashioned in outlook. The bedroom furniture and the carpets, curtains and decor were pleasing, pretty and feminine rather than avant-garde, and there was no need to alter any of it. Helen was carrying through her ideas about the kitchen, though. Work was in progress to remove all the old Formica units and replace them with pinewood cupboards and work surfaces in a more modern material. It was a mammoth task and she couldn't wait for it to be completed.

She was enjoying her work at the estate agency immensely. One of her duties, now that she was becoming more established at the firm, was showing would-be buyers around a variety of properties, from grey stone cottages similar to Aunt Alice's (Helen still found it incredible to think of this cottage as her own), to large detached houses and newly built estates. This was something she had always liked and at which she did well, having a persuasive, though not too pushy, approach. It was also helping her to become acquainted with the area in and around Pickering. She loved the country surroundings; the villages and farmlands and the gently rolling hills, and the wide variety of properties that were on sale.

Her boss, Alan Price, was very pleased at the way she had settled into the firm and with the number of sales she had negotiated. When Paula gave birth to a baby boy and decided that she would not be returning to work, he offered the permanent post to Helen.

Yes, it seemed that everything was going her way. She was enjoying her social life as well. She had made several new friends of both sexes but most of them were married couples. She knew it was rather unusual to have reached the age of thirty-three without having been married or, at least, engaged. She knew young women of her age who were already embarking on their second marriage and others who had been engaged once or twice. Was she too choosy? She really didn't know the answer to that, but she was not unhappy with her single status. Deep down, though, she knew that she did not want it to continue forever. She had been regretful for a while when her relationship with Alex had come to an end, but then her life had changed drastically and there had been so many other things to think about and to sort out.

Then Matthew had walked into her life. Never before had she experienced the certainty she now felt that this might be what she had waited for all this time. She felt happy and warm inside when she thought about him, but she did not allow herself to daydream because there were so many other things claiming her attention.

The work in the cottage was going on while

she was at the office. Fortunately there was an upstairs toilet, and while the bath was being replaced she would manage with a stand-up wash in the kitchen. It would be a great relief when it was finished. She hated the house being in turmoil; in fact, she disliked upheaval of any kind, but told herself it would be worthwhile when it was finished.

In the evenings, when she was not engaged in her musical activities she was still sorting out the remainder of her aunt's belongings. She had left her aunt's bedroom just as it had been when Alice was alive, with her ornaments, photos and her dressing table set in their original places. Her mother had stayed there when she came to visit, and it would be the guestroom for anyone else who came. She did not want to regard it as a shrine; she knew she must not remember her aunt in a morbid way. She still missed her, but life was for the living and her aunt would not want her to mourn forever. All the same, she felt that to remove all traces of Alice would be tantamount to eradicating her memory.

On the top of the wardrobe in what had been Alice's room there was a leather suitcase of the type that was not used much for modern-day travel. It was far too heavy for travelling by air or, indeed, to lug around on a train or a bus. This was one item that had not yet been investigated.

Helen stood on a chair and heaved the case down, staggering beneath the weight. She let it fall to the floor with a loud crash before clambering down herself. A cloud of dust flew up in the air, making her sneeze.

'You silly fool!' she chided herself, knowing that she should have waited until she had someone to help her, but she had a free evening and had wanted to tackle the last few items belonging to her aunt. Kneeling down, she dusted the lid then opened the case, which was not locked.

It contained several items of clothing, shoes and a handbag. The clothes in the wardrobes, which had gone to the charity shops, had been modern — or what Alice would have considered modern for a woman of her age — dating from the last few years. The articles in this case were much older, the sort that would now be called vintage. Helen guessed that they dated from the war years.

There were two dresses, one in a sort of crêpe material that Helen thought was called Moygashel. It was dark pink with padded shoulders and a pleated skirt and silver buttons on the bodice; the sort of garment that would have been a 'best dress' for special occasions. The other dress was more summery in silky rayon with a design of bright-red poppies on a white background.

There were two pairs of shoes; one was white and brown with Cuban heels, and the other was red with peep toes and what must have been some of the first wedge heels. There was some underwear too: a flimsy pink satin garment that Helen knew was a suspender belt, worn in the days before tights were invented. Helen thought what a bother it must have been and how uncomfortable, although she knew some women still wore such garments for various reasons. There was a pair of frilly pink panties and a nightdress of the same silky material that she thought was Celanese.

She felt sad, and rather guilty, too, at discovering such intimate items. She guessed that her aunt had enjoyed a passionate as well as a romantic and loving relationship with her young airman, something which would have shocked Alice's mother. She put them all back in the case feeling that she had stumbled upon something very private.

The handbag was a heavy boxy one of brown leather with a metal clasp. She opened it and took out an envelope containing a letter and some photographs. They were black and white photos, one of a bride and groom. At a first glance the young man appeared to be the one in the RAF uniform in Alice's box of treasures — but of course it could not be the same one. She turned it over and read the words *Jonathan and Rachel on their wedding day*. There was no date but the couple appeared to be in their early twenties. Jonathan — whom she thought must be Aunt Alice and Tony's son — was the image of his father as portrayed in his RAF uniform.

The next two photos were more recent. They were of babies, a boy and a girl, in what appeared to be their christening outfits. On the back were the words *Jennifer, aged six months* and *James, aged six months*.

Helen's heart gave a jolt. So she had been right after all — but it didn't make any sense. She then read the short letter that accompanied the photos.

Dear Alice,
We thought you would like to have these

194

photos. Maybe, one day, it will be time to reveal the truth, but for the moment it is better to leave things as they are.

With kind regards,
Robert and Pamela.

Curiouser and curiouser, thought Helen. What did it all mean? Her head was spinning with the mystery of it all. But she had other things on her mind which were a distraction from this problem. She would be seeing Matthew again in a couple of days. He was traveling to Scarborough on Saturday and would call to see her in the afternoon. He had suggested, tentatively, during his phone call, that she might like to accompany him there and assist him in his search to find somewhere to live. She was not sure how serious he was about the suggestion. Was he assuming she could take some time off work? As it happened her boss had already told her that she was due a few days' leave as she had now worked there for four months.

And so she had applied for three days off the following week. She would tell Matthew the news when he arrived. She would also tell him about her discovery of the letter and photos and ask his opinion. She was in a quandary as to what she should do. Clearly Robert Kershaw was involved in some way. But how?

Matthew phoned soon after she arrived home on Friday to say that he would arrive at her home at around one o'clock the following day, if that suited her.

'Perfect,' she replied. 'I'll prepare some lunch;

maybe soup and sandwiches. Will that do?'

He replied with the same word. 'Perfect. Thanks, Helen . . . Have you thought any more about coming to Scarborough with me?'

She hesitated for just a moment before saying, 'As a matter of fact, I have. I've got three days' leave due to me, so I'm free for Monday, Tuesday and Wednesday. But I wasn't sure how serious you were about it, whether you . . . really meant it.'

'Of course I meant it. I never say things I don't mean. That's great! I'll ring up and make a booking at a little place near the castle that's been recommended to me. I could have booked earlier but I wasn't sure that you would agree.'

Helen laughed, 'Well, I do. It'll be lovely to spend a few days in Scarborough.' She thought to herself that neither of them had wanted to appear too eager; they had both decided to be cautious.

'OK, then. See you tomorrow. I'm glad you're coming with me. Bye for now, Helen.'

'Bye, Matt. See you soon . . . '

He arrived almost on the dot of one o'clock. He kissed her cheek in a casual but friendly manner. 'Good to see you again.'

'You too,' she replied. 'Make yourself at home. I've made some ham sandwiches. What sort of soup would you like — tomato, oxtail, chicken . . . ? It's out of a tin, I'm afraid.'

'Really? I thought it would have been made by your own fair hands . . . Only joking! Tomato, please. You can't beat good old Heinz, can you?'

They dined casually in the newly fitted

kitchen. 'Very nice,' said Matthew, looking round approvingly at the pine units and the fresh yellow and white gingham curtains hanging at the window. 'They've made a good job of it. Your bathroom's very posh as well. You're all shipshape now, are you?'

'Yes, there's been quite enough upheaval. I can settle down in comfort now. I hate being in a mess.'

'So . . . what's new? How's the detective work going?'

'It's getting more and more mysterious . . . ' She told him about her latest discoveries, and when they had finished lunch she showed him the letter and the photos.

'There seems to be no doubt about those two young men,' he said, looking at the wedding photo and the one of Tony in RAF uniform. 'Father and son, you presume? And the babies, they are . . . ?'

'Jennifer and James Kershaw, Robert and Pamela's children. They are grown up now, both at college. They're lovely young people and Aunt Alice left them both some money. She used to babysit for them; she was very friendly with the family.'

'And do you see any resemblance there?'

'I'm not sure. I don't know them well enough.'

'But you are quite friendly with Robert and his wife?'

'Yes; they are in the church choir and in the operatic group as well. But they haven't so much as hinted at any connection.'

'Well, I think you will have to take the bull by the horns and ask them, or you will go on worrying about it forever. But before that we are going to have a lovely few days in Scarborough. Try to put it to the back of your mind for the moment.'

And Helen knew that that was what she really must do. She brought down her travel bag and they set off. Trixie was already settled with the next-door neighbours, who were willing to have her any time.

It was quite a short journey to Scarborough, not much more than half an hour. Matthew knew the place much better than did Helen. They came in on the back road, passing the railway station, then he drove up a steep hill that led towards the castle. They drove past an imposing hotel that stood on the headland overlooking the sea.

'Ours is less grand, I'm afraid,' said Matthew. 'Just a B and B, but my friend says they do a good hearty breakfast, which has to be a priority. Don't you agree?'

'Absolutely!' said Helen.

He stopped at a much smaller place where there was parking space for a few cars. 'This is it,' he said. 'Hilltop House. Well we can't disagree with that.'

A smiling, middle-aged woman answered the door at their knock and led them into a small hallway with just enough room for the reception desk. The place felt warm and homely with a richly patterned red and gold carpet on the floor.

'Mr Townsend and Miss Burnside,' said Matthew. 'I phoned earlier to reserve two single rooms.'

'Very good, sir. Rooms three and four, on the first floor. Here are your keys.' They were old-fashioned ones with the numbers written large on the heavy metal tags. 'I'll get my husband to carry your luggage.'

'No, it's OK, thanks,' said Matthew. 'I'll take them; we've not brought much with us.'

He had brought only enough for a few days, intending to bring the rest of his belongings — which were now at his mother's house — when he had found somewhere permanent to live.

'Very good, sir. I hope you'll be comfortable here. Folks usually are. I'm Mrs Porter by the way. Breakfast is any time from eight o'clock until nine. And I make a cup of tea in the evening if you would like one. So . . . enjoy the rest of your day and I'll see you later.'

Matthew carried their luggage up the stairs to their rooms at the front of the house. They overlooked St Mary's Church and churchyard on the opposite side of the road. The rooms were smallish but adequate with single beds and simple light oak furniture. They were both en-suite, with a cubicle containing a toilet, a washbasin and a small bath with a shower attachment. This was indeed a bonus. Many of the older hotels and B&Bs didn't yet provide this facility although more and more clients were starting to expect it. Mrs Porter was obviously keeping up with the trend and would no doubt reap the benefit.

'See you in a little while,' said Matthew, 'then we'll go and explore the town.'

Helen felt happy and excited at the thought of the next few days. She intended to travel back on Wednesday afternoon on the service bus, leaving Matthew to spend some time on his own before starting work the following Monday.

'What a lovely old church,' said Helen as they crossed the road on leaving the hotel, 'and a perfect setting for it as well. So picturesque; I've seen it on postcards, of course.'

The grey stone church of St Mary with its square tower was surrounded by trees in full leaf, with a well-tended graveyard, and a view of the rooftops of the old town and, in the distance, the sea.

'Anne Brontë is buried here,' said Matthew. 'Her grave is in the annexe a little further along. Let's go and have a look, shall we?'

Their walk took them past the churchyard, up to the ruined castle at the top of the hill. From there was a magnificent view of the curve of the South Bay, with the Grand Hotel, the most imposing one in the town, dominating the scene from its position on the headland looking out across the North Sea. There were still a few people on the golden sands making the most of the sunshine.

Matthew took her hand as they made their way down the steep path, then the steps that led down to the promenade. It was almost six o'clock, the time when visitors and residents alike had gone home for their tea or whatever they called their evening meal. This part of the town, usually a hive of activity, was almost deserted.

'This is — what shall I say? — the less salubrious part of Scarborough,' said Matthew. 'The posher part is on the other side of the Spa Bridge where there are the bigger hotels and gardens.'

'I'm not too bothered about 'posh',' said Helen. 'I'm just enjoying it, all of it. This part reminds me of the Golden Mile at Blackpool where the visitors all congregate, but there's a posher part there as well, up at North Shore.'

'It's the opposite way round here,' said Matthew, 'with Scarborough being on the east coast. The sun rises over the sea here, whereas in Blackpool that's where it sets.'

'Yes, there are the most glorious sunsets,' said Helen. 'If you're on the promenade to see them. We won't see that here.'

'Well, you can't have everything. On the other hand we could get up early and see the sun rise, if we felt inclined . . . '

Helen laughed. 'Probably not.'

Reaching the end of the north promenade they walked through a cliffside garden to the area near the Grand Hotel. A blue plaque on the wall marked the place where the Brontë sisters had stayed, in a small guest house which was there before the hotel was built. Nearby was the town hall with a statue of Queen Victoria in her later days.

'If I remember rightly there's a good fish and chip place near here,' said Matthew. 'I've just realized how hungry I am.'

There it was, tucked away in a corner, a small café with just a few tables. There was one other couple dining there. Helen and Matthew sat at a corner table covered with a green and white checked cloth, and they both ordered haddock.

Helen smiled. 'It's delicious.' She felt that she had never enjoyed a meal more than this one.

'Let's walk a bit further,' said Matthew when they had finished their food and he had paid the bill.

Dusk was falling and they headed back to the castle area where they found a quiet pub. They stayed for an hour or so, chatting companionably, as though they had always known one another, drinking a pint of bitter for Matt, and Helen's favourite Martini and lemonade.

'I'm so glad we met,' Matt said. 'To think that we've lived all this time without knowing one another!'

'Yes, I'm glad too,' said Helen.

Matthew took her hand as they walked back through the quiet streets to their lodgings. Mrs Porter appeared as she heard them enter the house.

'Would you like a cup of tea, or coffee? No extra charge; it's something I like to do for my guests if they want it.'

They looked at one another and nodded. 'Yes, thank you,' said Matthew. 'Tea for me.'

'And tea for me as well,' added Helen.

Mrs Porter opened the door to the dining room. 'Make yourselves at home. I'll be with you in a jiffy.'

At one end of the room a few tables were already set out for breakfast, and at the other end there was a settee and easy chairs, and a small television set. There were, however, no other guests in the room.

'How very kind of her,' said Helen. 'She certainly knows how to make her guests feel welcome.'

When Mrs Porter returned with a tray laden with tea and chocolate biscuits, they spent a pleasant few minutes in conversation before she left them on their own, saying that she would clear the pots away later.

'What a nice, friendly woman,' said Matthew. 'Do you know, I think I might stay here for a while until I find somewhere suitable to live. Even if I find a place in the next week I might not be able to move in straight away. Anyway, I'm ready to turn in now. How about you?'

'Me too,' said Helen.

They turned out the light and walked up the stairs, pausing outside the bedroom doors, which were next to one another.

'Goodnight, Helen,' said Matthew. 'We've had a lovely day.'

He looked at her, smiling in a fond and friendly way, then he put his arms around her and gently kissed her on the lips.

'Goodnight, Matt,' she whispered. 'I've enjoyed it too . . . See you in the morning.'

'Yes; about half past eight for breakfast? Is that OK? I'll knock on your door when I'm ready.'

'Yes . . . fine,' she replied, a little breathlessly.

Matt nodded then turned and entered his room.

Helen felt her heart beating faster. She smiled

to herself as she undressed and got ready for bed. That was a good beginning, but it was as well not to rush things . . .

14

There was the promise of a fine day when Helen
drew back the curtains. She washed and dressed
and was ready when Matt knocked at eight
thirty.

There were two other couples, middle-aged
people, seated at small tables when they entered
the dining room. They all smiled and nodded at
one another, saying 'Good morning'. Mrs Porter
appeared promptly, with a welcoming smile, to
take their breakfast order.

'Now, would you like tea or coffee? Brown
toast or white? Fruit juice or cereal, or both if
you wish. The full cooked breakfast is bacon,
sausage, fried egg, mushrooms and tomato; take
your pick of whatever you fancy.'

'Wow!' said Helen. 'I think we're spoiled for
choice.'

They finally decided, and Mrs Porter went
away seeming to remember it all without writing
it down.

'So, what shall we do today?' asked Matt. 'Any
ideas?'

'What about Peasholm Park?' said Helen. 'I
think I went there when I was a little girl but I
don't remember it.'

The church bells of St Mary's were ringing as
they set off. After they'd strolled through the
park they had a sandwich lunch at a small café
before driving up to Flamborough Head and

then, after a brisk walk that made their hands and faces tingle with the cold air, they sought the warmth of the car and drove on to Bridlington and then back north to Filey, stopping a while at each town for a walk along the promenade. They were both popular seaside resorts but they lacked the charm and the picturesque views to be found in Scarborough.

When they returned there it was early evening, and they were both feeling more than a little hungry. They found an Italian restaurant at the top end of Newborough. The place was not busy, so they lingered for well over an hour over their lasagne and ravioli, served with tasty garlic bread, and accompanied by a bottle of red wine. The delicious meal ended with Neapolitan ice cream and dark fragrant coffee.

Helen sighed contentedly. 'I'm having a lovely holiday, but we're supposed to be house hunting as well, aren't we?'

'We'll start in earnest in the morning,' said Matthew. 'It's ages since I enjoyed a break so much. I went on a camping holiday earlier this year with a mate from work; roughing it, you know, but it was great fun. This is different, though. Thanks for coming, Helen.'

'It's a pleasure,' she said, aware of his intense gaze. She reached for her shoulder bag. 'Now, let me pay my share. You can't pay for everything.'

He agreed as she was quite persistent. 'Now we'd better make a move, or we'll be overstaying our welcome.'

Dusk was falling as they drove back to Hilltop House. Matt said that he intended to read for a while, and invited Helen to join him.

When she went into Matt's room he was sprawled in the bed, leaning on a pillow. She sat on the basket weave chair which, with a couple of cushions, was quite comfortable.

'What are you reading?' she asked.

'Bernard Cornwell; one of the Sharpe novels. I've read them all before but they're like old friends to me now. What about you?'

She smiled. '*The Crowthers of Bankdam*. Have you heard of it?'

'Yes, I think so, a while ago. It's about a mill owner, isn't it?'

'Yes; since I came to live here I've been reading novels set in Yorkshire. I've read *South Riding* by Winifred Holtby and *Inheritance* by Phyllis Bentley; all about the Luddites and the history of the woollen mills. It's a great story. No doubt our ancestors were mill workers way back in the last century. I'm getting quite engrossed in it all. It makes a change from Jilly Cooper and Jackie Collins!'

They read in silence for a while. Although she was concentrating on the story, Helen's mind strayed now and again to Matthew and their friendship, wondering how — or when — it might progress a stage further.

'Do you fancy a nightcap?' he asked after a while.

'Yes, if you like. Do you mean . . . we should go down and have a cup of tea?'

'No, I've got something better.' He grinned as he opened a drawer and took out a hip flask of brandy. 'No posh glasses, I'm afraid. We'll have to manage with the ones in the bathroom.'

Helen laughed. 'I'll go and get mine then.'

When she returned he poured a half inch or so into each glass and added a little water from the tap.

'I've got a box of crackers as well,' he said. 'Help yourself.'

Helen found that the brandy helped to settle the butterflies in her stomach that she had been aware of since entering Matt's room. She glanced at his bedside alarm clock. It had turned eleven o'clock; time she was making a move. She stood up.

'Thanks for the nightcap, Matt; I'll say goodnight now — we have a busy day tomorrow.'

He stood up and, as he had done the previous night, put his arms around her and kissed her, a little more fervently, on the lips before she retired to her own room for the night.

*   *   *

Helen felt happy, but still a little apprehensive as she settled herself in her bed. She wasn't sure why she should feel nervous. She felt sure that her relationship with Matt would develop sooner rather than later, and this time she did want it to be just right.

After another substantial breakfast they set off early the next morning for the centre of town and the main purpose of their visit. Matthew parked the car in a side street off the top end of Newborough. There were a couple of estate agencies nearby and they stopped to look in the window of the first one.

'I'm thinking it might be better to rent rather than to buy, just at the moment,' he said. 'I know it might make sense to buy if I have the money for the deposit — which I have — but I think I shall wait a while and see how things go, with my job and . . . all sorts of reasons. Anyway, let's go in and see what they have to offer.'

There were several flats available for renting, both short and long leases. As was the case in all seaside resorts, many of them were in converted hotels or boarding houses, several in the area of North Bay and a few in the more select South Bay. Some had a sea view but that was not a priority for Matthew. The main criteria would be the condition and the general state of repair.

After looking at what was on offer, he decided, with Helen's help, on two flats that he thought sounded quite promising. Both of them were upstairs flats in large private houses rather than converted hotels. Accommodation in hotels would be geared to the basic requirements of holiday makers or those tenants who wanted a lower rental where they would get just what they paid for and no more.

Matthew found that Helen's help was invaluable. As she had been in the business for several years she was able to read between the lines of the agent's descriptions and their use of such words as basic or original, and compact — which meant pokey. He explained that the property was for himself — Helen was a good friend who had come along to help him — but he required two bedrooms, one being for relatives or friends who might visit; pleasant living accommodation, and central heating was a must.

Both flats were part of large — but modernized — Victorian houses; one in the Peasholm Park district, and the other at the opposite end of the town in a quiet square on the South Bay, near to the Italian gardens.

'Our property adviser, Joanne, will be available to show you round both properties this afternoon if that is convenient,' said the smartly dressed man whom they thought was the boss. 'Do you have transport, sir?'

Matthew said that they did, and it was agreed that Joanne would meet them outside the Peasholm Park property at two o'clock, then they would move on to the other flat in the south of the town.

After a stroll along the promenade and a sandwich lunch they went back to where the car was parked and drove off to the first address.

An efficient-looking youngish woman, possibly a few years older than Helen, got out of a small estate car when she saw them arrive. After they had introduced themselves she opened the double door, which had a stained-glass panel depicting flowers and butterflies, and led them into the house. From the squarish hall the wide staircase led to the upper floor where there were two bedrooms, one large and the other considerably smaller, and a fair-sized living-cum-dining room with a view towards Peasholm Park, the lake just visible between the trees. The flat was self-contained with a kitchen which was small but equipped with an electric cooker and a fridge; and a bathroom with a suite in the once-popular avocado green.

The flat was part furnished, clean and comfortable. All in all, Matthew was quite impressed, but it would not do to be too enthusiastic.

The rent was quite expensive and Matt was rather taken aback for a moment when Joanne told him the price. However, Helen told him — when the young woman left them alone for a moment — that it was the going rate for a flat of that size and quality.

'Yes, I like it,' he told Joanne, 'apart from the state of the garden, but let's look at the other one and see how it compares.'

In their separate cars they drove to the other end of Scarborough, to the quiet square where the other house was situated. Again it was a large Victorian villa. It was set well back from the promenade, but with a view from the upper windows of the Italian gardens in the distance, and the North Sea. The accommodation was similar, again part furnished, and the kitchen and the bathroom were adequate. But it was not so well maintained and Matt — and Helen, too — did not have the same feeling that they'd had in the first flat. The ambience in the other flat was warm and friendly and gave out the right vibes. Matt wondered if this was nonsense, but Helen told him later that it was true that houses evoked positive or negative feelings and that it was something she was often aware of when visiting a property.

Both flats were approximately the same

distance from Matthew's new place of work. The rent for the second flat was rather less, but he decided that it made no difference to the way he felt. However, he did not tell Joanne of his decision straight away, telling her, rather, that he needed time to sort out the pros and cons and that he would let them know the following day.

'Don't leave it too long,' she advised him. 'They are both desirable properties and I wouldn't want you to miss out.' He knew, though, that this was an estate agent's usual patter.

'I think you've already made up your mind, haven't you?' said Helen as they drove away.

'Indeed I have. I would never have believed it could be so easy. The moment I saw the first flat I had a good feeling about it.'

'Yes, it sometimes happens like that. On the other hand, you might search for ages and not find anything that you like.'

The afternoon had flown past and it was already approaching teatime.

'What would you like to do this evening?' he asked. 'Any ideas?'

'Not really,' said Helen. 'I'm having a lovely time, and I'm pleased that you've found a suitable flat so quickly. It will take a little while though before you can move in, with the contract and survey and everything.'

'Fortunately I'm in the right job, aren't I?' he replied. 'And I shall ask Mrs Porter if I can stay until everything is sorted out. Now, while we decide what to do this evening, what about fish and chips at that little place near the Grand?'

'Great idea,' said Helen. 'I'm ravenous — it must be the sea air.'

After another delicious meal, they decided they would go back to their digs and dress up a little, then stroll along the lower promenade and see what the Spa had to offer in the way of entertainment.

Helen put on her new floral top and a flared skirt in emerald green rather than the trousers she usually wore, and summer sandals with a higher heel, not designed for strenuous walking, but the Spa was not too far away. She felt that she wanted to look her very best tonight.

Matthew was smartly attired in his new navy-blue blazer, well pressed grey trousers and a blue and white striped shirt.

'You look lovely,' he said, 'but will you be able to walk in those shoes or shall we go in the car?'

'No, I'll be fine. It's a nice evening and not too breezy for a change.'

The wind had dropped and the air felt balmy and mild as they strolled across the bridge and along to the Spa buildings, hand in hand. They found that there was a concert in the theatre by the resident orchestra, of light classical music — known as 'easy listening' — and songs from popular shows and films.

'Just my cup of tea!' said Helen, and Matt agreed with her.

They were fortunate to find seats at the back of the stalls, as there was a crowd of people there already, many of them rather older than themselves, but there were younger ones there as well. They had already discovered that their taste

213

in music was similar, and as they enjoyed a drink in the crowded bar during the interval, Helen wondered if the evening could possibly get any better.

It appeared very dark when they came out after the brightness of the theatre, but as they walked along the promenade the overhead lights on the Spa Bridge shone on the midnight-blue sea, causing shimmering golden ripples. It was a truly romantic scene, but Helen's feet were beginning to ache as they walked up the steep slope to their guest house.

There was a light on in the visitors' lounge. But by mutual assent they went straight upstairs.

'Fancy a nightcap?' asked Matt.

'Why not?' said Helen. 'A fitting end to a lovely evening.' But they both knew that it would not be the end.

They talked about the events of the day and the flat which Matt hoped would soon be his, and the concert that had been a delight to watch and listen to. Then conversation turned to what they would do the next day, their last day before Helen returned home on Wednesday. Matt suggested a drive over the moors to Whitby, then a look at Robin Hood's Bay on their return journey.

'But tomorrow is another day,' he said. 'Today is not over just yet. Helen . . . may I stay with you tonight?'

He had been sitting on the bed and Helen on the one easy chair. He came over and knelt beside her, taking hold of her hands. He kissed her gently.

'May I, Helen?' he repeated. 'You know how I

feel about you? And I think you feel the same way, don't you?'

'Yes . . . yes, I do,' she whispered. 'And . . . of course you may stay.'

He kissed her again more ardently, then they both stood up, holding each other closely. 'I'll see you in a little while,' he whispered.

She felt a tiny bit apprehensive. She had known him for such a short time, although it seemed as though she had known him for ages. But it felt right, as though it was meant to be. There was a strong family bond between them, but not such a close relationship that it might cause problems.

When he came to her room she felt at once that she need have no doubts or regret. As though he understood how she felt, Matthew was tender and considerate and their lovemaking, although not abandoned, was mutually satisfying.

'I love you, Helen,' he told her. 'Be very sure about that.'

'I love you too, Matt,' she replied.

He left her after an hour or so. The single bed was not really conducive to a good night's sleep.

'See you in the morning,' he said. 'We'll have another lovely day. Sleep well . . . '

And so she did, after reliving for a few moments one of the happiest days of her life.

There was no embarrassment between them the next morning, only a kiss and a look of understanding. There were one or two important matters to be dealt with before setting off on the final excursion of their little holiday.

Matthew complimented Mrs Porter on another

delicious breakfast and asked if it might be possible for him to stay for another couple of weeks or so, depending on how long it took before he was able to take over the flat.

She seemed delighted to have his company — and his payment, of course — for a little while longer. The bed and breakfast business was one that fluctuated according to the season, and summer was now drawing to a close.

'The first thing to do,' said Matthew, 'is to call in at the estate agency and say that I will take the flat near Peasholm Park. Then I must go to my new place of work and assure them that I'm ready and eager to start work on Monday.'

There was quite a hefty deposit to pay on the flat, but Helen assured him that it was normal for a property of that standard. The business side of the day completed, they set off on the drive across the moors to the neighbouring town of Whitby, some twenty miles away.

Matthew parked the car a little way from the town centre as the streets were narrow and hard to negotiate and exploring was best done on foot.

It was Helen's first visit to the town, and she was captivated by the charm of it all; the sea breeze and salt-laden air; the cry of the seagulls wheeling round above their heads; the rooftops of the town huddled below, and the fishing boats along the harbour wall. And because she was with Matthew, his arm around her shoulders, the moment was filled with a quiet happiness.

On the journey back they stopped at Robin Hood's Bay, a picturesque village which consisted of a narrow street of old houses leading down to the sea. Here the incline was even steeper than the ones in Whitby. Victorian — or possibly earlier — cottages faced one another across the road, with here and there a little shop or a café catering for the numerous tourists.

'It's been another wonderful day,' Helen said as she settled into the passenger seat.

'It's not over yet,' said Matthew with a meaningful smile. 'What about this evening?' he asked after a few seconds. 'We said we'd go 'posh' one night, didn't we? Have a slap-up meal?'

'Yes, I know,' said Helen, 'but I really liked that Italian place we went to on Sunday. That's quite posh enough for me. What do you say? We can dress up a bit if we want to.'

'That suits me fine. It will be our last evening together for a while. But not too long, I hope?' said Matthew, smiling at her a little ruefully.

'No, not too long . . . ' Helen felt a momentary sadness at the thought of going back the next day.

'We're much nearer, though, than when I was living in Baildon. Now, let's get back to Scarborough. A cup of tea, I think, then a rest before we set off for our evening jaunt.'

After a refreshing cup of tea at a promenade café, Helen was glad to stretch out on her bed with a Ruth Rendell novel.

They had agreed to meet at seven o'clock. 'You look lovely,' said Matthew, his loving glance telling her all that she needed to know.

She had made an effort with her hair and make-up and was wearing the one dress that she

217

had brought with her, a 'just above the knee' shift dress in strawberry pink. A long rope of silvery links with matching earrings added the finishing touch. The warm weather had continued but turned chilly later in the evening, so she wore a lightweight cream jacket.

She smiled a little shyly at the compliment, aware of Matthew's intent gaze. She could hardy say, 'So do you.' She laughed it off.

'Oh. I can if I try,' she said jovially.

They decided to walk as it was not too far — just one hill to climb on the way back — and she insisted that her feet would be comfy in the sandals she had worn the previous night.

The waiter recognized them from their last visit and showed them to a secluded corner table. Music was playing in the background — a Neapolitan serenade, followed by Italian songs, old and new, sung by mellow-voiced tenors — as they made their choice from the giant menus.

It was a romantic setting, so right for their final meal of the holiday. Discreet lighting from red-shaded lamps and candles on each table floating in glass goblets; table lamps fashioned from Chianti bottles, and frescos of Italian scenes on the walls; the Colosseum in Rome to the canals of Venice; the picturesque villages of the Amalfi coast and the grandeur of the Dolomites.

'Have you visited Italy?' asked Helen.

'No, I haven't. Have you?'

'No . . . but I would love to go.'

'Then it's something for the future,' Matthew replied, smiling at her.

As it was their final evening they chose all three courses; a delicious crab soup; large pizzas with exotic toppings — 'Far superior to the ones that come in boxes,' said Matt — and what else to finish with but a neatly scooped bowl of gelato: pistachio, vanilla and strawberry, to represent the Italian *tricolore*.

After finishing a bottle of red wine and drinking strong fragrant coffee they walked back along the dark streets and up the steep hill to the castle area. By mutual consent, neither of them needing to say a word, they went straight up to Helen's bedroom. Their lovemaking was tender, then more ardent, as they knew it was their last time together for a while, but hopefully not for too long.

After breakfast the following morning Helen said goodbye to Mrs Porter and Matthew drove her to the bus station, there being no rail link to the village of Thornbeck. He kissed her gently on the lips then enveloped her in a bear hug.

'Thank you for everything,' he said. 'For helping me with the flat and . . . for just being you. I'll see you soon. I don't know just when, but I'll make sure it's not too long.'

'It's been wonderful,' she replied, blinking a tear away from her eye. There was really no need to feel miserable. 'I shall miss you, but I'll be busy at work, and at rehearsals . . . and I have some detective work to do. Wish me luck!'

'Yes, of course; your great-aunt Alice, my second or third cousin, or whatever she was. And her son? And grandchildren? More distant relations.'

'Who knows?' said Helen. 'I might be barking up the wrong tree, but I have a feeling I'm right . . . somehow or other.'

★   ★   ★

Helen had to admit to herself that it was good to be home again. Trixie was clearly pleased to see her, and Helen appreciated the security and comfort of her own little cottage. She wished that Matt could be with her, but he was not too far away, and she felt confident that they would enjoy a shared future. How could she feel miserable or lonely when she looked back on the happy few days they had spent together?

She found that it was good to be back at work, too, in the job she enjoyed so much. She decided not to waste any more time. She must pluck up courage and try to solve the mystery of Aunt Alice and her connection — for she was sure there was one — with Robert Kershaw and his family. She looked again at the photos of Jennifer and James as babies, and the one of Jonathan — Aunt Alice's son? — and Rachel on their wedding day.

She approached Robert at the end of their Friday choir practice. 'Robert . . . I wonder if I could have a talk with you sometime soon? There's something I want to ask you, and I must see you on your own — well, you and Pamela.'

'Yes, of course, Helen,' he replied, smiling at her kindly as though he might know what it was about. 'What about tomorrow? You don't work Saturday, do you?'

'Only in the morning.'

'Well, we close the garden centre at five o'clock and we have our meal around six thirty. So come along and dine with us. We'll be very pleased to see you, then you can tell us about . . . whatever it is, OK?'

'That's great,' said Helen. 'Thank you, Robert. I'll see you tomorrow then.'

The Kershaws' property was a mile or so out of Thornbeck, down a country lane. Helen had been there several times and was impressed by the thriving business. It had originally been just a market garden, selling vegetables, fruit and flowers to a wide area around Thornbeck. In addition they now ran a garden centre, keeping up with the modern trend, where they sold plants and shrubs and gardening equipment.

Robert and Pamela lived in a bungalow which had been modernized at the edge of their land. Helen drove there on Saturday feeling a little apprehensive about what she might — or might not — discover. Pamela had prepared a tasty chicken casserole, followed by their own strawberries with cream. They talked mainly of matters concerning the choir and the operatic group as they ate their meal; then Pamela stacked the pots in the dishwasher and they settled down in the sitting room with a cup of coffee.

'Now, what is it that is troubling you, Helen?' Robert smiled at Helen encouragingly. 'Pamela and I have an idea as to what it might be and, like you, we have not been quite sure what to do about it.'

Helen took out the photos and the letter from her handbag and handed them to Robert and Pamela who were sitting together on the settee.

'I found these among Aunt Alice's belongings. I discovered a while ago that she had a baby boy who was adopted. I know it doesn't seem to make any sense — the name is wrong for one thing — but I wondered if you might be . . . Alice's son. Or some relation?'

Robert smiled a little sadly. 'No . . . I'm not. But you are on the right track. Jennifer and James . . . ' He looked fondly at the photos of the babies, then he looked at Helen. 'They are Alice's grandchildren.'

'What? But . . . how?' Helen shook her head in bewilderment.

'It's a long story,' said Robert, 'and rather a sad one . . . '

15

Alice returned to Blackpool at the end of September 1943. She was reluctant to go; she could not think of it as going home. Her home was now in Baildon with her Aunt Maggie and Uncle Fred, but she knew that it was what she had to do. She could not be dependent on their kindness and support any longer. She had to go back to her home town, resume her war work and try to look to the future, not back into the past.

It was a tearful parting from her aunt and uncle and Sally, and when the train pulled away from Bradford station she settled back into her corner seat and stared unseeingly out of the window. Stoically she fought back the tears; the train was crowded and she did not want to make a fool of herself.

After a while she ate the corned beef sandwiches that her aunt had made and, despite the rocking of the train, she managed to drink the tea from her thermos flask.

Her sister, Lizzie, was there to meet her at North Station. Lizzie greeted her with a quick hug and a kiss on her cheek, not over-effusively, but Alice thought there was a glimmer of sympathy in her eyes.

'We were sorry to hear about Tony,' she said. 'It was tragic, but it's wartime, and you must try to put it behind you now, our Alice.'

Alice nodded numbly. Aunt Maggie must have written to tell them about Tony; Alice had never mentioned him. Lizzie grabbed hold of Alice's suitcase and they took a tram to the stop closest to their boarding house.

Her mother welcomed Alice with a fleeting kiss, curtly but not unkindly. 'So you're back then. Well, your job's waiting for you as far as I know.'

Ada was, as usual, busy in the kitchen. The house was still full of RAF recruits, one batch following after another. No reference was made to Tony, or to the baby either, then or later, but the memory of it was always there like a ghost in the room.

Alice went back to her work at the munitions factory. Her friends Doris and Freda were still there, and she was pleased to be put into the same section. The two of them knew why she had been away, but as far as anyone else was concerned the story was that she had been ill and had gone to the countryside to recuperate, and if there was any doubt in their minds no one said anything.

Winnie, of course, was not there as her baby boy, Joseph, had been born soon after Alice had gone to Yorkshire. He was a bonny, chubby-cheeked little boy, now beginning to notice things and to smile and gurgle. Alice was unable to stop her tears and the lump in her throat the first time she saw him, but she had known this would happen. Winnie was still living in her parents' home while her husband was away, and she was delighted to see her friend again.

'You should have been Joseph's godmother,' she told Alice, 'and that is how I think of you. I asked my cousin instead, and we had a nice christening, but I kept thinking about you. I hope it doesn't hurt too much, seeing Joseph?'

'Well, it does, of course, but I have to cope with seeing babies and try not to get upset. He's a lovely little boy. You must be thrilled to bits.'

'Yes, I am. I thought I wanted a girl, but when he arrived it didn't matter at all. But he's not always quiet like this, you know!' Joseph was sleeping peacefully in his carrycot. 'He has his moments, especially in the night when I want to sleep. He's on a bottle though, now, and Mum helps me quite a lot. It's best for us to live here while Keith's away. I can't wait for this bloomin' war to end and have him home again. We'll try to get a place of our own, a flat or some rooms to rent. It might be ages before we can afford a house.'

Alice settled into a routine at work and at home — where she still helped out with the suppers for the RAF lads — and she occasionally went to the cinema with her friends. Doris and Freda tried to persuade her to go dancing but she declined; there were too many painful memories.

Doris and Freda shared a flat over a shop in North Shore, not far from the factory where they worked. They felt sorry for Alice, knowing that she was not too happy living at home. Who could be happy with a tyrant of a mother like she had? After a lot of persuading she agreed to go and live with them in the flat and share the expenses.

There was plenty of room although it was by no means luxurious. Alice was happy to have her freedom at last, and although Ada grumbled there was nothing she could do about it. Alice was in her mid-twenties and able to please herself.

At last after almost six years the war came to an end. There was a time of great rejoicing, but sadness as well. Many lives had been lost and there followed a long period of austerity. Lizzie's husband, Norman, returned and resumed his work as a painter and decorator. Freda married her fiancé, an RAF sergeant whom she had met in the Winter Gardens, and went to live with his family in his home town of Oldham.

Alice and Doris were now the only two occupants of the flat. Neither of them had had a career as such before the war and had been doing compulsory war work for the last few years. Doris had formerly been a shop assistant, and she found employment in the large Woolworths store in central Blackpool.

Alice had always worked at home in the boarding house, but she too found a job as a shop assistant in a little general store on Central Drive, a main road leading out of Blackpool. The shop dealt in a variety of commodities: sweets and chocolate (though still on ration and hard to obtain), cigarettes and tobacco, newspapers, stationery and odds and ends of household goods. There was also a small post office. Alice settled in there very well. She enjoyed the work which was new to her and she regarded it a challenge. She soon discovered that she was very competent with the financial side of the business, and Mrs Dalton, the owner, began training her to work at the post office counter.

Alice and Doris lived together companionably. They were both even-tempered and there was rarely any discord between them. They went to the cinema together once or twice a week and, very occasionally, Alice would be persuaded to go dancing. This was something Doris had always enjoyed. She had never been short of partners during the war years, and the same was true now. She sometimes went on her own, leaving Alice at home listening to the radio, or reading, which she preferred over going to the dance halls.

Doris was concerned about her friend. She very rarely mentioned Tony but it was clear that the memory of him was still there, and of the baby she had been forced to give up for adoption.

Doris had had one or two casual boyfriends but was determined to wait until 'Mister Right' came along. Then, one evening in the Winter Gardens, she met him. He was not a complete stranger but someone she had known way back in her schooldays. His name was Desmond Forbes and he had been working as an electrician in the Manchester area. He had now returned to Blackpool to work with his friend, who had started a thriving business in the town. It soon became obvious to both Doris and Desmond that they had each met the person they had been waiting for. They were soon engaged and planned to marry in the spring of

1949. They were both in their late twenties and decided that there was no point in waiting any longer.

Desmond had served his apprenticeship as an electrician before joining the army at the beginning of the war. He was well qualified in his work and had managed to save up enough for a deposit on a small terraced house in Layton, a suburb of Blackpool.

Doris could not help but feel guilty at leaving Alice as the sole occupant in the flat. 'But I'm sure you'll soon find someone to share with you,' she told her.

'Yes, of course I will,' said Alice. 'Don't worry about it.' But she was putting on a brave face and was, in truth, not happy about the situation.

Doris and Desmond had a quiet wedding without a great deal of fuss at the Methodist church that Doris attended. Alice was the chief — and only — bridesmaid. She smiled happily, hiding her fears regarding the future. She was worried at the thought of being alone in the flat. She could not afford the expense on her own and did not want to share with someone she did not know. She had come to rely on the bolstering friendship of Doris, who had become a very close friend.

'Well, I reckon you can come back and live here if you're stuck,' said her mother. 'I dare say we can find you a room, although the holiday business is looking up again now.'

But Alice was determined that she would not go back. She had broken away from her mother's iron rule and had made a life for herself — up to a point. She still felt, though, that she needed the companionship of a true friend.

Over the years she spent a good deal of time with Winnie. Her husband had left the Merchant Navy at the end of the war, and after living in rented accommodation for a while they had managed to save up enough for a deposit on a semi-detached house in a residential area quite near Stanley Park, but it was rather more than they had wanted to pay, and the repayments were quite steep. Keith, however, was now earning quite a good wage at the General Post Office in Blackpool. He had worked there as a postman before the war and had now been promoted to an inspector. This meant that he sometimes had to work nights, and at other times he started work at five in the morning and finished at midday.

Their first little boy, Joseph, was now six years old, then in 1947 their second son, Daniel, was born; he was now two years old. Alice had become very fond of the two children. It had pulled at her heart strings at first, seeing Joseph as a baby, then a toddler. Her own son was much the same age and she could not help wondering about him. Where was he? Did he have a happy home with loving parents?

Gradually she had come to accept Joseph as a child in his own right and not to make comparisons with the child she had lost. He called her Aunty Alice and loved to spend time with her. Sometimes she would babysit for him, and later for the two boys on the rare occasions when Winnie and Keith were able to go out together for the evening.

Winnie was concerned about Alice's predicament with the flat, and she talked the matter over with Keith. They agreed that they would ask Alice to come and share their home, if she was willing to do so.

'She's a good lass,' said Keith. 'A bit quiet, mind, but I'm sure she'll fit in here very well with us and she'll help with the bills. I must admit we've been feeling the pinch since we had another mouth to feed. Not that I'd be without our Daniel. Two little lads, eh? Who'd have thought it? And you always said you wanted a girl . . . '

'I'm quite satisfied,' said Winnie. 'Don't get any ideas! OK then, I'll ask her; she's coming round tonight.'

Alice was quite taken aback when Winnie asked her if she would like to come and live with them.

'What! You mean you're inviting me to come and share your home? But you are a family; you and Keith, and Joseph and Daniel.'

'Of course I mean it, and Keith does as well. We've talked it over, and we think it would be a good idea if you will accept; good for you and of you as well.'

'But . . . you might feel that I'm intruding, if I'm there all the time.'

'Nonsense! You're not the sort of person to intrude, Alice. We have plenty of room. The bedrooms are a good size, even the smallest one which you would have. Actually, the house cost rather more than we wanted to pay, but we liked it so, so much. There's a nice garden for the boys to play in, and it's a quiet area. And with us having two boys there'll be no problem about sharing a room when they get older, as there would be if one of them was a girl. And we have two rooms downstairs, so you could have privacy if you wanted to be on your own for a while.'

'Well, I'm flabbergasted!' said Alice. 'And of course I'll say yes, and thank you very much for thinking of me. I must admit I hate living on my own now that Doris has gone, and I can't really afford it. I know I should have tried to find somebody to share with me, but I didn't do anything about it.'

'And we are finding the mortgage repayments rather hard,' said Winnie. 'But that isn't why we have asked you to come here. We won't charge you very much — we can come to some arrangement — but we feel it will be a help to us and to you as well.'

'It will be great,' said Alice with a wide smile. 'I can hardly believe it.'

'I think this calls for a little celebration,' said Winnie. She opened the sideboard and took out a half-full bottle of sherry. 'This was left over from Christmas. We're not big drinkers. Keith likes a pint now and again with the lads, but he won't mind if I enjoy the rest of this with you.' She found two glasses and a tin of shortbread biscuits. 'Anyway, cheers! Here's to us.'

'I'll be glad of the company,' said Winnie as they settled down in two easy chairs. 'Like tonight while Keith is on nights. I hate it when he's not there and I'm alone with the children.

Not that I'm scared, but it feels strange. And at other times he starts at five o'clock in the morning. I'm afraid I don't get up with him, but he doesn't expect me to. He just has a cup of tea and a piece of toast, then he's off. I make a meal when he comes home, at midday or early evening, depending on what shift he's on. You'll be ever so welcome to come and join us if you wish. Anyway, we can sort out the details when you move in.'

By the end of the summer of 1949 Alice had settled into her new home. She did not have many possessions. No furniture, but she had a small radio set, a record player and a fair collection of records, many of them reminders of the time she had spent with Tony. She also had a special box of mementoes which she looked at from time to time. She had some bright cushions and her own sheets and blankets and eiderdown. Her clothes, shoes and bags fitted into two large suitcases.

The third bedroom was quite a good size, containing a single bed, chest of drawers and dressing table, and Alice felt that she would be comfortable there. The front room downstairs was rarely used by the family except on special occasions such as Christmas. Alice was to have this room as her own for the times when she wanted to be by herself. There were comfortable chairs, a small table, a bookcase and a display cabinet where Winnie kept her best china tea set and mementoes of her and Keith's life together.

Alice arranged her selection of books on the shelves, and her ornaments — a china cat, a crinoline lady, a Coronation mug of the present king and queen, and a few photos, including one of herself and Tony — on the top of the bookcase and the mantelpiece. Her colourful cushions, including one that she had painstakingly embroidered years ago, made the room feel more like her own.

Winnie said that she could have a fire in the evenings if she wished — they would be allowed an extra ration of coal for her — or there was a small electric fire. They had made arrangements about her rent including payment for the lighting and heating, and Alice felt that she had definitely made the right move.

Winnie, noticing the photo of Alice and Tony, wished that her friend might try to move on — not to forget about Tony, but to realize that she might, one day, meet someone else with whom she could share her life. But Alice seemed to be contented with her lot. She enjoyed her work in the shop and sometimes went out in the evening with one or other of the girls who worked there. She visited her mother and sister occasionally, although Winnie felt that this was more of a duty than a pleasure. Above all she valued her growing friendship with Winnie. The two of them spent many happy evenings together when Keith was at work and the children were in bed. And she was very fond of Joseph and Daniel, to whom she was a very special aunty.

Keith suggested to her when she had been with them for a few months that it might be a good idea for her to apply for a position at the General Post Office where he worked as an inspector. 'I know you enjoy working at the post office counter,' he said, 'and I'm sure you are very competent. You would get more specialized training at a main branch, and they are continually taking on new recruits. It would be a chance for you to make a career for yourself, rather than being a shop assistant.'

Alice was happy at the shop on Central Drive, but she decided that Keith's idea was a good one and that it was worth a try. Keith put in a good word for her, and she started working at the main post office in Abingdon Street in the spring of 1950. The work was more challenging as this was a much busier office and there were continual queues of people drawing pensions and benefits, withdrawing or depositing money, sending packs or just buying stamps, and she was very tired at the end of the day.

Alice made friends there. She was becoming more confident and self-reliant, no longer as timid and shy as she had been in her younger days. She had turned thirty now but was still quite girlish looking with her trim figure and blonde hair which she occasionally had trimmed and set by a hairdresser instead of doing it herself. For a time she was friendly with one of the postmen, but the friendship ended as she was unwilling to commit to anything more permanent.

She watched the boys growing up and, despite her best intentions, she was unable to stop thinking of the child she had lost.

Joseph was now seven years old. He was a bright and happy little boy who enjoyed life to the full. He worked hard at school. He learned to read at an early age and seemed to have little trouble with any of the lessons. Alice enjoyed helping him to learn his spelling for the weekly test and listened to him reciting his times tables. He enjoyed games as well, particularly football. His dad was a keen supporter of Blackpool FC and, although Joseph was not yet old enough to attend the matches, he took part in lively discussions with his dad and watched with interest each Saturday as Keith checked his football coupon, always hoping for that elusive big win. Sometimes a couple of friends came round and they had a kick about with Keith in the back garden with Daniel, who was now toddling, trying to join in.

It was in the spring of 1953 that Alice began to feel that she was ready for a change. Joseph was now ten years old. Next year he would be sitting for his scholarship — or eleven plus — exam. His parents expected him to do well and move on to the grammar school.

As they so often did, Alice's thoughts drifted to her own child who would be roughly the same age. Where was he? What was he doing? Was he happy with his adopted parents? Did he know anything at all about her, Alice, or had his adoption been kept a secret? He, too, would no doubt be moving soon to a different school and she guessed he would be an intelligent boy, as his father had been. Alice did not know if his adopted parents were Yorkshire folk, and if they were, was the family still living in Yorkshire?

All these questions were running round and

round in her mind. Despite her intentions of leaving the past behind her, she knew that she could no longer do so.

16

Alice wrote to her aunt and uncle in Baildon, asking if she could come and stay with them for a little while. She did not say why, and they did not enquire any further, her aunt replying and saying that of course they would be pleased to see her again. They had exchanged Christmas cards and an occasional letter, but they had not met since she left after the birth and adoption of Alice's baby.

Winnie did not try to dissuade Alice. She guessed why her friend wanted to return to Yorkshire although Alice had not actually told her the reason. Winnie had noticed that Alice was preoccupied and, at times, seemed very sad. She had become very close to Joseph, and Winnie knew that her friend was thinking more and more of her own son and longing to know what had become of him. Winnie tried to put herself in the same position and knew that this was exactly how she would feel.

Alice's Aunt Maggie and Uncle Fred welcomed her unreservedly although they could not help but wonder why she had come to see them, after so long. Alice had told a white lie.

'I've not been too well,' she said. 'I've had a bad attack of gastric flu' — it was really more of a tummy upset — 'and it's left me very dispirited. I thought the country air would do me good.'

'Well, you stay as long as you like, love,' said Maggie.

Alice nodded. 'Thank you. I've got a fortnight off work . . . '

The smallholding that her aunt and uncle owned had prospered since the war years. They now reared a few turkeys as well as hens and geese, and cultivated more garden produce, vegetables, fruit and flowers which were sold to a wide area in West Yorkshire. The couple were well into their sixties now, but very hale and hearty with no intention of retiring for a while.

It was Alice's cousin, Sally, in whom she confided her real reason for returning to Yorkshire. Sally still lived in the same house in Baildon with her husband and two children who were now in their teens.

Alice went round to see Sally one afternoon soon after her arrival in Baildon. She knew that Sally would be on her own, her husband being at work, and the children — though not really children any more — would be at school. Alice wanted the information that she felt Sally might be more willing to disclose than would her aunt and uncle.

'It's great to see you again, Alice,' said Sally, greeting her warmly with a hug and kiss. 'Long time no see! You are looking well . . . hope that you are feeling better,' she added, looking at her a little more closely.

'Yes, I'm well again now, thank you,' said Alice. 'Life goes on, you know. I have a good job at the GPO in Blackpool now. I enjoy it although it's pretty hectic there at times. Queues a mile long and all kinds of customers to deal with. Still, it's been good for me, keeps me busy . . . '

They exchanged family news over a cup of tea. There was a moment's silence as their chatting came to an end and Alice decided that it was now or never. She must try to broach the subject that was uppermost in her mind.

Sally was looking at her thoughtfully. 'There's something on your mind, isn't there, Alice?' she said. 'Do you want to tell me about it?'

Alice sighed. 'Yes, I did have another reason for coming here. It's true — partly true — that I've not been well, but . . . I can't forget, Sally, about . . . what happened. I've tried, really tried, to get on with my life, but it's still there, all the time.' She told her about Joseph, that he was the same age as her boy would be, and she knew that she had to discover, if she could, what had happened to him. 'I'm sure you must have some idea, haven't you?' she said to her cousin. 'I do remember that it all happened so quickly. The baby . . . he was taken away from me, and I always felt that my aunt and uncle — and you — knew something about it.'

Sally looked a little uncomfortable. 'He was adopted, Alice,' she said. 'You knew that would happen and you agreed to it. I know it's hard, but it's been ten years. It's too late now to have second thoughts. He is happy and settled in his home . . . at least, I'm sure he must be . . . '

'So, you do know something, don't you?'

'I'm sorry, Alice. It wouldn't do any good to tell you. Surely, after all this time, you don't want to confuse the boy? It could cause all sorts

239

of trouble if you appear on the scene, if you try to contact them . . . '

'I won't, I won't!' Alice cried. 'I don't . . . I know I can't have him back, but I want to know where he is, just to satisfy myself that he's well and happy. And I know you could tell me . . . couldn't you?'

'I've been sworn to secrecy, Alice. We all have. Yes, Mam and Dad did know where . . . where the baby was going, and they knew he would have a good home. Can't you be content with that?'

'No, not really. Could you?'

'That's an impossible question, Alice. I understand how you must feel, but it might upset you even more if you find out.'

'Then that's a risk I will have to take. Tell me . . . please, Sally.'

Sally was quiet for a few moments before she replied. 'I know you will not leave me alone until I tell you. But you must promise that you will not cause any bother, or upset your little boy, or his adoptive parents.'

'Of course I won't,' said Alice. 'I just want to know. I want to see him, if possible. Yes, I know it may be heart-breaking, but I've got used to that, and I don't think it can make it any worse. Where is he, Sally? Please tell me.'

Sally sighed. 'Do you remember Mr and Mrs Fielding?' she said. 'They had a farm a couple of miles away — well, they still do — and are friendly with my mam and dad.'

'Yes, I think I met them while I was staying here,' said Alice. 'Go on . . . '

240

'Well, they had — have — a son, Ted, who married a girl called Mary. They had been married for a few years and were desperate to have a child, but . . . nothing happened. Anyway, you can guess what I'm going to say — they heard about you and that your baby would be adopted, and so . . . it was all arranged. Nothing 'hole in the corner' about it: the folk in charge were pleased that the baby would be going to a good home.'

'And where is he? Still in Baildon?' asked Alice, her voice breathless with emotion.

'No . . . Ted used to help his father on the farm, but when they adopted the baby — they called him Jonathan — they moved to a smallholding of their own, in Bingley. Just outside the town, I believe.'

'And they are still there?'

'Yes, as far as I know. Mam and Dad are still friendly with the Fieldings and they hear news of Ted and his family occasionally. It was very strange really — very nice, though — because a couple of years after they had adopted Jonathan they had a baby of their own. A little girl — they called her Pamela — but that's all I can tell you, Alice. I haven't heard any more about them, not for years. Mam and Dad felt that they had done the best they could for all concerned: for you and the baby and the Fielding family. Now . . . are you satisfied that I have told you?'

Alice nodded. 'I'm glad to know that he is in a happy home. Jonathan . . . that's a good name, one that I might well have chosen myself. And he has a little sister, that's nice.'

'Yes, we thought so too. Apparently it's not

uncommon. Looking after a baby seems to make a woman more fertile, somehow. Anyway, that was what happened.'

'Thank you for telling me,' said Alice. 'And I promise . . . I won't cause any trouble.'

She thought seriously about it, and it was all too irresistible. She knew where her son was living, so why should she not go there to see for herself? She persuaded herself that it would be enough to see him and to know that he was having a happy life. It was possible that Sally would be very annoyed, but what did that matter? It was Alice's decision and she knew she would not be satisfied until she had seen her son.

She did not tell her aunt and uncle what she had discovered. She told Sally, however, the next time she saw her what she had decided to do. As she had expected, Sally was shocked and rather annoyed.

'Alice . . . you promised me you would not do anything. I told you all that in the strictest confidence.'

'I didn't say that I wouldn't do anything; I said I would not cause any trouble and I promise you I won't. But I must go there; I must see for myself . . . '

'You mean . . . to go there for a day?'

'No, to stay there for a while, till I see how I feel. I'm sure I would like to live in Yorkshire again. I'm certainly not too happy in Blackpool now.'

'But what about your job in Blackpool? You have a good position at the post office there, haven't you?'

'Yes, but I'm sure I could get a transfer.'

'What? To Bingley? I doubt there's a main post office there.'

'But there is in Bradford. I'm sure I could get a transfer to there. It's not far away, is it?'

'No, just a few miles. Buses run to and fro all the time . . . but I think you're being very foolish, Alice. It might be too much for you. You could get very distressed.'

'Then that's a risk I have to take. It's no use, Sally. It's what I must do.'

Finally, when she could see that her cousin could not be dissuaded, Sally decided to give in and help her. Sally, of course, had to tell her parents of Alice's plan. They were far more philosophical about it but agreed that they would not say a word to their friends, the Fieldings, whose son and daughter-in-law had adopted Jonathan.

Alice returned to Blackpool, telling her mother and Lizzie that she intended to move to Yorkshire to start a new life there. She did not tell them the real reason, just that she was ready for a change, and that she felt that Yorkshire was where she belonged. It was where she had been born thirty-five years ago, and she felt that her roots were there.

It was easy enough to get a transfer to the main post office in Bradford, and Sally, as she had promised, helped her to find lodgings in Bingley with an old school friend of hers.

Sally's friend, Iris Shaw, had been widowed when her husband was killed in the Normandy landings, and she had never wanted to remarry.

Her son had married and moved away and so she had converted her semi-detached house into two flats. She felt that she would, therefore, not feel entirely alone or isolated with another person on the premises. Her previous tenant had recently left, so she was glad of Alice's presence in the upstairs flat and, of course, of the income which supplemented the wage she earned as a shorthand typist.

Alice could not believe how easily everything seemed to turn out just right for her. She took to Iris straight away. She knew the woman would not be a close friend to her, as Winnie had been, nor did she really want her to be. Alice knew that she had to keep her real reason for returning to Yorkshire a close secret to everyone she met. Words spoken in confidence might so easily reach other ears, and Alice had given a promise — to her aunt and uncle and Sally, and to herself — that she would not cause any disruption in the family that had adopted her son.

She settled down happily to her work at the main post office in Bradford. It was but a short distance away and the bus service was very good, with bus stops near to her new home and her place of work.

But how was she to find the Fielding family? Sally had been pretty sure that they were still at the same place but Alice had no idea where that might be. She broached the subject, quite casually, with Iris.

'I'd like to get some pot plants,' she said. 'You know — begonias, indoor roses, geraniums, that sort of thing — to make my living room a bit

244

more homely. There's such a lovely wide windowsill and they'd look lovely there. Do you know of anywhere I could get some? I love mooching round garden centres where they have a good variety.'

Iris smiled. 'Are you green fingered then? I'm afraid that I'm not. Jack — my husband — was the gardener, then my son, Jake, did what he could, but now . . . well, it's as much as I can do to keep it tidy. My next-door neighbour kindly mows the lawn for me and I put in a few bedding plants in the spring and hope for the best. Anyway, I just asked but I didn't give you a chance to answer — are you green fingered? I'd welcome some help in the garden if you feel like it. And you know you're very welcome to sit out in the garden, to sunbathe or to sit and read.'

'Yes, actually, I do quite enjoy gardening, although I haven't done any for ages. When I lived with my friend Winnie in Blackpool, her husband did all the gardening; he was quite an expert and I knew he didn't need any help. Winnie just left him to it. But I stayed with Sally's parents for a while, during the war . . . they ran a market garden, you know. Well, they still do, and I enjoyed helping out there.' She stopped abruptly, wondering if she might have said too much. Iris was unaware of her history, so it would be best not to say any more.

'Anyway, that's ages ago. I was asking you if you know of a garden centre where I could have a mooch around.'

'Actually, I do. There's one not very far away from here. It's run by some friends of mine; well, more acquaintances really. We attend the same church and we're all in the choir there. Ted and Mary Fielding, they're a nice young couple — well, youngish, you know, about our age. They have two children, Jonathan and Pamela.' She laughed. 'But that doesn't matter — you don't want to know their life story! I'll take you there if you like, perhaps on a Saturday afternoon, then you can have a mooch around as you say . . . and maybe we could buy some bulbs — daffs and crocuses — to plant in the garden, seeing as you've offered to help. Like I say, I've never bothered much before.'

'Yes, I'd like that,' said Alice. 'It's always nice to see the spring flowers after the winter. I'll plant them for you; I don't mind getting my hands dirty.'

Alice was finding it hard to speak in a normal voice; she was so amazed at the coincidence and her heart was beating so loudly, to her ears, that she was sure Iris would hear it.

'Well then, what about next Saturday?' said Iris. 'No time like the present.'

'Fine by me.' Alice tried to steady her voice. 'I'll look forward to it.'

'And there's something else,' said Iris. 'I mentioned the church I go to . . . I was wondering if you'd like to come along? I don't want to put pressure on you. I'm not a 'God botherer' and I know some people are not interested. But we're a friendly crowd and you'd be made very welcome if you'd like to join us.'

Alice could scarcely believe what she was hearing. 'Yes, I'd like that,' she answered a little breathlessly. 'I've not been for ages, though, not regularly. When I lived at the boarding house we were always too busy, though Mam made sure that me and my sister went to Sunday school. Then, well, I've sort of . . . lapsed, but I do believe . . . in God an' all that.'

'Will you come then, on Sunday morning, and see if you like it? Like I said, I sing in the choir, but I'll introduce you to some friends, and then after the service we have a cup of tea in the church hall. You can just try it and see how you feel. If it's not your sort of thing then fair enough.'

Alice was almost too flabbergasted to reply. She could not believe how easy it had been to trace the whereabouts of her son. And the following weekend she would be seeing the couple who had adopted him and . . . maybe . . . the boy as well.

17

To say that Alice was nervous was an understatement. As Saturday approached she could hardly contain her feelings, a mixture of apprehension and almost dread. Was she doing the right thing? Should she, after all, have left well alone as she had been advised to do? But she had set the wheels in motion and now she had to go on with it. She could not rid herself of the tension in her chest, and butterflies were dancing in her stomach as Iris drove her to the garden centre. Alice spoke very little, but Iris did not seem to notice her discomfiture.

The place that the Fieldings owned was rather more than a garden centre. It was also a market garden; they cultivated a range of vegetables and there was an orchard with apple and pear trees, and they also grew soft fruit, all of which was distributed to the shops and markets round about.

But it was the garden area that was of interest to Iris and Alice. There was a vast variety of plants and shrubs for the amateur gardener or, indeed, for those who took it rather more seriously. Alice's tension subsided a little as she strolled round the grounds with Iris, her interest totally absorbed in the riot of colour and verdant foliage that surrounded them. Iris had grabbed a large two-tiered wire basket on wheels on which to store their purchases.

Alice chose two begonias, a red one and a pink one, which looked very healthy with flowers already in bloom and many buds still to open; a cyclamen in a dark mauve shade and two indoor chrysanthemum plants, one yellow and one a russet brown shade of autumn, which was fast approaching.

Alice turned as she heard a man speaking to Iris. Could this possibly be the man who had adopted her little boy? Her question was answered as she heard Iris say, 'Hello there, Ted. We've decided to pay you a visit. I'm not much of a gardener, as you know, but this is my friend, Alice, and she offered to give me a hand in the garden. Alice, this is Ted Fielding, the owner of this lovely place.'

Alice looked up. He was a tall man, dark-haired with a youngish-looking face, which was prematurely lined, no doubt with spending so much time in the open air. He smiled cheerfully as he shook her hand.

'How do you do? I'm pleased you've come to see us. Can I be of any assistance?'

Alice felt a little strange and hoped she would be able to answer him cheerily. 'Hello, pleased to meet you,' she murmured. Then, a little more bravely: 'These are for me' — she indicated the pot plants — 'for the windowsill in my sitting room; I'm lodging with Iris, you see. And . . . and I think she wants to choose some bulbs for springtime, don't you, Iris?'

'Yes, that's right. What have you got, Ted? I'm rather a novice, as you know. Daffs maybe, crocuses, tulips?'

'Come along and I'll show you.' He led them to an indoor area where there were more pot plants, cut flowers, garden ornaments — animals and figures made from stone rather than the usual gaudy gnomes — and a variety of bulbs.

With Ted's help they chose crocuses of white, gold and purple, a selection of three different kinds of daffodils — or to be more accurate, narcissi — and some pink and white hyacinths.

'That will keep you busy,' said Ted. 'Have you got space for them all?'

'Yes, there's nothing in the borders till I put the bedding plants in. I've always been afraid that bulbs would not come up when there's nothing to see.'

'Make sure you put them in the right way up,' said Ted with a smile.

'Oh, Alice will make sure of that. Thanks for your help, Ted. I shall see you in the morning as usual. Alice is coming with me tomorrow, aren't you, Alice? I've been telling her that we're a friendly lot at All Saints and we'll make her welcome.'

'Sure,' said Ted. 'Can you sing, Alice?'

'No, not really,' she replied. 'Only in the bath!'

'We could do with some more ladies in the choir, couldn't we, Iris? We're quite 'go-ahead' at All Saints. Some churches insist on an all-male choir, but we welcome the ladies . . . and youngsters as well, boy choristers, you know. They're not up to the standard of York Minster but they do very well.'

'Yes, Ted's little boy is a chorister, isn't he, Ted?' said Iris.

Alice's heart gave a leap and she had to hold herself in check for fear of crying, or laughing, or goodness knew how she might react.

'Yes, Jonathan's ten,' said Ted. 'He joined a few months ago and he seems to like it, especially the pocket money he gets when we sing at weddings.'

'Oh, very good,' murmured Alice. 'Yes, I'll look forward to coming tomorrow . . . and thank you for your help.'

She was relieved when they were back in the car and on their way home, with Iris doing all the talking.

'They're a lovely family,' she said. 'Actually, their little boy — well, he's ten now — was adopted, and then a couple of years later they had a little girl. A complete surprise as they'd given up hope of having any of their own. Pamela's a lovely little girl and, strangely enough, she does look a bit like her brother.'

Alice kept to herself for the rest of the day. Both women felt that they needed time alone as well as the pleasant times they spent together. *After all, I'm only the lodger*, Alice told herself.

The next day they went to All Saints Church as planned. It was on the outskirts of the small town, midway between Iris's home and the garden centre.

'Sorry I have to leave you,' said Iris, 'but I'll introduce you to my friends Kate and Peggy — they both belong to the ladies' fellowship group where we go on a Wednesday. They'll look after you, and after the service we go for a cup of tea in the church hall. All right?'

'Yes . . . yes, thank you,' said Alice, feeling a little nonplussed.

Kate and Peggy were two friendly ladies who did, indeed, make her feel welcome.

'Our husbands don't often come to church,' said Kate. 'Only on special occasions, but we're always here.'

'Pleased to meet you, Alice. Iris told us she had a nice person lodging with her. It's good when you find someone compatible to share your home, isn't it?'

'Yes, we get along very well,' said Alice. 'We're both busy with our jobs during the day, of course . . .'

'Perhaps you might like to come and join our ladies' fellowship group?' said Peggy. 'It's on Wednesday evening.'

'I'll . . . think about it,' said Alice, feeling overwhelmed with their hospitality.

There was no time to say any more as the vicar announced the first hymn and the organist played the introduction to 'Praise, My Soul, the King of Heaven' as a cue for the congregation to stand. Then the choir, led by the vicar, processed round the church and down the central aisle to the choir stalls.

Alice watched surreptitiously as the young choir boys processed past the pew where she was sitting. There were eight of them, looking angelic in their white surplices with a ruffle at the neck. She knew that one of them was Jonathan but she did not dare to peer more closely. Following behind them were ten men and eight ladies, making a well-balanced choir. She recognized

Ted Fielding from their first meeting the previous day, and Iris nodded and gave a little smile as she passed by.

The service, like the first hymn, was traditional. It was a good while since Alice had attended church but she found that she remembered the order of service and the responses and did not feel like a fish out of water as she had feared she might.

The vicar, the Reverend Hugh Pritchard, she guessed was in his mid-fifties. His sermon, 'Who is my neighbour?' based on the parable of the Good Samaritan, was thought provoking as a sermon should be but delivered in a kindly way; he was by no means a rabble-rouser.

When the service ended, Kate and Peggy took Alice under their wing and she accompanied them to the nearby church hall. A trio of women were clearly busy in the kitchen, putting out cups and saucers near the service hatch, and boiling water to fill the large aluminium teapots.

The hall began to fill up as more of the congregation came in for a cup of tea and a chat.

'Some of 'em go home to see to their Sunday roast,' said Kate. 'But Peggy and me, we've got our husbands well trained, haven't we, Peg? They keep an eye on the dinner for us.'

'Well, they're supposed to,' said Peggy. 'Alec's sometimes fallen asleep over the *Sunday Express*! But we can't grumble. They're good lads, aren't they, Kate?'

'Aye, so they are. Our kids have flown the nest, and we're jolly lucky as both Alec and George came through the war unscathed. Poor Iris

— she lost her hubby, as you probably know.'

'Er . . . yes, she told me,' said Alice. 'I lost someone as well. We weren't married but I still . . . remember him.' She decided then that she had better say no more.

Iris joined them along with another lady. 'This is Mary,' she said to Alice. 'You met her husband, Ted, yesterday at the garden centre.'

The two women shook hands and Alice noted that Mary was a pretty and pleasant person, probably a few years older than herself. And she was now the mother of Jonathan. Alice knew that she must keep a tight rein on her feelings but, she told herself, she had got herself into this situation whether it was a wise decision or not and now she must deal with it, without revealing the truth to anyone.

The next moment Ted appeared with two children whom she knew at once were Jonathan and his younger sister Pamela. Her heart missed a beat and she had to hold on tightly to her cup of tea to stop it clattering in the saucer. The lad was quite tall for his age and dark-haired and . . . yes . . . she could see the resemblance to Tony. His sister had fair hair and resembled her mother, Mary.

Ted introduced them casually. 'These are our two, Jonathan and Pamela. This is Alice, she's staying with Aunty Iris.'

'Hello,' she replied. 'I saw you in the choir . . . Jonathan. Do you enjoy singing?'

'Yes, it's OK . . . Mum,' he turned to Mary, 'Peter's got a new rabbit. He says we can go and see it . . . can we?'

'Yes, you can, but you must be back for dinner at one o'clock. And it's Sunday school this afternoon. And take care of Pamela . . . '

''Course I will. Come on, Pam . . . '

The two children scampered off and Alice felt her heart beat steadying.

'He's a sensible lad,' said Mary. 'Peter lives a few doors away and he's in the choir with Jonathan. Pamela's been helping in the crèche while we're in church, looking after the toddlers with Mrs Mayhew. She'd like to be in the choir, but it's just for boys, until they get into their late teens. Don't know why but it seems to be the tradition, like it is in the cathedral.'

'It's a good choir,' said Alice. 'I was quite impressed.'

'Would you like to join us?' asked Mary. 'Joyce is leaving soon — they're moving away — so there'll be a vacancy.'

'Oh . . . I don't know. I've only just started coming to church. One thing at a time, eh?'

'Yes, of course,' said Mary.

'Well, I think we'd better be moving,' said Iris. 'I've left a joint of beef cooking slowly in the oven. It's only a small one, so I don't want it cremated. See you soon, Mary. Bye, Ted . . . '

'Pleased to have met you, Alice,' they both said.

'See you again soon.'

'Come and have dinner with me today,' said Iris as they drove home. 'I've got used to dining alone, but it'll be nice to have company.'

'Thanks,' said Alice. 'I'd like that.'

The vegetables were all prepared, and Alice

helped by setting the table and afterwards with the washing-up. It was the first time the two women had eaten a meal together, other than the odd cup of tea. They both appreciated their independence, especially as Alice was, in point of fact, a lodger. But from that time on, they did share the occasional meal, either in Iris's or Alice's quarters, and so their friendship developed. As Alice's did with the community at church.

Alice knew, though, that she must never say a word to anyone, even in the strictest confidence, about her real reason for being in Bingley. She still found it incredible that she had found her son so easily, but she knew that now she must be content to watch him grow up and develop just as she would watch any other child within the circle of her friends.

Ted and Mary Fielding became friends rather than just acquaintances because of their shared interests. Alice was drawn into the fellowship of the church. She pretended a certain reluctance at first, not wanting to appear too eager, but she knew that, had she been just an ordinary newcomer to the parish, she would have been glad of their overtures of friendship. And so she started to go more regularly to the church services. She and her sister, Lizzie, had been confirmed and made members of the Church of England, at their mother's insistence, when they were both in their teens, and so Alice was welcomed as a communicant. And a while later, after a friendly audition with the organist and choir master — just to make sure she could sing in tune — she joined the church choir.

She also attended the weekly ladies' fellowship group, which met on Wednesday evenings. Life was busy with her work at the post office, which she enjoyed but found somewhat exacting. Dealing with the general public day after day was not easy, and she was often tired, more mentally than physically, at the end of the day.

Although Alice had been a rather shy girl when she worked in the boarding house, by now her personality had blossomed. Although she could never be termed the life and soul of the party, she was friendly and easy to get along with. Occasionally she would take the train to Blackpool to spend a weekend with her mother and her sister and family, although they never visited her in Bingley.

Ada had found boarding house life too strenuous as she got older, so she had sold the property and now lived with Lizzie, Norman and Megan in their semi-detached house not far from the promenade.

But Alice was now settled into the Yorkshire environment with friends, a reasonable income and the freedom to do as she wished. She watched Jonathan grow from a young boy into a teenager. He was a friendly, high-spirited lad and as she followed his development she could see that, more and more, he resembled his father. She could see nothing of herself in his features, which was just as well, although no one would have thought anything about it. When he was a young boy he had called her Aunty Alice, as was the custom with friends of the family, then later she became just Alice.

The situation did not hurt Alice as much as she had thought it might. She knew that this was what she had chosen to do, to watch her son grow up as an outsider, and she had to be content with that.

As for herself, she had one or two casual friendships with men she met through her work, but she never allowed them to develop into a real romance. She could not explain why, even to herself, except that she was content the way she was. Alice was quite contented lodging with Iris, but she knew that someday she must move on to buy a little place of her own. With that goal in mind she was saving as much as she could from her wage, which had risen as she was given more responsibility. She did not think she would ever marry. She was happy — or as happy as she could be — with her single status. She had never forgotten Tony, her first and only real love, but she was able to look back now with fond memories rather than the anguish she had suffered at first.

In 1961, when Jonathan was eighteen, he went away to an agricultural college for two years. He had showed a keen interest in the work at the market garden, and Ted was pleased that he was anxious to learn about more modern methods and the advances that had been made in horticulture. Ted hoped to develop and extend the business and, eventually, hand it over to his son.

His sister Pamela also went away, two years later, to a domestic science college. Her mother,

Mary, was an excellent cook and Pamela was following in her footsteps. They now sold a variety of homemade jams, marmalade, lemon cheese, pickles and chutney at the garden centre. Pamela was not certain what she would do when she finished her course — work in the family business or look further afield — but that was something to consider in the future.

In 1965 Alice's mother, Ada, died after an attack of pneumonia. Alice was sad — her relationship with her mother had mellowed in the later years — but she could not say that she was heartbroken. When the boarding house had been sold she had lived with Lizzie, Norman and Megan in the semi-detached house that Ada had bought with the proceeds. It was only right, therefore, that the house should now be left to Lizzie, as it had been her and her family's home for many years. Ada, however, had acted in a proper manner and the bulk of her money was left to Alice. She now had enough capital to put down as a deposit on a place of her own.

She had no difficulty in obtaining a mortgage once she had found a little house that was to her liking and — more importantly — one that she could afford with repayments that were not too steep. She knew she could not buy a semi such as Iris had, nor did she need three bedrooms, which was what Iris's house had had before its conversion. After a month or so of house hunting she found a terraced property which had a small — very small — garden at the front, and a paved yard at the rear. There were two fair-sized bedrooms and a compact bathroom and toilet upstairs. There was a small sitting room downstairs and a rather large living room at the back and a tiny kitchen, such as was usual in houses of that type. It was well-maintained and the decorating was all right to be going on with. It was partly furnished as the old lady who had lived there had died and the house was sold with contents.

Iris was sorry to see her lodger go, but the house was only a few minutes' walk away and they would meet socially as before. Alice made the place comfy with her own possessions and settled down to living alone.

The old lady's son and daughter had made sure their mother had the 'mod cons' that were necessary to living in the sixties, so there was a small fridge, an electric cooker and a small washing machine in the outhouse which had once held coal. There was no central heating — that was still a luxury for most ordinary folk — but there were quite modern gas fires downstairs, and Alice had a fan heater to take the chill off upstairs. She considered herself fortunate and would improve her property as time went on.

18

Jonathan had developed into a handsome young man; at least he seemed so to Alice's eyes as he grew to resemble Tony more and more. As with most lads of his age he started to take more interest in girls as he reached his mid-teenage years. She did not enquire about his friendships; to do so would seem inquisitive, and she had kept her vow that she would not get too involved with the family, beyond her friendship with Ted and Mary. They were just two of the several friends she had made, both at work and during her leisure time.

It was not until he had finished college and was working in the family business that he met the young lady whom Alice guessed might be 'the one'. Her name was Rachel, and Jonathan had met her through his sister, Pamela. Rachel was studying at the catering college near Leeds along with Pamela and occasionally came home with her friend to spend the weekend in Bingley. Her home was in the Midlands, rather too far to travel for a short break. The students were allowed only a few weekends at home during term time, the holidays being longer, of course, at Christmas, Easter and the summer break. Alice, seeing the two of them together, thought that they seemed well suited to each other and clearly very happy in each other's company.

Jonathan had also formed a friendship with a

fellow student, a young man called Robert Kershaw. He, too, lived a fair distance away from the college, being from a village near Norwich. He also came home on occasions with Jonathan, and so, of course, he met Pamela. A happy coincidence that both Jonathan and Pamela should meet their future spouses through a family connection.

As time went by the four of them became close friends, although they all had their respective careers to pursue.

Pamela decided, when she finished her college course, that she wanted to be independent, for a while at least, from the family concern. She could have continued to help her mother with the homemade produce that was sold at the garden centre — and Mary had half expected that this was what she might do, but she was very understanding when Pamela told her mother of her plan. A new restaurant had opened in Bingley and Pamela, who had done well at college, applied for the position of pastry chef and, to her surprise and pleasure, was appointed.

The market garden, which had started in a comparatively small way with Ted and Mary, was now progressing by leaps and bounds as Jonathan became more and more involved in the business. Ted did not mind, in fact he was pleased, that his son was showing so much enthusiasm and introducing new ideas. Ted, and Mary too, were now in their late fifties and although they still enjoyed the work they were finding that they were not as agile and as 'raring to go' as they had once been. This was especially true of Ted. He had always been a hands-on sort of boss, taking his fair share and more of the manual work, and now he was suffering from time to time with pains in his back, the early onset of rheumatism.

Mary enjoyed her work and was expanding the range of jams and marmalades, chutneys and pickles, and had introduced a new range of coleslaws and potato salads. She had engaged a young woman to help her and they took their produce to local markets a couple of times a week. But she, too, was beginning to feel the strain. She did so wish that Pamela would change her mind and throw her weight with the family business, but, unselfishly, she had decided that her daughter must be free to follow her own course.

But things were about to change. Jonathan was keen to try a new venture. While he was at college he had taken a course in landscape gardening. So had his friend Robert — in fact, Robert had shown an aptitude for the work more so than Jonathan, and was now working for a firm in the Midlands.

Jonathan mooted the idea with his dad, saying that he intended to start just in a small way.

'By heck, you've got grand ideas, haven't you?' he said. 'But you go ahead, lad, if you think it will work. But don't expect me to be heaving rocks and such like around. You'll need somebody to help.'

'Of course, Dad,' said Jonathan. 'I've already mentioned it to Robert and he's willing to come and join us up here.'

'Well then, give it a try, lad, and let's hope it's a success.'

Robert was not altogether happy in his present job, and besides, his heart and his thoughts were now more and more drifting towards Yorkshire and his girlfriend, Pamela. They did not meet as often as they would wish, and so Robert was quick to seize the opportunity to come and work with his friend. He soon found lodgings in Bingley and Pamela was delighted that they were now able to meet frequently and make plans for the future, for they now both realized they had met their life partners.

Jonathan watched his sister and his friend happily continuing their relationship, and wished that Rachel was there with him. She was working as part of a team preparing school dinners in Birmingham, but was not happy working on the school meals staff. She was qualified and some of the women who were not resented her authority. Also, she and Jonathan were missing one another, so when he suggested, tentatively, that she might like to come and work with his mother and help with the growing demand for Mary's homemade produce, Rachel agreed readily. She, too, found lodgings in Bingley, and the two young couples started to look ahead in earnest.

'We need a new name,' Jonathan told his parents. The market garden, which had now branched out considerably, was always known just as 'Fieldings'. 'What about 'Fresh Fields'? It's short and snappy and includes part of our name.'

'All right, Jonathan, why not?' said Ted. 'It will

be yours one day, yours and Pamela's, of course.' For now Pamela, too, had come to work at the family firm.

As the sixties drew to a close they were branching out in all sorts of ways. They had opened a tearoom as the number of visitors was growing week by week. Pamela had left her position at the restaurant and was now in charge of the café at Fresh Fields. They served tea and coffee and soft drinks and a variety of sandwiches, scones, sausage rolls, cakes and tarts, baked on the premises. More staff were engaged in all the various enterprises as time went on, and Ted and Mary were looking towards retiring and leaving the business in the hands of their children. Ted, who was the only child, had inherited the quite considerable sum that his father had made on his dairy farm. Much of this had been invested in Fresh Fields, but there was still enough left to satisfy their personal needs.

Jonathan and Rachel were the first of the couples to marry. Rachel's home was in Wolverhampton, and so it was only to be expected that the wedding would take place in the parish church she had attended. There were so many relatives who had to be invited and could not be expected to travel to Yorkshire.

Alice did not expect to be invited. She was regarded as a friend of the family, but it would be only close relatives who would be making the journey to the Midlands. It felt surreal to her to be watching with interest, but not involved, in the preparations for her son's wedding. The hurt she had felt at first had gone, but she still felt a bond with him. How could it be otherwise when she had given birth to him? And still no one knew the truth. It had been kept hidden for the last thirteen years, since the time she had come to make a new home in Bingley, and it was unlikely now that anyone would ever know.

The marriage of Jonathan and Rachel took place in the summer of 1966. Pamela, along with two of Rachel's sisters, were bridesmaids, and Robert was Jonathan's best man. As was the custom then, many photos, in the form of slides, were taken, then shown with a projector and screen in the church hall in Bingley. And so everyone who had not been there, including Alice, could share in the happy event.

Pamela and Robert were married the following year. That ceremony, of course, took place at the church in Bingley. The roles were reversed, with Jonathan acting as best man and Rachel as chief bridesmaid — or matron of honour — to Pamela. This time Alice, along with Iris and a few close friends from the congregation, was invited.

Both young couples managed to buy a house, albeit with a substantial mortgage, quite near to Fresh Fields where they all worked. Ted and Mary were pleased at the way the business was progressing with the input of new ideas by the younger generation, but they still looked to Ted as the head of the concern. He was now approaching sixty and Mary just a year younger, and they intended to hand over the reins before long to their son and daughter and their respective partners.

Both couples wanted to have a family of their own. There was great rejoicing when in 1968 Rachel gave birth to a baby girl whom they christened Jennifer.

'My grandchild,' thought Alice, not a little perplexed, as she was present at the baptism, and watched the vicar make the sign of the cross on the little one's head.

Rachel and Jonathan's second child, a boy whom they named James, was born two years later in 1970.

'You have two beautiful little children,' Alice told Rachel when she met her one day as she was shopping. 'You must be very proud of them. You . . . and Jonathan.'

'We are indeed,' said Rachel. 'And I think that James will be just like his daddy. Don't you think so, Alice?'

Alice peeped into the pram where the three-month-old child was sleeping. 'Yes, I think so,' she said. 'The same dark hair, of course, and . . . I can see he'll have the same nose.' She felt a tightening in her throat as she then looked at Jennifer, now aged two and a half, hanging on to the handle of the pram. 'And this little one is just like her mummy, aren't you, lovey?' Jennifer was blonde-haired and dainty, as was Rachel.

What a lovely, pleasant lady Alice is, thought Rachel as they went their separate ways. *I wonder why she's never married. She'd be a lovely grandma.*

Pamela was starting to feel a little crestfallen seeing Rachel with her two lovely children.

'There's plenty of time,' Robert tried to

console her. 'Jonathan and Rachel have been married longer than we have.'

'Only a year longer,' Pamela replied. 'I do hope there's nothing wrong — that I can't conceive, I mean. And we've done nothing to prevent it happening.'

'True!' said Robert. They had decided to let nature take its course and not to bother with any kind of contraceptive measures. They were both in their mid to late twenties, Robert being slightly older, and agreed that this was probably the ideal time to start a family. But there was no sign of it so far.

Pamela, although a teeny bit envious, was not at all bitter at the situation and she loved her little niece and nephew. She and Robert were always happy to look after the children if Rachel and Jonathan wanted to have a night out together, just the two of them. Their two homes were not very far apart, within easy walking distance, or only five minutes or so by car.

In the autumn of 1970 Jonathan and Rachel were invited to attend the wedding of Rachel's younger sister which would take place in Wolverhampton in the church where they had been married four years earlier. They would have to stay overnight with relations and they decided that the children were too young to accompany them — but it would all depend on whether Robert and Pamela would agree to look after them overnight. The wedding was at 2 p.m. on the Saturday.

'Of course we will,' said Pamela. 'You know we're always delighted to have them. Just the one night, or do you want to stay a bit longer?'

'Oh no,' said Jonathan. 'We'll set off early on Saturday morning and come back sometime on Sunday, ready for work again on Monday. I must admit it's a little inconvenient because we're usually busy at the garden at the weekend, but we can't miss Carol's wedding.'

'No, of course you can't,' said Robert. 'You go and have a good time. It's very rare that you have some time off. The only thing is we have no cot for James . . . might it be better if we come and stay at your place, then the children will be in their own beds?'

'That's a splendid idea,' said Rachel. 'That is, if you don't mind. James is only six months old, rather too small to sleep in a bed. Fortunately, he sleeps through the night, and he's on a bottle now.'

'We'll take good care of them,' said Pamela. 'I shall look forward to it. It will be good practice for me.' She gave a wry smile.

'Don't worry,' said Rachel. 'Your time will come . . . ' Pamela was to recall those words a few weeks later.

Jennifer was almost two and a half now, beginning to talk coherently and clearly an intelligent little girl. James was six months old and recognizing people that he saw regularly: his mummy and daddy, of course, and he always smiled when he saw his Aunty Pamela and Uncle Robert. And so Jonathan and Rachel had no qualms about leaving their children in their close relatives' capable hands.

It was quite a novelty to Jennifer when Aunty

Pamela put her to bed. They had explained that her mummy and daddy had gone away but would be back the next day. James was oblivious to what was happening, but content so long as he was fed and kept clean and with people who were familiar.

Jonathan and Rachel had said that they would be back sometime on Sunday afternoon.

'Don't rush back,' said Pamela. 'Make the most of your time with your family.'

Rachel did not often see her parents and siblings and it was a nice change for them to have some time on their own, knowing that their children were being well-cared-for.

'Mummy and Daddy coming soon?' asked Jennifer at around four o'clock on Sunday afternoon.

'Yes, they won't be long, darling,' said Pamela. 'I'm sure they'll be back at teatime, then we'll all enjoy that cake you've helped me to make.'

She turned to Robert. 'I thought they'd be here by now but the roads may be busy. It's a lovely day.'

'I can hear a car now,' said Robert, moving to the window. 'Oh . . . no, it's not them. It's a police car.' He lowered his voice. 'They seem to be coming here . . . ' He cast a worried glance at his wife. 'I'd better go and see what they want.'

A police sergeant and a young woman constable were standing at the door.

'Excuse me, sir,' said the sergeant. 'Is this the home of Mr Jonathan Fielding?'

'Yes, so it is,' said Robert, 'and his wife Rachel and . . . their two children.'

'And you are . . . ?'

'I'm their brother-in-law. My wife, Pamela, is Jonathan's sister.' Robert knew by this time that something was wrong.

'I see . . . May we come in, sir? I'm afraid we have some distressing news.'

Robert led them into the living room. 'Pam,' he said to his wife. 'Would you take Jennifer into the kitchen — or somewhere — for a little while? I rather think . . . it's bad news.'

Pamela went cold as she saw the serious faces of the policeman and woman. 'Come along, darling,' she said to Jennifer. 'Come and help me to get out the cups and saucers . . . '

'Sit down, sir, please,' said the sergeant. 'There is no easy way of saying this. There has been an accident on a minor road near Wolverhampton. From what we can make out, Mr Fielding swerved to avoid a car that was coming in the other direction. He hit a tree and I'm sorry to say that Mr Fielding died instantly. His wife has suffered serious injuries and is now in a hospital in Wolverhampton.'

Robert had to use all his self-control to hold back his tears and to find a voice. 'That's dreadful. They were just returning from a wedding. Rachel's sister . . . Have her parents been informed?'

'Yes, sir, they have. Her parents' address was in her handbag. And Mr Fielding's parents; they live near here, do they?'

'Yes, they own a garden centre, Fresh Fields. Well, it's more a family concern. We all help to run it. We'll tell them. Pamela and I will tell

271

them . . . about Jonathan.' He gave a deep sigh and shook his head. 'It seems unbelievable. I just can't take it in. And we are looking after their two children . . . What a shock it will be for Rachel's parents too. I do hope she will pull through — only to find her husband has gone, of course. Oh . . . ' He gave another heartfelt sigh. 'Life can be so cruel sometimes.'

'Yes, sir. Indeed it is.' The young police woman spoke feelingly. 'This is the job we always dread, breaking the sad news to relatives.'

'Would you prefer it if we told Mr and Mrs Fielding?' asked the sergeant. 'We try to be as tactful and gentle as we can.'

'No, thanks all the same. I'll go,' said Robert. 'The sight of a police car is always a shock. And we'll take care of the children for . . . well, as long as is necessary.'

The sergeant and constable left, and Pamela came hurrying from the kitchen, tears streaming down her cheeks. 'I heard that, well most of it,' she said, 'but I can't believe it. Our Jonathan . . . It just doesn't make any sense at all.'

'I know, darling.' Robert put his arms round her. 'What about Jennifer? She didn't pick up on anything?'

'No, she's playing with her doll and talking away to herself, bless her. And Rachel . . . she's in hospital?'

'Yes, but with severe injuries. We can only trust and pray. Listen, love: I shall have to go round and tell Ted and Mary. Will you be OK for a little while with the children?'

'Yes, James is still asleep and Jennifer will help

me, in her own little way. I shall have to pull myself together. Oh, Robert . . . how dreadful it is!'

He held her close for a moment, kissing her forehead. 'I won't be long,' he whispered. 'I must go and break the news to your parents.'

Pamela tried to occupy herself in the kitchen, mechanically buttering the bread and preparing what would have been a snack meal for Jonathan and Rachel when they returned.

Jennifer looked up at her. 'Mummy coming soon?' she asked. 'And Daddy?'

'In a little while, darling,' she replied, not knowing what to say, and finding it hard to speak for the lump in her throat. 'But you will be staying with me and Uncle Robert a bit longer. Is that OK?'

Jennifer smiled at her. 'Yes, OK. Will you read me that story again tonight about the little pigs?'

'Yes, of course I will . . . ' Pamela continued making the sandwiches while Jennifer played happily. James woke up and needed changing and feeding. She felt as though she was in a world that was unreal, that this was happening outside of her, to someone else.

By the time Robert returned about an hour later, Pamela had made a meal of sorts, which she certainly did not feel like eating, but she knew they must carry on as normally as possible for the sake of the children. Robert told her that understandably her parents were devastated to hear the news, and seemed too stunned to take it in.

'We knew from a young age that Jonathan had

been adopted, and I know they regarded him as their own child, just as much as I was,' said Pamela. 'And to me he was just my big brother. We fell out now and again as kids do, but we were really very close. They told him — and me — when we were old enough to know, that Jon was adopted: chosen they said, because they wanted a little boy. I suppose it's the best thing to do, just in case he found out some other way.'

Robert nodded. He guessed that his wife's thoughts were running the same way as his own. What would happen to Jennifer and James if Rachel did not recover? There would be only one solution . . .

Sadly, Rachel did not regain consciousness. She died the same night and both families, hers and Jonathan's, were left feeling bereft and helpless. It was too much to take in. One day they were celebrating a happy occasion, and the next day their lives were blighted by this double tragedy.

But life had to go on, especially for the sake of the two children. There was no question as to what would happen to them.

'They will stay with us, of course,' said Robert. 'We'll adopt them; it should be straightforward. They know us very well and they're happy with us. And I know you will agree, Pam?'

'Of course I do — I already love them as though they were our own . . . with us not having any.' She looked pensive. As time had gone on it seemed more unlikely than ever that she would conceive. There were complications, and the doctor had told her it was unlikely they would have a child of their own.

'The poor little loves, though,' she said. 'James is too young to understand, and we'll have to hope that Jennifer's memories will fade. We'll tell them, though, won't we, when they're old enough to understand?'

'Of course we will,' said Robert, 'and for now they must be our priority.'

Jennifer looked puzzled sometimes. 'Mummy and Daddy coming soon?' she asked.

And Pamela, not wanting to lie, or to tell the bald truth, said that they had had to go away, but Uncle Robert and Aunty Pamela were looking after them now. They moved back, of course, into their own house, taking the children's equipment with them and making a nice comfy bedroom for the two of them.

19

Fresh Fields was closed for a couple of days, then opened with a skeleton staff. Arrangements had to be made for a double funeral. It was agreed by both families that this should take place in Bingley, where the couple had made their home.

The news travelled around the parish in the community via the inevitable grapevine. It was Iris who broke the news to Alice. She called on the Tuesday evening when Alice had returned from work and had eaten her evening meal.

'I'm afraid I have some very sad news,' she said. 'You'd better sit down, Alice. It's really almost too awful to believe . . . '

Alice sat down. 'Go on, tell me. What is it?'

'It's Jonathan — you know, Jonathan Fielding from the garden, and Rachel. They've both been killed in a car crash.'

Alice felt herself go cold and she gave an involuntary scream. 'Oh, no . . . how dreadful. But they can't be . . . they can't both be dead . . . ' She knew at the back of her confused and whirling mind that she must try to control herself as much as she was able. There was no one here who knew the truth and they must certainly not find out now.

'Yes, it's dreadful,' said Iris. She crossed the room and put her arm round Alice. 'I'm sorry to give you a shock but there was no other way of telling you. Just think how awful it must be for the family. It's bad enough for the rest of us who just knew them as acquaintances. You've gone quite white, Alice. Would you like me to make a cup of tea?'

'Yes, please,' Alice murmured. 'If you don't mind. I must admit, it's shaken me up.'

She tried to compose herself as Iris went into the kitchen to make a cup of tea, the thing that everyone did at times of crisis — as if a cup of tea could erase the pain in her heart.

'Here you are, drink this,' said Iris, returning with two mugs of tea. 'I've added a drop of brandy, I hope you don't mind. It was in the cupboard and I guessed that you might use it on occasions such as this. It's good to settle you down when you've had a shock.'

'Yes, thank you,' said Alice. She sipped at the warm, comforting beverage.

'When is the funeral?' Alice asked, her hands around the mug of tea to stop them from trembling.

'I don't think they know yet,' said Iris. 'There's a lot to sort out first: an inquest, post-mortem. I'm not sure. But it will be here, at the church they attended. Rachel's family will come up here, no doubt. It's just too awful to think about.'

'And those dear little children,' said Alice. 'James is only about six months old, isn't he? And Jennifer, she'll be old enough to know that Mummy and Daddy aren't there, won't she? Are they with Robert and Pamela?'

'Yes, they are. I don't know for sure, but I have a feeling that they may adopt the children, which would be a good solution all round . . . Jonathan was adopted, you know.'

'Yes . . . I did know,' answered Alice quietly.

'But Ted and Mary have never made a secret of it, either to Jonathan or to anyone else. It's the best thing to do, I think, rather than the child finding out from someone else.'

'Yes, and how dreadful for Jonathan's . . . parents, Ted and Mary. Life is so unfair sometimes, isn't it? It makes you wonder why such things happen.'

Iris nodded. 'I suppose we're fortunate if we get through life without some sort of tragedy happening to us. So many were killed in the war, including my Eric . . . '

Alice was relieved when Iris left and she was alone with her thoughts and her grief. She felt cold and numb inside but she knew that life had to go on. She must go to work each day, try to behave normally with her colleagues and friends and keep her sorrow hidden deep inside her.

The funeral was held almost three weeks later. Alice sat unobtrusively halfway back in the church with Iris. The church was almost filled to capacity. Jonathan and Rachel had been a popular couple, well known in the parish and the area, and from their work in the family business. The family members sat at the front, all except for Jennifer and James who were being cared for by neighbours.

Alice tried to keep a tight rein on her emotions as the coffins were wheeled in, side by side, both covered with bright seasonal flowers — chrysanthemums and dahlias in rich hues of gold, red and purple. The vicar gave a fitting eulogy to the young couple and Alice tried to listen although her thoughts were wandering far and wide. Jonathan, her dear son whom she had never been able to acknowledge, was now with Tony, his father, who he resembled so much. Would they know one another? It was all a mystery too deep to contemplate.

In heavenly love abiding
No change my heart
Can fear

Alice tried to find comfort in the words of the hymn, but there was a lump in her throat and tears welling in her eyes. She was sure she was not the only one who was moved by the poignancy of the service, but her personal sorrow must remain deeply hidden.

The graveyard was at the back of the church, and Alice stood with Iris at the back of the group as the vicar spoke the final words of committal and the coffins were lowered into the grave. It was a still autumn day, pleasantly warm for the time of year. Some of the leaves had already fallen, crunching beneath their feet, and the sun glinted through the tapestry of russet, crimson and gold on the branches above them.

'At least it isn't raining,' Iris whispered to Alice. 'It so often does at times like these, and I suppose a ray of sunshine is rather comforting.'

Alice nodded numbly, feeling that nothing could ease the ache in her heart. Then a little grey squirrel bounded fearlessly across their path, chasing a fallen leaf, and she found herself giving an involuntary smile.

The vicar had already said that those who wished to do so were invited to go along to a nearby country inn where light refreshments would be served.

'Shall we go to the Coach and Horses?' said Iris. 'It might look odd if we don't, being fellow members of the choir and knowing them quite well.'

'Yes . . . yes, I suppose we should,' replied Alice, feeling that she would far rather go home, but if she did that she knew she would wallow in her grief. It might be better for her to mix with her friends and try to come to terms with what she knew had to be endured.

A buffet meal, the usual fare for such occasions — various sandwiches, meat pies and sausage rolls — was laid out on long tables covered with white cloths. Waitresses poured out the tea or coffee, and there was a bar where just a few of the men were ordering stronger drinks.

Alice really disliked these occasions, the get-together following the interment, even when she was not directly involved. It seemed sometimes that there was too much jollity and bonhomie, as though the mourners were determined to look ahead cheerfully, despite the loss of their loved ones. She was glad that there was not too much laughter and loud chatter today, more a feeling of quiet sadness and tranquillity. She nibbled at a chicken sandwich and sipped at her tea, not joining in very much with the conversation going on around her, but the others did not appear to notice her lack of involvement.

There was one person, however, who had noticed Alice, and that was Robert Kershaw. He knew her as a rather quiet, unassuming middle-aged lady — early fifties, he guessed — very pleasant and friendly. He had enjoyed chatting to her whenever she came into the garden centre, and he knew her from the church they all attended. He had assumed that she would be here today. He had gathered that she was a lady who did not divulge too much about herself, however well one got to know her. She often looked pensive, a little sad maybe, but who could know what problems and worries people often kept hidden. Never, though, had he seen her look so sad and distracted as she did today.

The group of women she was sitting with were chatting — not jovially, but rather more solemnly as fitted the occasion — but Alice appeared to be taking no part in the conversation. After a few moments he saw her rise and take up her handbag and go into the ladies' washroom. When she came out, some ten minutes later, it was obvious that she had been crying. No one else was near her and he saw her dab at her eyes with a hanky and put it in her bag. Then she stood for a moment, looking out of a nearby window that overlooked the garden area.

Robert did not hesitate. He knew, whether it was right or not, that he must go and speak to her. Something was telling him to do so, even though it might seem intrusive. He got up, saying quietly to his wife that he wanted a word with Alice, and went over to her. He touched her arm gently and she turned to look at him.

'It's a sad occasion, isn't it, Alice?' he said. 'I hope you don't mind me speaking to you. I just felt — somehow — that you needed someone to talk to. Forgive me if I'm wrong . . . '

She smiled very sadly. 'Do you know, Robert, that's exactly what I need. I didn't realize it till now, but . . . thank you.' She took hold of his arm. 'Come and sit with me, on our own. There's something I've got to tell you.' There was an empty sofa nearby and they both sat down.

'Funerals are always sad,' Alice began, 'and I would have been sad anyway. Jonathan was a fine young man and Rachel . . . she was lovely.' She paused, looking directly at Robert. 'It's so dreadful for all of you, and . . . for me as well. You see . . . ' She looked away from Robert and then, staring down at her tightly clasped hand, said, 'Jonathan was my son . . . '

Robert gasped, as he leaned forward to take hold of both her hands. 'Oh, my dear Alice. I'm so sorry . . . ' Suddenly it all made sense and he realized that he was not really surprised to hear this.

'That's why I came to live here, to find him,' she said. 'It doesn't matter how I found out, but I did, and I knew it was what I had to do. But I knew that I must not upset his family life. No one must know who I was, and I've been content to see him growing up into such a grand young man.'

Robert squeezed her hand. 'You're a very brave lady,' he whispered, leaning towards her. Then, aware that people might be watching, he

282

drew back. He could see his wife watching him curiously from across the room. She raised her eyes questioningly and made as if to rise, but he shook his head and waved his hand in a tight, dismissive gesture. Pamela nodded, obviously realizing that there was some sort of problem, and stayed where she was.

'I met Tony in Blackpool when he was billeted with us during the war,' Alice told him in a quiet and flattish, unemotional sort of voice. 'We fell in love. I'd never had a boyfriend before — I was really a very shy girl — but Tony meant everything to me, as I believe — I know — I did to him. We would have got married after the war, but he was transferred to another camp — Blackpool was only a training area — and I never saw him again. He was a wireless operator, and he was killed in a raid over Germany . . . like so many were,' she added. 'I had his home address, and when I contacted his parents his mother wrote and told me what had happened to Tony.' She was quiet for a moment, then went on talking rather more bitterly. 'My own mother was ashamed of me. She packed me off to stay with relations until the baby was born, and I was persuaded — well, forced really — to have him adopted. I went home but I never settled down in Blackpool. So, I came and made a new life for myself here.'

'I think you are very brave,' Robert said again. 'Thank you for telling me. I know it can't have been easy for you. And then . . . for this to happen. It is so tragic for you as well as for us.'

Alice smiled sadly. 'Jonathan was the image of

his father, Tony. I couldn't see anything of myself in him.'

'He must have inherited your kindness and your gentle nature,' replied Robert. 'He was a great friend, and then he became my brother-in-law. And . . . as you no doubt realize, Pamela and I are taking care of the children.'

'Yes, of course. They're such dear little children . . . How are they? Do they miss their mummy and daddy?'

'They are very young, which is fortunate, I suppose. James will be too young to remember and Jennifer . . . well, she's asked about them a few times and we've said that they've gone away for a while. We can't tell them the truth, not yet, but we will eventually. We are going to adopt them: there shouldn't be any problems there, and Jennifer, bless her, is already seeming to look upon Pamela as a mummy figure.'

'My grandchildren,' said Alice pensively. 'I've loved seeing them grow, from a distance, just as I loved seeing Jonathan grow up. At least there is part of Jonathan still here with us.'

Alice closed her eyes for a moment, then looked straight at Robert. 'You must go back to Pamela and the rest of your family. She'll wonder whatever is going on. Thank you for listening to me, it has helped quite a lot.'

'Thank you again for sharing it with me,' said Robert. 'Do you mind if I tell Pamela? But no one else, of course. My wife and I have no secrets from one another.'

'That is how it should be,' said Alice. 'Of course you must tell her. But it must still be just between the three of us.'

Robert rose and gently kissed her cheek before going back to the family group. Alice took a deep breath, trying to compose herself. She then got up and returned to the little group of women with whom she had been sitting.

Iris looked at her with concern. 'Are you all right, Alice?' she asked.

'Yes . . . well, to be honest, not really,' replied Alice. 'It's been a sad day, hasn't it? I had a headache; that's why I went to sit on my own and then Robert came and talked to me. I think I'd like to go home now, though.'

'Yes, so would I,' agreed Iris. 'I'll give you a lift home. As you say, it's been very sad. I don't like funerals, whosoever it is, but this was particularly poignant.'

Iris dropped Alice off outside her home. 'Now, are you sure you're all right? You look a bit peaky to me.'

'Yes, I'll be fine. I'll take some pills for this headache — it's still there, I'm afraid — and take things easy. I'll see you at choir practice. Thanks for your concern, Iris. I'll be fine.'

She knew that she had to be, but it was a relief that she had told Robert of her great secret. She had never intended doing so, but she felt now that it was right. Life must go on. The old adage was a cliché, but very true. She must go back to work, carry on with her normal day-to-day activities just as the rest of Jonathan and Rachel's family had to do. But she could not help but feel that life could be so cruel. She had found her son and watched him grow to

285

maturity, only to lose him again.

Robert approached Alice at the end of the choir practice later in the week. They sat down together in a pew at the back of the church. 'Pamela and I would like you to come and have a meal with us, very soon,' he said. 'I told her . . . about you and Jonathan. She was taken aback at first, as I was, then she realized that it all made sense; your friendliness and your interest in the family. Although we are quite sure that no one else has noticed and no one will ever hear about it from us — we can assure you of that. Pamela is deeply sorry for you, especially as you have to keep your feelings all to yourself.'

'Yes, I admit it's not easy,' said Alice. 'I have my work to keep me busy, and my home to look after, and lots of friends . . . I'm grateful for your friendship, Robert.'

It was decided that Alice would share a meal with them on the following Tuesday, after work.

'I'll look forward to it,' she said. 'I'd better go now. Iris always runs me back home and I don't want to keep her waiting. I can see she's busy chatting, though, to Pamela and Dorothy.'

'Yes, Pam said she would keep her talking for a little while. See you soon, Alice. God bless . . . we'll be thinking of you.'

Pamela had prepared a tasty chicken casserole on the following Tuesday evening, which they enjoyed with a bottle of white wine, and there was an apple crumble to follow.

'The children are both tucked up in bed,' she said. 'That's what we usually do, then we can have our meal in peace.'

'How are they?' asked Alice. 'They've settled down all right?'

'Yes, they're as good as gold,' said Pamela. 'Jennifer looks a bit confused at times, but she is used to us and she's been no trouble at all. We will tell them when they are old enough to understand. We feel that it would be the right thing to do. It's fortunate, in a way, that they are so young.'

'And the adoption is going through,' added Robert. 'There were no complications, with us being close relatives . . . It's still very sad, though . . . ' He shook his head. 'But our main concern now is for the children.'

They took their coffee through to the sitting room after the pots had been stacked in the dishwasher. 'We treated ourselves to that when I was working at the garden,' said Pamela. 'I'm not going back there now, of course. I'm a stay-at-home mum.' She gave a wry smile. 'That was what I intended being, eventually, but it just didn't happen for Robert and me. Anyway, here we are with a ready-made family, and we just hope and pray that we can do our very best for them.'

'I know you will,' replied Alice. 'They are lovely children. It's been quite a thrill for me to see them beginning to grow up, even though I had to keep my interest secret . . . as I must still do.'

'Pam and I have been wondering if we should tell Ted and Mary the truth now,' said Robert. 'We think it is admirable the way you kept your distance. You could so easily have upset the apple

287

cart if you had been so inclined.'

Alice shook her head. 'I never wanted to do that. Jonathan had two lovely parents and I was really happy about that. That was what I had wanted to find out, that he had a good home . . . No, I suppose it might not do any harm now to let Ted and Mary know. So long as it goes no further. I don't want to be the talk of the town.'

'You wouldn't be,' said Robert. 'Actually, we're thinking of moving away from Bingley, making a fresh start. We feel it might be good for the children, as well as for us.'

Alice looked crestfallen. She hadn't expected that at all. She had lost Jonathan. Was she now to lose his children who were, after all, her grandchildren, possessed of her blood running through their veins?

Robert noticed her discomfiture. 'I know what you are thinking,' he said. 'We may not move too far away and, of course, we would still keep in touch with you.'

'We feel it would be better for my parents as well,' said Pamela. 'We want somewhere smaller. My mum and dad are not doing as much now in the garden: they've had a lifetime at it and I'm busy now with the children — they must be our priority — and, of course, we no longer have Jonathan and Rachel working along with us. We intend to put Fresh Fields up for sale and see if we can find somewhere suitable for us.'

'You might even consider moving along with us!' said Robert. Alice gave a start of surprise.

'I don't mean to live with us,' he said, 'but I heard you say, not long ago, that the work in the

Bradford Post Office is somewhat intense.'

'So it is,' she replied. 'I often have a headache at the end of the day. All those endless queues and people's problems, I feel completely drained sometimes. I had been wondering, actually, if a sub-post office might suit me better . . . Won't people think it odd, though, if I move away at the same time as you?'

'Why should they?' said Pamela. 'We don't need to make an issue of it. Anyway, it might not be for a while yet. We haven't really started looking for somewhere else, and this place could be on the market for ages. You can never tell what snags there might be.'

Robert drove Alice back home an hour or so later. 'It's very kind of you to consider me,' she told him. 'I'm still very sad, but it has helped a lot knowing that you know all about my . . . past. It was considered shocking at that time to have an illegitimate child, but folk seem to be a bit more tolerant these days. There are still very few people who know about it though, and . . . I would rather keep it that way. But tell Ted and Mary: it's only right that they should know.'

Robert kissed her cheek. 'God bless, Alice. Pam and I are very pleased to have your friendship. We'll keep you informed about what is happening.'

As it turned out everything seemed to fall into place quite quickly. There was no problem in finding a buyer for Fresh Fields; in fact, several people were interested. Robert and Pamela travelled to various locations in Yorkshire to find a suitable place, not too large, but not too small.

They found what they were looking for after only a few weeks. A small market garden with potential for development in the village of Thornbeck in the North Riding, not far from the small town of Pickering, and on the main road leading to Scarborough. There was living accommodation nearby, and a small bungalow was found for Ted and Mary about a mile away.

As for Alice, she was able to get a transfer from the Bradford office to a much smaller post office in the town of Pickering, just a short bus ride away from Thornbeck. And she fell in love with the cottage in Bluebell Cottages overlooking a little stream. It was available to rent and although she would have preferred to buy, she decided it would do very well for a start.

Robert and Pamela and their newly adopted children moved to their new home in Thornbeck the following January and Alice followed them there a week later.

20

'And the rest you know,' said Robert when he came to the end of his story.

Helen had listened along with interest, astounded at some of the revelations. A lot of it she had sort of guessed at, but she had been shocked to hear now Alice had lost Jonathan so tragically after finding him.

'Poor Aunt Alice,' Helen said now. 'How very, very sad; to lose her young man, Tony, and then for their son to die . . . what a tragic story.'

'You don't need to feel too sorry for your aunt, Helen dear,' said Pamela. 'She made a good life for herself here. She settled down and made a lot of friends and she was very contented. In the end I would say she was happy.'

'Yes . . . ' Robert gave a little chuckle. 'We wondered if there was a sort of romance going on between her and Donald Jenkins — you know, the gentleman who owns the antique shop. They spent a lot of time together, but they were both very circumspect people and they didn't give anything away. His wife died about seven years ago and, as I say, your aunt and he were very friendly.'

'I wonder why they didn't get married?' mused Helen.

'Oh, well, they were both in their sixties, and both of them had a nice home of their own. And maybe they were concerned about what people might say — you know — have a quiet laugh about it. Really, we would have been pleased,' added Robert, 'but they were very private sort of folk.'

'Alice may have told him her big secret, about Jonathan, but she never wanted anyone else to know, even after all these years.'

'So, Jennifer and James never knew that she was their real grandma?' added Helen. 'They still don't know?'

'No, they don't, but Pam and I have been wondering whether they should know now. When Alice gave birth to her baby boy she was made to believe — by some folk, mainly her family — that it was a shameful thing and, I suppose, she never really rid herself of that stigma.'

'Yes . . . I suppose so,' said Helen. 'Jennifer and James were very fond of her, though, weren't they?'

'Yes, very much so,' said Pamela. 'But they already had a grandma and a granddad — well, two of each at the start. We didn't see Robert's parents all that often, but my parents moved up with us when we started our business here. Although, the ironic part is that they were not really blood relatives at all. Jonathan my adopted brother, although Mum and Dad loved us both just the same. And Jennifer and James — well, they had none of our blood, Robert's and mine, in their veins, but it has made no difference. They are our dear son and daughter.'

'Yes, we told them when they were old enough to understand. Jenny had a vague recollection of Jon and Rachel, but it had faded, and James had never known anything else — he was only six months old when we lost them. I must say, we've been very lucky. We are their mum and dad, and I'm sure they never think of us in any other way.'

'You said your parents knew, though, about Alice?'

'Yes, Alice agreed that we should tell them, and they were delighted to find out that Alice was Jonathan's birth mother. They had always liked her very much. My parents both died a few years ago,' added Pamela. 'They were several years older than Alice but they never minded that Alice sometimes acted as babysitter for the children when they were not available. They did it between them, very amicably. And Alice became a surrogate gran . . . even though she was actually the real one.'

'Yes, of course,' said Helen thoughtfully. 'Very odd when you come to think about it, but, as you say, it clearly worked very well. And I'm so pleased to know that Aunt Alice had a happy life here, in spite of all her heartaches.'

She smiled, a little bewildered by all the revelations. 'So . . . your Jennifer and James are actually blood relatives to me, aren't they? We share the same . . . let me see . . . ' She thought for a moment. 'The same great-grandparents. There was my great-grandma Ada, then there's my gran, Lizzie, my mum, Megan, then me. And the other line is Ada, Alice, Jonathan . . . and then Jennifer and James. So that makes them my . . . what? Sort of cousins, I suppose, twice or three times removed.' She shook her head. 'It's all too complex to work out, but it's nice to think that we are related somehow.'

'I really think we ought to tell them now,' said Robert. 'They know they were adopted, and now that my parents and Pam's are no longer with us, we should tell them about Alice. They were a little puzzled as to why she left them the money, but very touched by it.'

'And Matthew is a sort of relation of theirs too, like he is to me,' said Helen. 'He laughs at me for trying to work out what relation we are to one another. We're still not at all sure.'

'It doesn't matter, does it?' said Pamela. 'You and Matthew obviously get along very well together.'

'Yes, that's true,' said Helen with a fond half-smile. 'I shall have a lot to tell him when I see him again. He was quite amused at me doing my Miss Marple act, but it's been a happy outcome, not like trying to track down a murderer.'

'Something else has occurred to me, though,' she went on. 'Wasn't it rather coincidental that Alice found employment at the post office here? It seems too good to be true that she should walk into the perfect job straight away.'

'Well, it wasn't quite like that,' said Robert. 'Alice worked in the post office in Pickering for a while — I'm not sure how long, maybe a couple of years. She got a transfer there from the Bradford office without any difficulty. And with it being quite a smallish community in Thornbeck she got friendly with Clive and Edith Meadows who ran the village store-cum-post office. And when they needed a new assistant, Edith asked Alice if she might be interested. Alice jumped at the chance to be working so close to her home. She travelled on the bus to Pickering each day. It's not all that far but the bus left quite early and they are not all that frequent. Alice never learned to drive, of course. She was never interested in doing so and it was ideal for her to be working in her own village, where she knew nearly everyone. Then she went into partnership with Edith when Clive died. And they remained friends ever after. Alice had many friends, of course.'

'And it worked out well for her with the cottage, didn't it?' said Helen.

'Yes, she rented at first, then the landlord decided to sell, and she was able to afford to buy it, so that's what she did.'

'Gosh! What an amazing story.' Helen thought for a moment. 'Who was it who said that fact could be more unbelievable than fiction? And what a tale I will have to tell Matthew when I see him again. And my mum and gran, of course. I think mum would have preferred me to leave well alone, to let bygones be bygones. And my gran, Lizzie — she was Alice's sister, of course — she certainly didn't want to dig up the past.'

'Did she — your gran — never know why Alice had come back to Yorkshire?' asked Robert.

'No, I don't think so. And if she guessed she would never have said so. Poor Alice was more or less cast out of the family because she had become pregnant, and so it was a closed book after that. So they would know nothing of all that Alice discovered, about finding Jonathan and the tragic aftermath. But I will have to tell my mum and gran, of course. I find it incredible that Aunt

Alice kept the secret to herself for so long, apart from you two and Pamela's parents.'

'Yes, it was what she wanted,' said Robert. 'But I think the time has come now for us to tell our two. It's only right that Jennifer and James should know the truth, especially now you are here on the scene — a distant cousin, or whatever. I'm sure they'll be pleased at that.'

'And Matthew as well,' said Helen. 'Matt and I are feeling it's a sort of miracle — or fate, maybe — that we've met up after all this time. We didn't even know that we existed, hundreds of miles apart.'

'We shall look forward to meeting him,' said Robert. 'He has certainly put a sparkle in your eyes.'

'It's early days. My mum and dad haven't met him yet. So there'll probably be a meeting of long-lost relatives in the near future. Anyway, I had better be making my way home now. Thank you for the lovely meal and for giving me the answers to all my questions. How nice it is to have a happy ending. I know there has been a lot of tragedy along the way, but that's life, I suppose. I'm so glad that our families are connected by this. Jennifer and James — two more distant cousins. I can hardly believe it.'

Pamela put her arms around Helen and kissed her cheek. Then Robert did the same. 'I'm pleased it's all in the open,' he said. 'And I think Alice would be pleased too. She just didn't want folk gossiping but I don't think it matters now; and everyone who knew Alice realized what a lovely person she was. They certainly won't condemn her now. It will be a nine-day wonder, then forgotten.'

'Sleep well, Helen, dear,' said Pamela. 'Your mystery has been solved and we can all look forward to the future.'

21

Helen found it difficult to concentrate for the next couple of days, her head still full of all the surprising revelations she had learned. She phoned Matthew the following day, but it was such a long and complicated story that she could not possibly tell it all over the phone. She just told him that all was well, that she was very happy, and that her detective work had been on the right lines, but not entirely so.

'Intriguing!' said Matthew. 'I can't wait to hear the full story . . . and I can't wait to see you again. I'm missing you so much.'

'Same here,' she said. 'When do you think . . . we can meet?' She did not want to appear too eager. It was still early in their relationship, although she did feel very sure about him.

'I shall be busy settling into the flat — quite soon, I hope. I'm still not sure when I shall be given the key — these things take time, as you know only too well. I love you, Helen,' he whispered. There was no one else to hear but it made the words more meaningful. 'And I'll see you just as soon as I can.'

'I love you too,' she whispered. 'Bye for now. Good luck with your move and everything.'

They were able to meet two weeks later, by which time Matthew had moved into his flat. Everything was still in chaos, his belongings not yet all stored away, but at least he had a bed to sleep in and a workable kitchen. The rest could wait as he was eager to see Helen again.

He drove there on the Saturday morning — they took it in turns to be free on that morning — and arrived in time for lunch which Helen had prepared: just a simple salad as they had agreed to have their evening meal at the local inn.

When Helen saw him again and experienced the ardour yet tenderness of his greeting, she knew that she need have no doubts about him or about where their relationship was going.

After lunch they settled down on the settee and she told him the story about Jonathan, his children, Jennifer and James, and how Robert and Pamela Kershaw fitted into it all.

'Wow!' he exclaimed — as he had done several times already — when she came to the end of her tale. 'How amazing! Very tragic for your poor aunt to lose her son after managing to find him, but at least there was a happy ending. So I have two more cousins — are they cousins? — that I knew nothing about. Goodness, Helen, you've certainly opened Pandora's box!'

She laughed. 'Yes, I'm still trying to get my head round it. I suppose Jennifer and James are cousins somehow, but don't ask me to work it out. I haven't told Mum and Dad yet about what I've found out. It's only right they should know — and my gran, of course. She was quite annoyed when I started meddling, as she put it. She thought it should be left alone, but I'm sure she'll be interested to know what her sister discovered . . . and that Alice had a happy life in the end.

'I'm convinced she was happy, Matt. She never seemed down-hearted to me. But she never breathed a word about her big secret.'

'But she left you some clues, didn't she? I think she wanted you to know, eventually.'

They spent a happy couple of days together, and at the end of the weekend, when they said goodbye, they both felt even more certain about their feelings for one another.

They had decided to travel to Blackpool the following weekend, so that Helen's mum and dad could meet Matthew, who was a second cousin — or something of the sort — to Megan. And surely her gran, Lizzie, would be interested, despite herself, to meet her long-lost relation?

'Mum and Dad have three bedrooms, so there will be plenty of room for both of us,' she told Matt with a sly smile. 'I've told her that we are friendly, but . . . well, you know how it is.'

'Indeed.' Matthew laughed. 'But I'm really looking forward to meeting them all.'

They both managed to wrangle a free Saturday morning, so Matthew called for Helen around nine o'clock and they set off on the journey across the Pennines to the west coast.

Megan and Arthur made Matthew very welcome as Helen had known they would. Megan looked appraisingly at the young man and liked what she saw.

'I'm delighted to get to know you,' she said. 'It's dreadful, isn't it, how families can lose touch with one another? Let me see . . . my mother, Lizzie, and your mother, Sally, are first cousins, aren't they? But I'm much older than you,

Matthew — we're a generation apart.'

'That's because I was what you might call an afterthought,' said Matthew, laughing. 'My parents were in their forties when I was born.'

'But it's made no difference,' said Helen. 'Matt's mum thinks the sun shines out of him.' She glanced at him fondly. 'But don't try to work out what relation we are to one another. It's too complicated.'

'Well, it's great to see the pair of you,' said Helen's dad. 'Your mum's cooked a good old Lancashire hotpot and then we'll have a proper natter.'

'Matthew wanted to meet you, of course,' said Helen. 'But there's another reason for our visit. You know what I'd discovered about Aunt Alice, Mum?'

'Yes, of course I do . . . and you were determined to find out more, weren't you?'

'Yes . . . and I've found out about an incredible story. Aunt Alice discovered her son . . . but it's a long story.'

'Then let's have our dinner, and you can tell us all about it,' said Megan.

So, after a satisfying meal of hotpot followed by home-made apple tart, they settled down in the comfortable sitting room with a cup of tea.

'Now, let's hear your story,' said Megan. 'I knew you'd get to the root of it all by one means or another.'

Helen nodded. 'I thought I was on the right track, and that Robert and Pamela Kershaw had something to do with it . . . '

Helen told them the whole story of Alice's

discovery and the happiness — then the sadness — that followed.

'So you have two more relatives, Mum, that you did not know about,' Helen said in conclusion. 'Jennifer and James Kershaw, two very nice, friendly young people.'

'Wow!' said Arthur. 'What a story! And you say that these two still don't know about it, that Alice was really their grandmother?'

'That's right. They still have no idea, although I think they were rather curious about why Alice took such an interest in them. Robert says he is going to tell them very soon. It was Aunt Alice, you see. She didn't want there to be any gossip about her in the village. It was still a problem to her, the guilt and shame she was made to feel at having a baby when she wasn't married.'

'Yes, poor Alice,' said Megan. 'My grandma Ada was a woman of rigid principles, and she tried to make my mother feel the same. Poor Alice must have gone through hell with the pair of them. But I think your gran has mellowed somewhat with age, Helen. We shall have to tell her, of course.'

'Yes, but I think I'll leave that to you, Mum, after we've gone back,' said Helen with a smile. 'And don't feel too sorry for Aunt Alice. She had a bad time, especially with trying to keep it all to herself when Jonathan died, but she found happiness in the end. Apparently she was enjoying a pleasant friendship with the man who had the antique shop in the village. They were very discreet about it, but who knows? There may have been more to their relationship than

302

met the eye. Anyway, I felt really glad about it. She deserved to be happy. You've told Gran we're here, I suppose?'

'Yes, she invited us for Sunday dinner tomorrow. Then I suppose you'll have to set off back to Yorkshire?'

'Yes, work for both of us on Monday,' said Matthew. 'But this is really exciting for me, meeting you all.'

'And tonight we thought we'd have a trip round the illuminations,' said Arthur. 'Megan and I haven't seen them properly for years, only a glimpse from the end of the road. Residents seem to take them for granted, but it's a grand show.'

'That'll be great,' said Matthew. 'I've never seen them.'

'We won't take the car, though,' said Megan. 'It'll be nose to tail and stop-start all the way along the prom. We'll get a bus to Squires Gate, then a tram back all the way to Bispham.'

'Then we'll call for fish and chips on the way back and make a real night of it,' said Arthur. 'We Blackpudlians can enjoy ourselves when we try.'

Helen and Matthew took a brisk walk along the clifftop path following their substantial meal. Megan and Arthur's home was only a few minutes' walk from the sea, handy for both buses and trams into the town centre, although they both had their own car.

It was mid-September now and the breeze for which Blackpool was renowned was very much in evidence as they stood by the sea wall, looking out over the Irish Sea.

'It's what we call Lights weather,' said Helen. 'Sometimes the wind is so strong that the tableaux here take quite a battering. It has been known for them to blow down.'

They were standing at the rear of the huge framework which held the various scenes of fairy tales, circus acts, deep sea creatures and adverts for Blackpool, the leading seaside resort, all of which would be illuminated in their full glory in a few hours' time.

'Well, at least it's flat here,' said Matthew, 'not all up hill and down dale as it is in Yorkshire. But does the wind ever stop blowing?'

'Not often,' said Helen with a laugh. 'Let's have a look round the shops before we go back — there are some good stores here. And I'm ready for a cup of tea.'

'Your parents are great,' said Matthew, as they enjoyed a satisfying brew in the café at British Home Stores, 'and I think they like me.'

'Of course they like you,' said Helen. 'You're one of the family, don't forget, although we knew nothing about you till recently.'

'And I shall soon be a much closer member, I hope,' said Matthew, putting his hand over hers.

They smiled at one another in mutual understanding. Marriage had not yet been mentioned openly, but it was in both their minds.

Helen grinned. 'You have still to meet my gran, Lizzie! But don't worry, her bark is worse than her bite, as they say.'

They set off that evening as dusk was falling, taking a bus through the suburbs of the town to

Squires Gate, the southern Blackpool boundary, where the illuminations started, stretching some five miles northwards to Bispham.

There was a queue at the tram stop but seats for everyone on the tramcar. A ride on a tram was a first for Matthew, as was the sight of the Blackpool Illuminations. He and Helen sat hand-in-hand watching the fairyland of multicoloured lights twinkling overhead. There were gaudy butterflies and exotic birds flashing from the lampposts. Flowers and fairies and sea creatures and giant 'diamond' necklaces, brooches and tiaras festooned across the promenade. They passed trams on the opposite track in the shape of a rocket and a Mississippi show boat. The highlight of the extravaganza was the series of tableaux on the cliffs at Bispham, which they had seen, unlit, earlier in the day. Circus acts, zoo animals, characters from fairy stories, witches and dragons and giants, and a spectacular scene with the tower in the centre, extolling the delights of Blackpool as a holiday resort.

'Wow! That was quite some show,' said Matthew as they left the tram, trying to adjust their eyes to the comparative darkness after the dazzle and glitter of the lights.

'Aye, it's been called the greatest show on earth,' said Arthur. 'A slight exaggeration maybe, but it certainly takes some beating. To be honest, it's years since we saw them, isn't it, Megan?'

'So it is. I remember we used to take Helen when she was a little girl . . . Anyway, fish and chips now as a final treat.'

Their home was only five minutes' walk away

from the tram stop, and they called at the local chippy for haddock, chips and mushy peas. Megan dashed on ahead to warm some plates.

'I know they taste good eaten out of the paper,' she said, 'but it's a bit tricky to cope with the fish. Anyway, we'd better show Matthew that we know how to behave.'

He laughed. 'I'm having a great time. I think Blackpool's a fantastic place . . . and that's summat coming from a Yorkshireman!'

The fish and chips were cooked to perfection, crispy batter and golden-brown chips eaten by the fireside with mugs of strong tea.

They half-watched a variety show on the TV, then Arthur and Megan said goodnight, leaving the young couple on their own. Matthew had been allocated the small bedroom and Helen would be in her old room. Helen was quite sure that her mother knew the score, but it was best to stick to the rules.

'Sleep well!' said Megan as she said goodnight to them. 'You will be meeting my mother tomorrow, Matthew. Don't worry, though, she says she's looking forward to meeting you.'

Helen and Matthew did not stay downstairs for long. After a few kisses and warm embraces they both knew they were exhausted after an eventful day, and they each retired to their own quarters.

'Sunday dinner at my mother's,' said Megan the following morning after they had breakfasted on bacon sandwiches. 'It'll be a slap-up meal. She still knows how to cook a good roast, but we'd better go a bit early so that I can give her a hand.'

Lizzie lived alone in the house to which they had all removed when her mother, Ada, had retired from the boarding house. Then Megan had married and moved away. Helen was born, then Ada had died. It was a comfortable semi in the same area, quite near to the sea, and Lizzie had no thoughts of ever moving.

She opened the door to them looking flustered, but soon took off her floral apron and showed them into the front room, which was used only on special occasions. They took off their coats and sat on the old-fashioned but comfortable three-piece suite that had belonged to Ada. It almost filled the room apart from a display cabinet and a small table by the window.

'I'm up to my eyes in it,' said Lizzie, 'but I can spare a few minutes.' She looked at Matthew and nodded.

'I reckon you must be my cousin Sally's lad.' She smiled then and her eyes brightened, making such a difference to her face.

'Well, I'm real pleased to meet you. Eeh . . . it's dreadful, I admit it, the way we've all lost touch with one another. But this one here . . . ' She motioned towards Helen. 'She seems to have got us all together again.'

'That's because I went to live in Yorkshire, Gran, in Aunt Alice's cottage. I had to go and find our relations; it was the right thing to do.'

'Yes, happen it was: I'm not denying it now.' Lizzie nodded sagely. 'And I hear that you two have got very friendly.' She smiled rather coyly at Helen and Matthew.

'You could say that . . . er . . . Aunt Lizzie,'

said Matthew. 'Is that what I should call you? I think you're a sort of aunt, aren't you, being my mother's cousin?'

'Yes, it'll do, lad. I don't really mind what folks call me, so long as it's nowt rude. Well, our Helen's had a few boyfriends but none of 'em seemed to be right for her. Happen she'll not be so choosy this time.'

'Gran, honestly!' Helen felt herself blushing a little. Really, Gran was the limit. And she'd only just met Matthew.

But Matthew just laughed. 'Oh, I think things are going OK. And I've been married, you know. I'd waited too long . . . and then I made a mistake. No harm done, though. Helen and I hit it off straight away.'

'Well, what will be will be,' said Lizzie, using one of Matthew's mother's expressions. 'Now I best get on with our dinner. Megan can come and give me a hand.'

'And I'll set the table,' said Helen. 'Dad, you can show Matt round the garden.'

'He seems a grand lad, our Helen,' said Lizzie as they were all busy in the kitchen. 'Don't you go messing things up this time.'

'I won't, Gran,' said Helen with a trace of annoyance. 'But just leave it for now. Matt and I have not talked much about . . . the future.'

'Yes, don't go scaring him off, Mother,' added Megan.

'Oh, I can see when summat's right, and these two are right for one another,' said Lizzie. ''Tisn't as if they were first cousins. Our queen married her second or third cousin, didn't she?'

'We've come to tell you something, Gran,' said Helen, changing the subject. 'Not about Matthew. I found out about Aunt Alice . . . and her little boy. I know you thought I should leave it alone but . . . '

'But you didn't, eh? Well, if our Alice had wanted me to know I reckon she'd have told me, but it was such a long time ago and she'd been made to feel so guilty . . . poor lass,' she added with a sad smile. 'So . . . she found him, did she?'

'Yes . . . but it's a long story. We'd better have our dinner first, Gran, or we won't be able to eat when we're talking.'

The meal was served in the room at the back of the house, which was larger than the front room, and was the one in which Lizzie normally spent all of her time.

Helen had put on the best cream damask cloth and proper napkins — not paper ones — with the best cutlery, used for Christmas and other such occasions.

The roast beef was cooked to perfection, with Yorkshire pudding — in Matthew's honour — roast potatoes and mixed vegetables, to save on pans. Apple crumble and custard followed, after which Lizzie made a pot of tea.

'We'll go in the front room and you can tell me your tale,' she said. 'We'll see about the washing-up later on. But I haven't got a dishwasher like some folks I could mention. It's not worth it when there's only me.'

'We'll all help, Gran,' said Helen.

They settled down with cups of tea on their laps. The story took some telling, although Helen tried to make it as succinct as possible: especially with Lizzie's frequent interruptions.

'Wait a minute, you've lost me now. The little lad was called Jonathan? Then they had another little girl? And he never knew that he was her son? They never told him? Well! I never.'

She looked really sad — Helen thought she could see a tear in her gran's eye — when she heard that Jonathan and his wife had been killed.

'Oh! Poor Alice. It might have been as well if she'd never found him . . . and you say that the children, Jennifer and James, never knew she was their grandmother?'

'They don't know yet, but Robert and Pamela are going to tell them the truth quite soon. Aunt Alice was such a private person, you know, and she didn't want any gossip about it.'

Lizzie was silent for a moment. She shook her head sadly. 'No, I can see that she wouldn't. The poor lass! She had a rough time of it. Our mother was a real tartar, and I had to go along with her, no matter what I really thought. Things were different then, though. It was a disgrace to 'have to get married' as they put it. And folks didn't know so much then as they do now, about preventing babies coming. Not that that makes it right,' she added. 'All the same, I don't think our Alice committed such a dreadful crime.'

Lizzie stared into space, as though lost in thought. 'It was wartime. Those poor lads were homesick and lonely, and facing all kinds of dangers. And they did love one another, our Alice and that Tony. You could see that . . . there were some fine young men billeted with us.' She gave a pensive smile.

A thought flashed through Megan's mind. Something that she remembered, and she guessed her mother was remembering it too.

Lizzie shook her head as if to clear her mind. 'Well, I suppose I'm glad you found out, Helen. Alice and me, we did patch things up between us as time went on, but she never breathed a word. And she seemed contented enough with all her friends in Thornbeck.'

'Yes, she was happy, Gran. I feel sure of that,' said Helen. 'Apparently she had a 'special friend', the man who owns the antique shop. Robert thinks they were possibly a little more than good friends, although we will never know. She's left us a legacy, though, hasn't she? Relations we never knew we had, and long-lost relatives to get in touch with.'

Lizzie nodded. 'Yes, we must make amends. I'd be so pleased to see my cousin Sally again.'

'And my brother and sister, Charlie and Susan,' said Matthew. 'Although I must admit I don't see them very often now.'

'Happen some of us could meet up at Christmas?' said Lizzie. 'Maybe here, or in Yorkshire?'

Megan was pleased to see her mother so enthusiastic, especially as she had wanted to let sleeping dogs lie.

'We'll see what we can sort out, Mother,' said Megan. 'We've met Matthew and that's a very good start.' She smiled at her new-found cousin or whatever he was.

'And we really must be heading back soon,' said Matthew. 'I've to see Helen safely into her

311

cottage, then drive on to Scarborough.'

They set off around five o'clock, after another cup of tea and a piece of cake.

'I reckon we'll hear wedding bells soon,' said Lizzie as they waved goodbye.

'Don't speak too soon, Mother,' said Megan. 'It's early days, but I think we'd be pleased to welcome him as a son-in-law, wouldn't we, Arthur?'

Her husband agreed wholeheartedly.

'That went well,' said Matt, as they took the road across the Pennines. 'I can see your gran is a bit of a force to reckon with, but I think I've got on the right side of her.'

'You charmed her, all right,' said Helen. 'She's more amenable than I've seen her for ages.'

It was dark by the time they arrived back in Thornbeck. Matthew did not linger long as he still had a journey of more than half an hour to Scarborough.

They kissed and embraced lovingly, not wanting to say goodbye but knowing that it was inevitable and that it would not be for too long.

'It's been a lovely weekend,' said Matthew, 'and it's been so nice meeting your family. Can't say just when I'll see you again, but we'll phone one another and let's hope it won't be too long. Take care, Helen, love.' He smiled at her for a moment in a sort of silent wonder.

'I'm so glad we found one another,' he said, almost breathlessly. 'Sometimes I can't quite believe it.'

'Same here,' she replied, hugging him again. 'Drive carefully now, Matt. See you soon . . . '

22

Helen missed Matthew. It would be good if he were there all the time, but she was too busy to be miserable, both at work and in her leisure activities. Business was quite brisk at the estate agency, although the boss said there would probably be a lull around the Christmas and New Year period. The choir at St Michael's was practising special music, firstly for the harvest festival and then for Christmas. Harvest would be celebrated the following week, the first Sunday in October, then Christmas would be upon them in what would seem like no time at all.

Robert Kershaw told Helen that he and Pam had decided it was time to tell Jennifer and James the truth about Alice — and they both wanted Helen to be there when they broke the news.

'Are you sure?' asked Helen. 'Isn't it a private family matter?'

'And who are you but part of their family?' said Robert. 'If it hadn't been for you coming to live in your aunt's cottage and finding all the clues to her story . . . well, who knows? We might never have got round to telling them about Alice, and it's only right that they should know.'

James was in his final year at university and Jennifer had completed her training and been fortunate in finding a post as a junior school teacher in the market town of Helmsley. She was living in digs there but the journey home to Thornbeck took only half an hour or so. She would be home for a couple of days at the end of October when it was the half-term break and, fortunately, James would be having a short break from his university course. Jennifer had passed her driving test and now had a little runabout Mini, by no means new but it served its purpose. James was still dependent on public transport but was determined to catch up with his sister soon.

Helen had been invited round for a meal on the Saturday evening: she was not meeting Matthew that weekend. Jennifer and James did not seem surprised to see her. They knew that Helen had become a close friend of their parents, and they both liked her very much.

After a satisfying meal of a homemade steak and kidney pie, followed by an apple meringue pudding, they settled down in the lounge with coffee and mints.

'Quite an occasion, Mum,' said Jennifer. 'Is it something special we are celebrating?'

'You could say that,' replied Pamela. 'You are both home, of course, which is always a reason to celebrate, and we invited Helen along because we have something important to tell you.' The brother and sister looked at their parents enquiringly.

'It's about Alice,' Robert began. 'Helen's great-aunt and the lady whom you two became very fond of.' He paused. 'You two have known for a long time, of course, that we adopted you because your birth parents were so tragically killed. And you also knew that your father,

Jonathan, was adopted when he was just a baby, by Pamela's parents. He knew that as well but he never knew, or tried to find out, who was his birth mother. Well . . . ' He paused again, before saying, 'It was Alice.'

Jennifer and James both gasped. 'I don't believe it . . . ' breathed Jennifer, but of course she did. 'That's incredible.'

'And did our . . . father, Jonathan, not know?' asked James.

'No, because Alice wanted it to be that way,' said Pamela. 'She was a very private sort of person, as you know. She had found her son, and she had the pleasure of seeing him grow up — he was about ten when she found him. And she seemed to be content for it to stay that way. She didn't want to upset the apple cart, so to speak, and she knew he'd had a good upbringing with lovely parents. They knew, eventually, but not at first.'

'And then he was killed,' said Jennifer. 'Oh! How dreadful for poor Alice!'

'Yes, it was dreadful,' said Robert. 'And that was the time that I found out her secret: she was so distressed at the funeral. But Alice was a very brave woman. She carried on with her life here; she had lots of friends and she took consolation in watching you two grow up. That was why we asked her to babysit for you and to take part in your activities and your interests.'

'Yes, she was lovely,' said Jennifer. 'Just like an extra grandma — which was what she was, of course.'

James looked at Helen. 'And you are her

great-niece,' he said. 'So . . . you are some sort of a relation to us, aren't you? What are you? A second or third cousin?'

Helen laughed. 'I couldn't possibly work it out. It would take a genealogist to do that. It's certainly very complicated. And since I came to live in Yorkshire I've met Matthew, another relation I didn't know I had. And we have become . . . well . . . rather friendly.' She smiled fondly at the thought of Matthew.

'We saw you with him a few weeks ago,' said James. 'He looks a nice sort of chap.'

'I can assure you he is,' said Helen. 'I was devastated when Aunt Alice died, but what a legacy she has left behind! I think she would be very happy to know how things have worked out.'

'And maybe she does know,' said Pamela quietly. 'Who can tell?'

'I think this calls for a celebration,' said Robert. 'Get out the glasses, Pam, and I'll open a bottle of prosecco.'

'Here's to us all,' said Robert, raising his glass. 'To us and to our family members in other parts of the country. And . . . God bless Alice.'

They all raised their glasses, repeating 'God bless Alice' before taking a sip.

Helen felt a tear pricking her eyes, but the few tears she shed would be tears of happiness as well as sadness as she remembered her dear aunt.

'When I think about it,' said Jennifer, 'I suppose I am not really all that surprised. Well, I was stunned at first, of course.'

'And so was I,' called her brother.

'But . . . Alice was always so special to us, to me and James, and we really did come to think of her as a member of our family.' She turned to Helen. 'And there was something about you, too, Helen. I can't explain it, but it was so easy to get to know you and to talk to you. And I think there is a family resemblance too, inherited from Alice. We're both quite small — like Alice was — and fair-haired.'

'And very pretty too,' said Robert. 'And James, here, has inherited Jonathan's sharper features and dark hair.'

Pamela looked a little pensive.

Jennifer broke in quickly, 'But James and I have had a wonderful mum and dad. I can't think of you any other way. My memories of . . . Jonathan and Rachel are so hazy, and James does not remember them at all.'

James nodded. 'I suppose it was a typical story of that time, wasn't it? Two young people falling in love in wartime. How very tragic, but I suppose there must have been many more just like them.'

'Hundreds and hundreds,' said Robert. 'I don't remember this war. I was born towards the end of it, as Jonathan was. Tony was part of a bomber crew; a wireless operator. Alice told me when the truth came out. I suppose he knew that he might not survive the war, so many planes were shot down over Germany. And Alice said she knew too. She had a feeling when she didn't hear from him for ages that the worst had happened. Then Tony's mother wrote to tell her.

Alice was a very brave lady, but there must be many more just like her.'

'I was born well after the war,' said Helen. 'I've heard a little about it from my mum and gran, but Aunt Alice never mentioned it. It was only since coming to live here that I've found out the facts of it all. But the good thing is that I've found all of you.' She smiled round at them, Robert and Pamela, Jennifer and James.

'And Matthew as well,' said Robert with a sly grin at her.

'Oh, yes, Matthew too,' she said with a happy smile.

23

Helen and Matthew met most weekends, either at her cottage in Thornbeck or at Matthew's flat near Peasholm Park in Scarborough. Occasionally Matthew drove via the moors to stay overnight with his mother in Baildon. He had felt a little guilty at leaving her, but she was an independent woman and was pleased that he now seemed to have found the right person with whom to share his life. They had all agreed that very soon Sally must be reunited with her relatives in Blackpool. The weeks seemed to fly by so quickly, and it would probably be Christmas time before they could arrange a meeting.

Autumn had arrived with a change in the weather and a change in the scenery around Thornbeck and the outskirts of Scarborough. Helen delighted in the colourful glory of the scenery: the gold and russet and crimson of the leaves on the trees in the village and in Peasholm Park before they shrivelled and died, forming a crisp carpet underfoot. The cottage gardens and the urban flower beds were ablaze with the bright hues of dahlias, chrysanthemums and scarlet geraniums.

Their time together was precious, amounting to the Saturday afternoons when they had both finished work for the weekend, and the whole of Sunday, before Matthew drove back — or Helen drove back to Thornbeck — in the early evenings.

Helen, of course, was forced to play truant from her position in the church choir on the occasions she visited Scarborough, but no one seemed to mind.

At times it was very cold and blustery on the east coast, but Helen was used to the gales at Blackpool, and she and Matthew sometimes braved the weather, wrapping up warmly as they walked round the headland. The coastal path led from the south bay round to the north above which stood the ruined castle where seagulls wheeled and screeched in the chilly air. Then they would enjoy a meal of fish and chips at the little café near the Grand Hotel, and on Saturday evenings they would dine at their favourite Italian place that they had discovered in their early days together.

They both knew that they were destined to spend their lives together and so, one Saturday evening in early November, Matthew kneeled down in front of her in the cosy little living room and asked her to marry him.

'Of course,' she said, and their kiss held all the promise of a loving marriage, one that they both knew was meant to be. They were both in their mid-thirties, with past mistakes behind them, knowing — God willing — that this would last forever.

'I haven't bought a ring,' he told her. 'We will choose it together, then I know it will be what you want, and then we can tell everyone.'

'Perhaps not just yet,' said Helen prosaically. 'There's rather a lot going on and my parents are wanting to arrange a get-together at Christmas.

So . . . shall we announce it then? It would seem like a good time, don't you think?'

'Whatever you want, darling,' he replied. 'You have said yes, and that is all that matters. Now, what about a glass of prosecco to celebrate . . . and then an early night?' He grinned at her, and she nodded approvingly.

'What a good idea!'

It was true that there was a lot going on, particularly for Helen. She was not especially busy at work. Her colleagues had told her that it was usually a fairly slack time around Christmas, as she remembered it had been in the Blackpool office. She was very busy, however, with her social activities.

The church choir was practising anthems and special music for the Christmas services including highlights from 'The Messiah' to be performed at the evening service on the third Sunday in Advent. This was a first for Helen. She was familiar with the music but had never taken part in a performance of Handel's most popular work. It was quite a challenge for her, and she knew that her voice, which she had considered to be tuneful but not particularly outstanding, was improving with more constant use.

There were also rehearsals for *Iolanthe* with the Light Operatic Society, which had been going on for some time. Helen was dancing and singing in the fairy ring but also understudying the part of Iolanthe.

The operetta was to be presented in the village hall on the Thursday, Friday and Saturday at the end of November. Olga, the lady who was cast in the title role, suggested to Helen, during the rehearsal at the beginning of November, that Helen might like to take over the role for one of the performances: she suggested Friday.

Helen was overwhelmed. 'But . . . I thought the idea was for the understudy to take over in the case of flu . . . or something unavoidable.'

'Yes, that is so,' said Olga, 'but you have worked so hard in the chorus and standing in for the pianist; I think you deserve a bit of recognition. I've spoken to Jim and Maureen and they agree.' They were the husband and wife who were producing and directing the performance.

'Well . . . that's really generous of you,' said Helen, although she was starting to feel a little apprehensive at the thought. 'But . . . do you really think I could do it?'

'Of course you could. And it seems a shame to learn the part and not perform it. You'll be fine, really. And I've done my fair share of leading roles over the years.'

'But I'm only a newcomer . . . '

'A very popular one,' said Olga, 'and you've fitted in so well here you deserve a reward.'

'Thank you,' Helen gasped. 'Oh, Gosh! I never really thought I'd have to do it.'

Helen's family — and Matthew of course — would be coming to Thornbeck for one of the performances, and Helen had assumed it would be on the Saturday. However, when they found out that Helen was to take over the title role on the Friday night they knew that they must make arrangements to get there, somehow.

'Don't bother about trying to put us up at the

cottage,' said Helen's mother over the phone. 'Your gran wants to come as well: she seems highly delighted at the idea, so could you book us in at one of your local inns? That one where we had Alice's funeral seemed very nice. I know that Matthew will be staying with you, won't he?'

'Yes, if he can wrangle the Saturday morning off work,' said Helen. 'What about Dad?' she asked. 'School doesn't finish till half past three, does it? It'll be a rush for you.'

'Oh, your dad will sort it out,' said Megan. 'He's head of department, you know, so he says he'll be able to delegate. And I can leave Anne in charge of the book stall. We're looking forward to it. Helen, love — you've certainly made your mark in Thornbeck, haven't you?'

'Yes, I'm very happy here,' said Helen. 'I miss you all, of course, but our family seems to be getting larger and larger, doesn't it?'

'Yes, we're still thinking about Christmas,' said Megan. 'Some of us must try to get together. Anyway, bye for now, love. Good luck with your rehearsals.'

Helen was given a chance to practise the scenes in which she appeared — there were not too many of them, compared with some of the other leading characters — and the producers were well satisfied with her. And at home she continually practised her solos, accompanying herself on the piano.

Then, before she had time to think any more about it, the last weekend in November was upon them.

Rooms had been booked at the Cherry Tree

Inn for Helen's parents, and for her Grandma Lizzie. They would stay for the Friday and Saturday nights and return home on Sunday. They would watch the performance of *Iolanthe* twice, on the Friday and Saturday evenings. It had been planned that, in the beginning, they should watch only the third performance, but they simply had to be there to see Helen in her moment of glory.

Helen had been allowed to finish work a little earlier that evening and by six thirty, when she arrived at the village hall, she was finding it hard to control her emotions — the butterflies dancing in her stomach and the fear that she was not ready, that she didn't know the words, that she would make a fool of herself. She tried to take herself in hand.

'Don't be an idiot. You're word perfect. You'll be fine.'

Then Matthew was there at her side, wishing her well, and she felt better at once.

'You look stunning,' he said, looking at her flimsy white dress and the circle of flowers on her blonde hair, which she had allowed to grow over the last few weeks, and which now hung loosely almost to her shoulders.

'Your mum and dad and gran are here and we're all rooting for you. Good luck, darling . . . oh, no! Thespians aren't supposed to say that, are they? Break a leg, or whatever.' He kissed her gently on the lips.

Helen went over to talk to some of the other fairies, finding that the worst of her nervousness had passed. At seven twenty-five the producer stood in front of the curtain and the audience stopped their chattering.

'Good evening, ladies and gentlemen,' he said. 'Just one announcement. The part of Iolanthe this evening will be taken not by Olga Mayhew, but by her understudy, Helen Burnside. Now, sit back and enjoy the performance.'

The small orchestra struck up with the haunting first few notes, and after the fairies had tripped hither and thither Iolanthe was summoned by the Fairy Queen from her exile at the bottom of a stream to rejoin her fairy sisters. Helen felt the warmth of the audience, as well as the cast members, embracing her and wishing her well, as indeed it turned out to be.

The audience was delighted with the performance, and although bouquets were not normally presented until the final night, there was an exception made that evening.

The producer handed Helen two bouquets. He spoke to the audience. 'I am sure you will agree that Helen has risen to the occasion this evening.' And to Helen, as he kissed her cheek, 'Congratulations, my dear.'

The audience applauded agreement as Helen read the cards on the flowers. One read: *From Olga and your sisters in the fairy ring. Here's to many more leading roles.*

The other was from Matthew. *For a very special fairy and an even more special human being. With all my love, now and always, Matt.*

Helen was quite overcome by the messages, but smiled happily, blinking back tears of gratitude. She had enjoyed her one night of stardom but she knew that she would be pleased to continue her role in the operatic group as a member of the chorus, helping out where she was able.

She was pleased to hear the words of praise and encouragement from her family and her fellow cast members, but she was glad to return with Matthew to the comfort of her little cottage.

'No doubt there will be a knees-up of sorts tomorrow night,' she told him, 'but all I want now is a bit of peace and quiet.'

He kissed her forehead tenderly, knowing that she was physically and mentally exhausted. A few moments later she was asleep.

Saturday evening's performance of *Iolanthe* was something of an anti-climax to Helen after her efforts of the previous evening. However, she was able to relax and enjoy herself in the subordinate role. The audience was again most appreciative in their applause and cheers as the finale almost raised the roof.

Helen and Matthew went on to the party at the home of a man called Barry, who had played the part of the Lord Chancellor, and his wife Mavis, a member of the fairy ring. A family reunion — or, to be more correct, the first meeting for some — took place on Sunday. Following their attendance at St Michael's Church for the morning service, they all met at the Cherry Tree Inn for lunch. There were Helen and Matthew, Megan, Arthur and Lizzie, Robert and Pamela Kershaw and Jennifer and James, who had both come home for the weekend to attend the final performance of *Iolanthe*. They were sorry not to have seen Helen's moment of glory, but the main purpose of the weekend was to meet some unknown relatives, mainly Lizzie, the elder sister of their lifelong friend Alice, who, incredibly, had turned out to be their grandmother.

It could have been a rather embarrassing situation, but Arthur Burnside and Robert Kershaw, who had found they got along famously together, made sure that everyone was at ease.

Megan had been concerned about how her mother might react, remembering how adamant she had been that the past was best forgotten and that Helen would be well advised to leave it all alone. But, of late, Lizzie had mellowed considerably, even going so far as to admit that poor Alice had had a rough time: giving birth to an illegitimate baby had been bad enough, with all the shame and rejection she had suffered, but to find him again, then lose him so tragically, was a dreadful shame. Lizzie had found herself feeling so sad and sorry at what her sister had had to bear.

They enjoyed a Sunday lunch of roast chicken and all the trimmings, followed by the inn's speciality, bread and butter pudding served with fresh cream, plus drinks of their choice, and Arthur insisted on footing the bill.

Introductions were made when they all sat down, the main one being between Jennifer and James and Lizzie, who had not officially met amid all the activity of the previous evening.

Megan noticed that tears welled up in her

mother's eyes as she shook hands, then, impulsively kissed the cheeks of Jennifer and James.

'Well, I never thought I'd see the day,' she exclaimed. 'My sister's . . . grandchildren. Let me look at you,' she said. Lizzie took hold of Jennifer's arms, standing back a little from her. 'D'you know you're the image of our Alice when she was a lass. Same colouring; Alice was fair like you and you've got the same nice smile. I'm sure Alice must have noticed the resemblance. But she wouldna remark on it, would she?'

'No, she didn't,' said Jennifer. 'We never knew, James and I, until recently. Alice was just a very dear friend. We loved her very much, just as though she was one of the family: an extra granny. We were flabbergasted, weren't we, James? But it all makes sense now.'

James nodded. 'Yes, she was very special to us. But we're not sure, are we, Jen, whether we would have liked to know the truth when she was alive . . . or not?'

'And you, young man,' said Lizzie, turning to James. 'I guess you might be the image of your dad, Jonathan, our Alice's son?'

'Yes, so I'm told,' said James. 'I've no memories of him at all and Jen's memories are only hazy. Mum and Dad told us the story when we were old enough to understand. What a dreadful thing to happen for everyone, and more so for Alice I dare say. But Jennifer and me, we've had a wonderful life, thanks to Mum and Dad.' He smiled at Robert and Pamela. 'Haven't we, Jen?'

Jennifer nodded a trifle sadly, thinking of Alice.

'Aye, it was a sad affair, right from the start,' said Lizzie. 'I remember Alice being friendly with that young corporal. Tony, he was called. Good-looking lad, dark and slim; a lot like you, James, from what I remember. Aye, I reckon they were very much in love but our mam raised the roof when she found out what had happened. Of course it was different in those days. She made Alice feel like a trollop. She couldn't get over the shame of it, our mam. But it was wartime and there must've been hundreds — thousands probably — in the same boat.' She sighed. 'Things are a lot different now. Not that I hold with it, mind you, all this free and easy carry-on, couples living together before they're wed.' She grinned, though. 'But I'd better shut up, hadn't I, before I say too much?'

'Yes, let's get on with our meal, Lizzie,' said Arthur, her son-in-law, good-naturedly. 'Everything's turned out splendidly.' He raised his glass of beer. 'Cheers everyone,' he said. 'Here's to the future.' They all raised their glasses. 'Cheers,' they repeated, and there were smiles and laughter all around.

Following the excitement of the *Iolanthe* weekend, Helen and Matthew spent the next weekend quietly together in Scarborough, where they set out on an important expedition to choose an engagement ring for Helen. Although he was, at heart, a Yorkshireman who liked value for money, Matthew insisted that the ring should contain some diamonds, the traditional gem for such an occasion, and eventually she settled for a sapphire, surrounded by a ring of smallish diamonds, one that she knew would not break the bank.

The young assistant wished them both every happiness and they went out feeling happy and excited and full of hope for a glorious future together. They had decided to tell their family members the news at Christmas, and Helen said she would not wear her ring until then. Her parents, and Matt's mother, must be the first ones to know, although it was doubtful that anyone would be surprised.

They dined that early December evening at their favourite Italian restaurant and — just for that evening — Helen wore her ring. Their usual waiter was quick to notice. They were regulars and very popular customers, and he brought a bottle of the best red wine — on the house — to celebrate the event.

They spent a quiet Sunday together, and Helen insisted that she must drive back before darkness fell, as the nights were now drawing in rapidly. She was a competent driver but still wary of the twists and turns on the country roads.

They said a loving 'goodbye for now', happy to meet again at least once before Christmas.

24

Christmas Day fell on a Tuesday that year, an odd time really, as many businesses carried on working until Monday afternoon, with the workforce returning on the Thursday, and no weekend to make the break a little longer. Helen and Matthew were fortunate as their offices closed down at Saturday lunchtime, not opening again until Thursday 27 December, making it a nice long weekend, which was what they needed for their somewhat complicated arrangements.

This Christmas Lizzie and her cousin, Sally, were to meet again after a period of . . . well, neither of them knew quite how long, probably more than forty years.

Sally had been invited to stay with Lizzie at her home in Blackpool, and Matthew would drive to Baildon on the Sunday to pick up his mother, taking her back on Wednesday, which was Boxing Day. Helen thought to herself that Sally, by that time, would have endured quite enough of her Grandma Lizzie. Although, she chided herself, Gran had been much more understanding lately, and she knew that the two elderly ladies would have a great deal to talk about.

Helen would drive her own car to her parents' home on the Sunday and meet up with Matthew when he had delivered his mother safely to her cousin's home. Sleeping arrangements had proved to be rather a problem, however. Helen's brother, Peter, his wife, Linda, and their two children always spent Christmas in Blackpool and although there was not a great deal of room in the semi-detached house they had always managed, with Helen giving up her room to her brother's family and sleeping in the small box room. This year there was Matthew to accommodate as well. Megan and Arthur were quite modern and liberal-minded parents: they had guessed that Helen and Matthew's relation- ship had developed and was by now much more than the casual friendship it had been at the start. Even so, Megan knew that she could not allow Helen and Matthew to share a room, nor, she guessed, would Helen want her to suggest it. So it was agreed that Matthew should sleep in the box room — there was a comfortable single bed in there — with Helen sleeping in the room that had always been hers and still was when she came to stay. A look of complete understanding passed between mother and daughter as this was discussed, both of them knowing that love would find a way but that protocol must be observed.

'What about Peter and his family?' Helen had asked.

'We've booked them into a little B and B not far away,' said Megan. 'We know Mrs Roberts, the landlady, very well. They take just a few guests for Christmas — elderly couples who are on their own, and they provide an 'all-in' tariff, with Christmas meals and all the trimmings. But Peter and Linda and the children will just have their breakfast there and then come here to spend the days with us.'

'Great idea,' said Helen. 'But what about Father Christmas? Will he know where to go?'

The children, David and Lindsay, were still young enough to have faith in the old gentleman. 'Lindsay has written him a letter telling him where they will be hanging up their stockings,' said Megan with a laugh. 'Peter and Linda have always told them Father Christmas fills the stockings, but that the bigger presents are given by Mummy and Daddy and other relatives. That was what we always told you and Peter.'

'Yes, I remember,' said Helen. 'Some children think that Father Christmas will bring them whatever they want. Quite a strain on their parents' bank balance if they go along with the idea. I know that Peter and I were delighted with the little things that Santa left, and I know we wrote thank-you letters to all the others. Except for you and Dad, of course, but I think we learned to appreciate everything.'

'And I'm sure that Linda and Peter are trying their best with their two,' said Megan. 'Anyway, that's what is going to happen.' She counted on her fingers. 'There'll be ten of us for Christmas dinner. I must get a good-sized turkey . . . '

It was a happy family gathering at the home of Megan and Arthur on Christmas Day. Peter and Linda and the children had driven from Skipton the previous day and arrived at the parental home mid-morning. The gifts that Santa had brought — sweets, chocolate bars and sugar mice, Matchbox cars for David and miniature dolls and dolls' house furniture for Lindsay

— were exclaimed over and put to one side for the ritual opening of family presents. Lizzie and Sally arrived mid-morning as well, and Sally was introduced to the family she had heard about but never met.

Megan had one eye on the turkey and kept dodging back and forth to the kitchen to see that all was well.

When gifts had been exchanged and the pile of wrapping paper and tinsel cleared away, Helen and Matthew looked at one another and nodded.

'Listen, everybody!' said Matthew above the chatter and laughter. 'Helen and I have something to tell you, haven't we, Helen?'

Helen smiled lovingly at Matthew, then looked joyfully at the rest of them. She held out her hand, displaying the diamond and sapphire ring. 'Matthew and I are engaged to be married,' she said as Matt put his arm around her and kissed her cheek.

There were cries of delight and hugs and kisses all round.

'Well, I can't say I'm surprised,' said Megan. 'We're very pleased, aren't we, Arthur?'

Her husband agreed, saying, 'Actually we made sure we were ready for the announcement.' He opened the sideboard cupboard and brought out a bottle of prosecco. Glasses were filled and a toast made to the happy couple.

'God bless you both,' said Megan. 'This is wonderful news.'

'Well, I must say, it didn't take you long,' said Lizzie in her usual brusque fashion, then adding, 'but I'm real pleased, that I am.'

'I knew as soon as I saw the pair of 'em together,' said Sally. 'Isn't it grand, eh, how things have worked out?'

'And I think we should remember Aunt Alice,' said Helen quietly. 'We all miss her, but . . . she is really the one who brought us together, Matt and me.'

They all nodded and raised their glasses again.

'Hear, hear . . . '

'Thanks to Alice . . . '

'God bless her . . . '

'And now I really must get on with the dinner,' said Megan. 'I think everything's under control, but I don't want anything to go wrong, seeing as it's such a special occasion.'

'I'll help you, Mum,' said Helen, jumping up from the settee.

'And I'd better lend a hand an' all,' said Lizzie, half rising.

'No, you stay where you are, Mother,' said Megan. 'I'm sure that you and Sally still have a lot to talk about.'

'Aye, we've talked ourselves hoarse,' said Lizzie, sitting down again, 'going down Memory Lane.'

'And now we've something else to look forward to,' said Sally. 'I reckon you and me will be seeing a lot more of one another in the future, eh, Lizzie?'

'You can set the table, please, love,' said Megan to her daughter, 'while I make the gravy and the stuffing. It's out of a packet, I'm afraid, but it should be nice. There's crackers and hats — I got some real posh ones from the market 'cause I know the children like them — and fancy serviettes with snowmen and Father Christmas. There are ten of us, so we'll have to extend the table . . .'

'Don't worry, Mum. I'll see to it,' said Helen cheerfully.

When all was ready they sat down to the traditional meal: turkey with cranberry sauce, sage and onion stuffing — which everyone seemed to prefer to the chestnut variety — roast potatoes, sprouts, carrots and peas. For dessert there was Christmas pudding — made by Marks and Spencer, rather than Megan herself — and rum sauce.

Lindsay wore a silver fairy crown, David a pirate hat and the rest of them were kings and queens, clowns and jesters.

When the crackers had been pulled and the meal was well under way, conversation led, inevitably, to the forthcoming wedding.

'Well, I hope you're not going to keep us waiting too long,' said Lizzie. 'Sally and me, we're knocking on a bit you know.'

'You speak for yourself,' retorted Sally, with a laugh. 'I was near your Alice in age, and you'll be . . . how old?'

'I'm seventy-eight and I'm not ashamed to say so,' said Lizzie, 'so you'd best get a move on, you two. Where's it going to be?'

Helen and Matthew looked at one another questioningly, then nodded.

'We don't want a long engagement,' said Matthew. 'There's no point in that.'

'No, neither of you are exactly spring

chickens, are you?' said Lizzie.

Helen was used to her gran's forthright remarks and did not retaliate. 'It will be in the spring,' she said. 'Probably early May. We're going to have a word with the vicar of St Michael's very soon.'

'So it will be in Thornbeck?' said Megan. 'Well, yes, I suppose that makes sense.'

'It's where I live, and it's the church I attend,' said Helen. 'I know a lot of people will have to travel, but it would be the same wherever we chose. But there's no one who's a thousand miles away.'

'It'll be a real gathering of the clans, won't it?' said Lizzie. 'More relations to meet; your other son and daughter, Sally, and their families.'

Lindsay, who had been listening intently and clearly understanding it all, piped up then. 'Can I be a bridesmaid, Aunty Helen?'

Helen had not really given much thought to the matter, but she answered at once. 'Of course you can, love.'

'But I don't want to be one of them page boys,' said her brother. 'They look daft; anyway, I'm too old.'

They all laughed and Matthew, who had taken to both the children, said, 'Perhaps you could be an usher, David. That's someone who hands out the hymn sheets to the guests. It's an important job. Would you like that?'

'Yes, please.' David, who was a friendly little boy, and not at all shy, nodded happily.

The two elderly cousins, Lizzie and Sally, were as excited as anyone.

'I'm thrilled to bits,' said Sally, 'but, like I said, I'm not surprised. My son and your granddaughter, Lizzie. Who'd have thought it a year ago? We'd nearly forgotten about one another and now we're not only cousins, we're . . . well, I don't know what we are.'

'You'll be a mother-in-law, and I'll be a grandmother-in-law, I suppose,' said Lizzie with a wan smile. 'Well, it'll be an excuse to buy a new hat, won't it?'

25

The wedding took place on the first Saturday in May 1991 at St Michael's Church in Thornbeck. Helen and Matthew had said initially that they did not want a lavish wedding, just a quiet ceremony with family and close friends, but when they started to sort out the guest list they both found that there were not only relations but friends, both old and new, who simply must be invited. There were Helen's work colleagues, some of whom had become friends more than workmates, and it was the same with Matthew and his colleagues — you could not invite some without the others. There were friends from way back; school friends with whom they had kept in touch over the years. Matthew had asked his long-time friend Brian to be his best man and Helen had asked her old school friend, Barbara, to be a bridesmaid. She had already promised her niece, Lindsay, and she decided to ask Jennifer Kershaw to be the third one, thinking that two adult bridesmaids and one child would be the ideal number.

Jennifer was delighted to be asked. They had long since stopped trying to work out their relationship with one another, but the same blood of Aunt Alice ran in their veins. James was to be a groomsman along with David, Helen's nephew, and would be able to give the little boy a helping hand if needed.

It could not have been a more glorious day for the spring wedding, and the village of Thornbeck was an ideal setting. The gardens of Bluebell Cottages, the terrace where Helen lived, were a vista of heavenly blue, complemented by early wallflowers of yellow and russet. The same flowers bloomed in the churchyard of St Michael's beneath the cherry trees of pink and white and the oak and ash trees displaying the fresh green of springtime.

Despite their desire for a quiet wedding without a great deal of fuss, there were more than fifty guests assembled in the church for the simple ceremony. Helen had chosen an elegant dress of white satin with a boat-shaped neckline and fitted bodice — no frills or flounces — and a short veil held in place by a coronet of small white flowers and seed pearls. Her small bouquet of lemon roses and freesias matched the pale yellow of the bridesmaids' dresses, the ideal colour for a springtime wedding. The men wore lounge suits rather than morning dress, but many of the guests had gone to town with their outfits, believing that a wedding was one occasion on which you ought to dress up. Feathery and flowery hats, flowing skirts, lace jackets and gaily patterned chiffon dresses added a touch of gaiety to the event, although it was a reverent and moving service conducted by the Reverend Martin Crosby. After the singing of the final hymn, 'Lord of all Hopefulness', and while the wedding party were occupied in the vestry with the signing of the register, the organist played a selection of melodies from one of

Helen's favourite musicals, *The Sound of Music*.

No bride could have looked happier than Helen when she walked down the aisle with Matthew to the strains of Mendelssohn's familiar music, followed by Barbara and Brian, the best man and bridesmaid, then James and Jennifer, and finally the younger brother and sister, Lindsay and David, who beamed proudly having successfully completed his task of usher.

After the photographs were taken in the ideal setting of the churchyard garden, and the confetti was thrown, all the guests made their way to the Cherry Tree Inn, which was the venue for many occasions throughout the years, both happy and sad.

The wedding breakfast was quite a traditional menu, but well-cooked and proficiently served to each guest by the waiters and waitresses. Everyone enjoyed the prawn cocktail, roast chicken with all the trimmings and the sherry trifle, followed by coffee with cream and mints. The toasts were drunk in champagne. Arthur declared that he had only one daughter and he wanted to give her and her husband the very best start to their marriage.

There were the traditional speeches by the best man, by the bridegroom (on behalf of his wife and himself) which as always roused a cheer, and then by Arthur, who said how delighted he was to welcome Matthew into the family, although the young man was, of course, already a member of the extended family but one whom they had not met until recently.

'And that all came about because of a lady, whom we call Aunt Alice,' he said. 'You all know the story by now, about how Helen found out about the secret that Alice had hidden for so many years. A tragic story, in some ways, but I am sure you will all agree that this has been a wonderfully happy ending. Helen and Matthew met and fell in love, and that is why we are all here today, to wish them every happiness and God's blessing on their future life together . . . to Helen and Matthew.'

They all raised their glasses and toasted the couple.

Then Arthur added, raising his glass again, 'One more toast — to Aunt Alice who is no longer with us. But who knows? Maybe she is with us in spirit.'

'To Aunt Alice.'

'To Aunt Alice,' they all echoed, and many tears of sadness, as well of joy, were shed, as those who had known Alice remembered her.

The two-tier wedding cake was cut — and another photograph taken — then the guests dispersed, to mingle and chat with relations and friends they had not seen for a while, or, in some cases, to be introduced to relations of whom they had been unaware until recently. Jennifer and James were bemused at meeting people they had never known existed, but who were, in some mysterious way, related to them.

Lizzie and Sally stayed together, having become firm friends over the last couple of days.

'Poor Alice,' said Lizzie, shaking her head. 'I wasn't very sympathetic at the time. In fact, I was real nasty to the poor lass. It was our mam's fault, of course. She was so ashamed that a daughter of hers should bring disgrace to the family. And it was all swept under the carpet, never mentioned again when Alice came back home. We'd no idea she'd tried to find her son. And when Helen found out about it, I was dead against her digging up the past, but I think Megan was a bit more understanding. Anyway, I have to confess I was wrong. There's been a happy ending to it all.'

'Aye, it was the same with me,' said Sally. 'Alice came to me all those years ago, and said she wanted to find her son. I told her to leave well alone, she'd only stir up a hornets' nest, but she wouldn't listen. We fell out about it and I never saw her again. I was wrong an' all. I suppose you might call it Fate. She had to find him, although it brought her as much sadness as happiness, poor lass. But like you say, it's ended happily. And you and me have got to know one another again.'

'I believe they're staying on in the cottage,' said Lizzie. 'She's made it very nice and cosy, although it's a long way for Matthew to travel to Scarborough and back each day.'

'It seems so to us, but they reckon nothing of it, these young folk,' said Sally. 'Our Matthew's used to travelling long distances. And Helen's keeping on with her job, I believe.'

'Aye, for the time being,' said Lizzie, 'but I reckon they haven't got much time to waste. Helen's thirty-four now, and if they want a family, they'd best get a move on.'

343

'Oh, I'm sure they'll do that,' said Sally with a smile, 'without any prompting from us . . . '

'I hope I live long enough to see my new great-grandchildren — well, at least one,' said Lizzie. 'I only had one child. I hope they don't keep me waiting too long.'

'Go on with you,' said Sally. 'You're not all that old. Just a few years older than me.'

'Don't rub it in,' said Lizzie. 'I'll be eighty next year. I can't believe it, but there it is.'

'Aye, time flies,' remarked Sally. 'But it's not that old by today's standards — there's more and more living to be a hundred. It'd be nice to get a telegram from the queen . . . '

'God bless her,' added Lizzie, 'I reckon she's got enough problems of her own, poor lass. You never know what your kids are going to do, do you?'

'No, that's true, but you and me, we've done all right . . . '

In the middle of the afternoon the bridal couple departed in Matthew's car to drive to Bradford airport where they would board a plane to take them to Paris, the most romantic place in the world for a honeymoon. Helen looked radiant in her 'going away' outfit of primrose yellow shift dress and jacket. As was tradition, she tossed her wedding bouquet into the crowd of well-wishers, and it was caught by Jennifer, who blushed and looked a trifle coy. She had brought someone with her to the wedding: a young teacher called Barry who taught at the same school. She said they were good friends, but his smile at her gave promise of rather more.

But time would tell . . .

There was the usual shower of confetti, kisses and hugs and laughter as the pair got into the car and drove away.

'Paris . . . ' said Sally thoughtfully. 'How lovely. I've never left these shores, and I don't suppose you have either, have you, Lizzie?'

'No, not me,' said Lizzie. 'I don't know as I've ever wanted to. I've been quite content with Blackpool, especially since we gave up the boarding house and we were able to appreciate it a bit more. Aye, it's a grand place when all's said and done. They can keep their Monte Carlo and Sorrento and all them places. And that reminds me; we must decide when you're going to come and visit me again . . . '

Helen and Matthew's five-day honeymoon was idyllic. The flowering trees were in full bloom and the Tuileries gardens were a riot of colour. They drank coffee or wine at boulevard cafés, went up the Eiffel Tower, sailed along the Seine in a river boat and even watched a rather risqué performance at the Moulin Rouge. They had known from the start that they were compatible and returned home even more certain that they had found their soulmates.

Lizzie's wish was granted. Helen and Matthew's first child, a girl, was born in the May of 1992, just over a year after their marriage. A small family group attended the baptism at St Michael's Church a couple of months later. They asked Jennifer and James to be the only two godparents, Helen believing that it was the duty of Matthew and herself, more than anyone, to bring up their child in the Christian faith and to set a good example. Who could tell what the future might hold? Sad times as well as happy ones maybe; all they could do was to promise to do their best.

They had pondered about the name they would give the little girl. They had both thought of Alice, but eventually settled on Alicia, followed by May, the month of her birth.

'Alicia May,' said the vicar, making the sign of the cross on the little one's head. He then walked down the aisle with the baby in his arms to show her to the congregation, who were there for morning service.

Lizzie felt an unaccustomed tear in her eye, which she hastily brushed away. She had been feeling a little unsteady of late but had tried to banish her fears. There was an incentive now to live a few more years. She could not remember a time when she had been as thrilled as when her dear little great-granddaughter was born. It was a pity she wasn't able to see her every week, as she would have done had they been living locally, but she hoped that Megan and Arthur would include her whenever they went on a visit to Thornbeck.

And it was grand to have met up with Sally again. They were now good friends — which they had never really been before — as well as cousins; and they kept in touch by phone between their meetings. Sally visited her for two weeks in the summer of 1992, and again in 1993, when Matthew, who had driven his mother to Blackpool, broke the news that Helen

346

and he were expecting another baby in December.

'I daresay you'll be wanting a lad this time, won't you?' said Lizzie.

'We don't mind at all,' said Matthew, 'but if it's a boy we know we'll have to move eventually so they can have a room each. But we're happy in the cottage and it's too far off to think about moving just yet.'

'Well, I doubt if I shall be here to see the next one born,' said Lizzie, when Matthew had driven away.

'Don't talk daft,' said Sally. 'You're good for another few years yet.'

'I know what I know,' said Lizzie darkly, 'but I can't complain. God's been very good to me, letting me live to see the first one. Sometimes I think it's more than I deserve.'

Sally glanced at her anxiously. Lizzie looked pensive, but then she shook her head and gave a little laugh. 'Aye, I'm a silly old fool, aren't I? Take no notice; I'm just being maudlin. Come on, it's nearly time for *Coronation Street* . . . '

Epilogue

Lizzie died at the beginning of December 1993, a month before her eighty-fourth birthday. She had told no one about the lump she had found in her breast, trying to tell herself it would go away. Like her mother before her, she did not have much patience with illness. It was probably a blessing, all her family agreed, that she was taken ill with pneumonia in November and passed away within a fortnight.

'God bless her,' said Megan. 'It's a pity she didn't live long enough to see her next great-grandchild; but I know she would not have wanted to face an operation. Just like her not to have told us . . .'

Megan was sad, but she knew that her mother had been much happier during her last few years on earth and had mellowed more than anyone would have thought possible.

There was a great deal of clearing away and sorting out to be done. It was the day before the funeral and Megan was in what had been her mother's bedroom. She sighed as she opened the wardrobe door and saw all her mother's clothes hanging there. Much of the stuff was rather old-fashioned but still in good order; it must all go to the charity shop.

She closed the wardrobe door and, without really thinking about it, she idly opened the bottom drawer of the dressing table. It held scarves, gloves and underwear; that was perhaps the saddest of all. There was a tin box too: a Coronation souvenir, which had probably held biscuits, of George VI and Queen Elizabeth. She opened it, not quite sure why she was doing so. They had already found her will in the bureau downstairs. The box contained mainly birthday and Christmas cards. Possibly the ones that were too special to throw away. Then Megan found a letter in an envelope which had a date stamp of 1943, only just decipherable, and was addressed to Mrs Lizzie Weaver, with the address of the boarding house where they had once lived. She took out the letter and started to read. She knew at once that it was a private sort of letter — a love letter? — but she felt no guilt at carrying on reading. Just as Helen had found and read a letter that Tony had written to Alice, this one was from the same era, and her mother was no longer there to know or to care. Lizzie could have destroyed it to keep it away from curious eyes, but she had not done so.

My dearest Lizzie, it began, and Megan knew instinctively that it was not from her father.

I miss you more than I can say and I can't tell you how much I look forward to seeing you again, because we both know, as we have known from the start, that this is not possible. We loved one another just for a little while, and what happened was inevitable. I can't believe that it was wrong. We were both lonely and troubled and so our friendship deepened into love. I have no

349

regrets, my dearest Lizzie, just very fond memories and I trust it is the same with you. We were just 'ships that pass in the night' as they say. And I hope that your husband comes through this dreadful war safely, and that you and little Megan will have a happy life together.

With my love,
Alan

Megan's thoughts flew back to the wartime days. Yes . . . she remembered the young airman whom her mother had called Alan. A quite ordinary young man from what she could recall, cheerful with a jolly laugh and smile, and he had been kind to Megan. She tried to recapture those days, but her memories were hazy. It must have been around the same time that Aunt Alice had been friendly with her Tony . . . and Megan had no recollection at all of that young man. Lizzie, from what she had gathered, had shared Grandma Ada's feelings of shame and disgust at Alice and the disgrace she had brought to the family. But sadly Lizzie, deep down, must have understood and sympathized with her sister? Though she would not have dared to say so, not at the time. But folks were a good deal more understanding and tolerant now, and Megan reflected that her mother, over the last few years, had become a much softer and gentler person.

Megan smiled sadly as she folded the letter and put it in the pocket of her trousers. She would destroy it later.

'God bless you, Mum,' she whispered, wiping

a stray tear from her eye.

Life was for the living, and very soon there would be a new grandchild for them all to love.